CONTROLLING INTERESTS

TRACIE PETERSON

BETHANY HOUSE PUBLISHERS
MINNEAPOLIS, MINNESOTA 55438

Cover illustration by William Graf
Cover design by the Lookout Design Group

Published by Bethany House Publishers
A Ministry of Bethany Fellowship International
11300 Hampshire Avenue South
Minneapolis, Minnesota 55438
www.bethanyhouse.com

Printed in the United States of America by
Bethany Press International, Minneapolis, Minnesota 55438

Library of Congress Cataloging-in-Publication Data

CIP data applied for

ISBN 0–7642–2064–0   CIP

Dedicated to my daughter Julie.

God gave you to bless me, to teach me patience and endurance,
to give me hope and joy and laughter.
God knew that as my second born,
you would be the continuation of a very special love.
I'll love you forever.

Books by Tracie Peterson

Controlling Interests
Entangled
Framed

RIBBONS OF STEEL*

Distant Dreams
A Hope Beyond
A Promise for Tomorrow

*with Judith Pella

TRACIE PETERSON is an award-winning speaker and writer who has authored over twenty-five books, both historical and contemporary fiction. Her latest book, *A Promise for Tomorrow*, follows the history of America's railroads and is co-written with Judith Pella. Tracie and her family make their home in Kansas.

Prologue

*D*enali Deveraux hiked up the long, rocky path. Her steps were quick and even, her heart keeping beat with the rhythm of her feet. Coming here always gave her a feeling of mixed emotions. Solitude and peacefulness exuded control over the luxurious lawns, but there was also an unspoken veil of loneliness and sorrow.

Spying her destination, Denali left the well-worn path and made her way across the thick carpet of new spring grass.

"Hello, Mama," she whispered, taking a seat on the cold marble bench. There was no response . . . but then Denali hadn't really expected one.

Granite markers couldn't speak.

ROSE DEVERAUX, read the etched marker. This was accompanied by the date of her birth, and alongside it was an artfully carved rosebud. Beneath these came the word *Died* and a date that was not so very long after Denali's own birth.

"I can't stay long," Denali said, her voice respectfully soft. "Aunt Chrys is waiting for me." Then, remembering the small offering she'd brought, Denali got to her feet and placed a single perfect red rose on the grave.

"I miss you," she said, touching the granite as lovingly as if it were her mother's own face. "Sometimes it seems like this is as close as I can get to you. They won't let me go into your old room, and while I think I understand the reason, I still say it's selfish."

A cool breeze blew across the grounds, causing Denali's waist-length cinnamon hair to whip across her face. She closed her eyes, wishing desperately that it might be her mother's touch.

"I wish you wouldn't have died," Denali whispered. Tears escaped her tightly closed eyes. "I wish I could open my eyes and find you right here with me, safe and alive . . . and happy. I know it would make me happy."

How many times had she stood here just like this? Wishing against all the possible wishes she could ever make that when she opened her eyes her heart's desire would come true. There wasn't anything in her possession that Denali would not give to have this single longing fulfilled. Balling her hands into tight fists, Denali gritted her teeth and tensed her entire body—concentrating, forcing every single thought into subjection. There just had to be a secret way for making wishes come true. Just one wish. That's all she needed. Just one.

But even before she opened her eyes, Denali knew her wish would not become reality. Even at the age of twelve, she knew death was forever.

Swallowing back the lump in her throat, Denali opened her tear-filled eyes and stepped back.

"I hope you can see me here," she whispered, her childish voice trying hard to sound brave. "I hope you can hear me." Again a gentle breeze stirred the grass. Denali liked to pretend it was her mother and God walking by. It comforted her heart, and that was all she cared about.

"Grandfather hates me," she continued. "I know I've told you that before, but it's true. I just wish I knew why. He never comes to the house anymore, and I know it's because I live there." Hot tears threatened to fall again. "Sometimes I'm so lonely. . . . I just want you to be with me."

In the distance, Denali heard the car horn being sounded. That was her aunt's signal that time was getting away from them.

"I have to go," she said, her voice raw with emotion. Falling to her knees, she awkwardly hugged the headstone and a strangled sob escaped her throat. The pain never seemed to go away. In fact, it only grew stronger with each passing year. Each passing reminder. Christmas. Birthdays. Mother's Day.

"I need you, Mama," Denali whispered, laying her head against the cold stone.

The horn sounded again, and Denali tore herself away. Getting to her feet, she brushed grass off her jeans and dried her tears.

"I love you," she said, blowing a kiss to where she'd placed the rose earlier. She glanced skyward and spread her arms, stretching them high to the heavens in an open embrace. "Don't forget me, Mama."

One

Denali Deveraux stared at the real estate listing in her hand and marveled that a simple piece of paper could reduce the home she loved to mere lines of rhetorical information. For all of her twenty-five years, she'd never known any other home besides this one. And now it was for sale.

"I don't understand why we have to leave Kansas City for Dallas," she told her aunt, tossing the piece of paper to the table.

Azalea Deveraux shrugged. "It's what Father wants." She picked up a platter of fresh fruit and offered it to her niece.

"And of course whatever Richard Deveraux wants, he gets," Denali replied sarcastically and plopped down in one of the dining room chairs. Just thinking of her grandfather brought a certain discomfort to Denali's already stressful morning.

Azalea's expression looked pinched; nevertheless, she continued to offer the fruit until Denali finally took the platter. Selecting some of the early season strawberries and cantaloupe, Denali put the fruit tray down and picked up her morning coffee. After a restless night considering the move her grandfather had demanded they make, Denali cherished the rejuvenating, steaming liquid.

"It just doesn't make good sense," Denali finally started in again. She put the delicate china cup down and crossed her arms. "Azalea, you know very well that the Kansas City office is every bit as productive as the Dallas location. He's only doing this to make me miserable." No amount of reasoning would convince Denali otherwise. She held the reins of Fun, Inc.'s Kansas City division, and the business was doing well. As a theme park architectural design firm, they had more than enough work, as well as a strong profit margin.

"I'm sure that isn't his reasoning, Denali," Azalea protested. "He's just looking out for his best interests. Besides, Chrys loves it there, and she already has a place picked out where we can live."

"So . . . Aunt Chrys has already found an apartment where you and she can live together, and Grandfather has his mansion in Highland Park. You two will have your uptown apartment, and I'll be left to figure out what I'm supposed to do with myself."

"But, Denali, you are twenty-five," her aunt reminded.

"I know that, and I'm not saying that I don't desire a place of my own. It's just that I love this house." She waved an arm in the air for emphasis. "This is the only home I've ever known." She stopped abruptly, trying to figure out how to put into words the things that were weighing down her heart. "Mother lived here. She was raised here with you and Chrys. It's one of the few connections I have to her."

Azalea grew sympathetic. "I know, sweet. I've always known that it was this reason, more than any other, that tied you to this place. But your mother isn't here, and you may never get the answers to those questions you have."

"Questions that you and Chrys, not to mention Grandfather, could answer for me if you would," Denali reminded her.

Azalea paled a bit and picked at the food on her plate. It was as it always seemed to be. She would rather focus on anything else than talk about Denali's past. Denali sighed and made a pretense at eating. The family wasn't compelled to give her the details of her past, but they were more than happy to dictate the details of her future. She tried to relax and not let everything close in on her. It wasn't like she couldn't give up the family business and stay on in Kansas City. But in truth, she wasn't completely sure that she could stay in Kansas City and not live at Cambry.

Cambry stood as a gracious estate in the lush Mission Hills area of Kansas City. The twenty-two-room house represented the only truly good thing about Denali's life. The home was lovely and elegant, with just the right touches of antique and modern furnishings to make the place unique yet comfortable.

Her aunts had a passion for travel, and the rooms of Cambry were positively filled with bric-a-brac from all over the world. There were fine Lalique crystal candelabrums and Sevres porcelain vases from France, as well as Waterford delicacies from Ireland. The china was Haviland, pure and simple. Passed down from their great-grandmother, the family would consider nothing else capable of properly attiring a table. Creamy white with a border of primroses and lavender ribbons, the Haviland china was a family legacy that spoke of decades of use—of parties long gone by, of family now passed on, of friends forgotten in the rush of life. The gold leafing on the rim bore wear, and indeed a couple of the plates were chipped by Great-grandfather Deveraux, who constantly forgot to leave his pipe elsewhere when called to the dinner table. Nevertheless, they continued the family lineage, passing from one generation to the next, bestowing grace and charm upon the Deveraux table.

On the floor were lovely but well-worn Persian rugs, which also had witnessed numerous celebrations and festivities. Denali herself had crawled upon them as a child and easily remembered her captivation with them. The intricate patterns of blue, red, and gold were enough to keep her imagination occupied for hours. Complementing these were lovely medieval tapestries that had been carefully negotiated for in Liberec and scandalously smuggled out of the country by Denali's great-grandfather. Stories abounded about this rugged adventurer who thought nothing of breaking the law if it meant gracing his wife with some trinket.

There were also one-of-a-kind artist renditions, as her aunts were tremendous supporters of new talent. Everything from wooden figurines to sculpted marble gargoyles were to be found, prized acquisitions from their protégés. It was hard to imagine which among these treasures would accompany them to Dallas and which would stay to be auctioned off or given to appropriate museums.

Denali's own antique bedroom set was a part of her grandfather's collection, and because no one dared to protest Richard's decision to sell the house and most everything within its walls, Denali would even lose her own bed. Added to this would be the matching dressing table and chair, highboy, and writing desk. Denali's world was on the verge of a drastic change, and she was helpless to keep it from happening. Looking around her now, she found a growing ache in her heart. How could she be truly happy anywhere else?

"I just don't agree with his decision," Denali stated flatly and gave up on her attempt to eat. "I've headed up the Kansas City office too long for him to tell me it's not holding its own. If he can't realize the benefit of keeping us here, let him look to his accountants for advice."

Azalea smiled sympathetically. "Denali, I learned a long time ago that it does little good to put myself into the center of any argument, especially one that has to do with either you or your grandfather. You are both cut from the same stubborn cloth. So was Rose."

Denali laughed bitterly. "That's the most I've heard regarding my mother's characteristics in fifteen years."

Azalea opened her mouth to speak, then closed her lips tightly and studied the gold trim on the china plates. Running her finger along the rim, she appeared to have little more than a disjointed interest in her niece, but Denali knew better and pressed the issue.

"Chrys isn't here to shut you up or remind you of how Grandfather forbade you to ever mention Rose's name in this house again. He's in Dallas, Azalea! Yet for all these years you and Chrys have raised me, you've both acted as though he might walk through the door at any moment. I'm tired of Richard Deveraux running my life, and I think now is as good a time as any to make a clean break." Denali slapped her napkin down on the table and got to her feet. "That's it. This is the sign I've been looking for. For twenty-five years I've been coddled and spoiled by you and Chrys but hated by my own grandfather—and all because my mother committed suicide after bearing me out of wedlock. And to make matters worse, I wouldn't have even known about my mother's suicide if I hadn't run across the note she left behind. Think of how much simpler it would have been to have told the truth rather than have me find the evidence of the deed when I was snooping as a child."

"Denali," Azalea said in a soothing voice, "think of what you'd be throwing away. You're a talented theme park designer. You have followed in your grandfather's footsteps and have made a name for yourself."

"He couldn't care less," Denali retorted bitterly. She smoothed down the jacket of her blue Christian Dior suit and shook her head. "I'm only his trained monkey. I dress the way he thinks I should. I drive the car he believes is appropriate for someone in my position. I even subscribe to the magazines he suggests. But not once—not in all the years of doing things his way and trying my best to earn his approval—have I ever had one positive word from him. Never mind positive," Denali said, staring hard at her aunt, "there's never been any word—period. Now, doesn't that strike you as a bit odd, Azalea?

"I mean, let's think about this for a moment." She saw Azalea squirm, rather like a child about to be interrogated regarding some missing cookies. "The man hasn't even seen me since I was ten years old. He refuses to have you even send him a picture of me. He doesn't know who I am—what I like, what I don't like. He sends down his edicts through Aunt Chrys and you and expects that life should go tidily along as he has deemed appropriate. And you know what?" She paused and actually smiled. "I'm tired of it. I'm tired of all of it."

"Now, Denali, don't go doing something stupid just because you're mad at your grandfather. I've told you before, he has never dealt well with your mother's passing."

"Neither have I, but no one seems to care." Denali placed both of her manicured hands on the oak table and leaned down to draw closer to her aunt's face. "I love you. I love Chrys, too, and I could have even loved that old man. But I won't go on being a nonentity in his eyes. I'm going to Dallas with you, but only to give him my resignation in person. Not that I think he'll care overmuch, but at least he'll finally have to deal with me."

Azalea's eyes widened, and her expression turned to one of sheer panic. "You can't do that, Denali. First off, he'll never see you. He'd never allow you to get that close. Secondly, what good will it do to dig yourself into this grave? You have to earn a living. You have to have the means to support yourself. You have your mother's stocks, but the dividends aren't enough to live on—not really."

"I have a master's degree in business, Azalea. I have ten years of experience in this field in one form or another. I've worked my way up from being a mail clerk at fifteen, to secretary, to office manager, to design assistant. I went to college and earned my bachelor's and master's, all while continuing to work at Fun, Inc. There isn't a part of that business I haven't tried my hand at. I've been noted by magazines and clients for my work, and I've earned a name for myself as the youngest woman in architectural history to single-handedly design a multi-million-dollar theme park. Richard Deveraux may be powerful, but he can't take that away from me. He can't simply rewrite the past because he doesn't happen to like what it shows him."

Azalea looked away at this. It was while she nervously folded her napkin that Denali realized that maybe her grandfather did have the power to rewrite history. Maybe that was why she found only dead ends on pathways that should have led her to answers regarding her mother. And not only her mother, but her father, as well. Had Richard Deveraux determined the past too painful to deal with—too awkward to display for the dirt-hungry public? And because it was too painful, had he merely erased it completely?

Swinging around, waist-length cinnamon-colored hair flying behind her, Denali left her aunt in the dining room and stormed back upstairs to the sanctuary of her room. She hardly thought of the hour or the fact that she would have to battle rush hour traffic in downtown Kansas City if she didn't leave the house in precisely ten minutes. She was hurt and angry, and worse yet, she was frightened. Some time ago she had taken to ignoring the signs and symptoms of her fear. And some time ago she had convinced herself that Richard Deveraux couldn't be as bad as she thought him to be. Thinking like that had gotten her through the rough times and helped her to focus on something other than the utter and complete rejection she felt by the one man who could have solved all of her mysteries.

She let the door slam behind her and stood frozen in place as she tried desperately to control her emotions. One by one, she reined in her feelings of sadness, betrayal, and desertion. What good would it do to bathe herself in those things? They wouldn't resolve her problems, nor would they give her answers to the questions she had. Taking a deep breath, Denali tried desperately to figure out what she should do.

"If I quit," she said aloud, "he wins. If I walk away with my tail tucked between my legs and my head hung low, Richard Deveraux has yet another trophy to tack up on his wall." She tried to imagine it there among his big game kills from multiple hunting trips around the world. Her aunts had told her of the well-preserved heads of elk, moose, panthers, and lions. There was even rumored to be the head of a full-grown elephant, tusks intact, placed on a commemorative mounting. How strange her heart, so shattered and broken, would appear amidst these prized kills of her grandfather's. But her heart was no less a victim of that man's brutalities than the animals had been. He had killed her emotionally just as surely as he had killed that elephant.

"Only I'm not a trophy he wants," she whispered, ignoring the tear that slid down her cheek. "He wants me hidden away where he never has to look at me again. Like a little boy who's accidentally killed a songbird, he wants to bury the evidence lest anyone find it and accuse him of his deed."

A soft knock sounded at her door, and Denali knew it would be her aunt. She hurried to her dressing table mirror and dabbed at her eyes in order to keep from smearing her lightly applied mascara. No sense in upsetting Azalea more than she already had.

"Come in," Denali finally called. She picked up a comb and pretended to fuss at pulling back her hair when Azalea entered the room.

"Denali," the older woman said softly.

Denali turned around to see her aunt. She looked so old and matronly in her high-collared blue dress. Chrys wore business suits and participated in the career world of Fun, Inc., but Azalea had always been frail of health. Her place was clearly in the home, where she was happiest playing mistress of Cambry and mother to Denali. At her aunt's worried expression, Denali's heart softened. Without thought, she put down the comb and went to embrace Azalea.

"I'm sorry I let myself get so upset," she apologized. "It's just that this whole move has me unnerved."

"I understand. I really do," Azalea admitted. "You're having to leave all of your friends and co-workers."

"He didn't even offer them jobs in Dallas," Denali said, referring to the ten people who were employed by the Fun, Inc., Kansas City office. "They all have families to support and mortgages to pay, and now they have no jobs."

"Yes, but you've given all of them very generous deals."

"No thanks to him. If I hadn't have taken the initiative and issued them hefty bonuses, Grandfather would have never offered them a cent. He doesn't care about anyone but himself," Denali retorted. Again the bitterness in her voice put a wall of anger between her and Azalea.

"Denali, you can't let him ruin your life. You can't. If you quit, I'm afraid it will anger him enough to go after you and see to it that no one in any design firm will have you on staff."

"But he hates me." She pulled away to face her aunt. "He does and you know it. So why does he insist on bringing me closer to him? Why does he want me in Dallas?"

Azalea's face went white, and she stammered to say something. "He . . . well, you see . . . he . . ."

And then, as if all the pieces were suddenly assembled and the puzzle was laid out in completion before her, Denali knew that quitting Fun, Inc. was exactly what her grandfather had hoped she would do. He wanted her to put up her defense and stay in Kansas City. He wanted her to fail, and with his help, she would do just that.

"Oh, Azalea," she said, dropping her hold on the woman. "You're trying to protect me, aren't you? You're trying to help me see that moving to Dallas is the only way I can remain employed without Grandfather setting out to ruin whatever I touch. That's it, isn't it?"

Denali walked to her bed and sat down in a state of shock. He would wait her out. He would let her quit in a blaze of accusations and anger. He would patiently watch as she went to work elsewhere, maybe even helping her to achieve a position. Then, when the time was right— when he was convinced that the highest amount of pain could be inflicted with the least amount of trouble on his part—Richard Deveraux would crush her. And if by some fluke she chose to stay on in Dallas, Richard would have the upper hand in overseeing her position and again would no doubt find a way to make her life miserable.

"I knew he hated me. I just never knew how much."

"We won't let him put you out," Azalea said, coming to sit beside her. "Chrys has already told him that we stand behind you, and while he may well have controlling interest in this company, we have our shares of stock, too, and a small say. He knows we love you, and he knows that we will provide for you even if he refuses to allow you your rightful place. That's why Chrys took the apartment. We're going to have you there with us until we can help you find a place you like for yourself."

This brought Denali out of her contemplative stupor. "You would have been welcome to live with him if not for me, isn't that right?"

Azalea seemed to suddenly realize that she'd said too much. "Now, Denali, don't make it worse than it has to be. I simply meant—"

"Don't!" Denali snapped and jumped up from the bed. "Don't lie to me. He wanted you both to join him in Highland Park, didn't he? He was counting on my desire to stay here in Kansas City. He never expected me to come to Dallas with you, did he?"

Azalea looked as though she might launch into a tirade about Denali's overactive imagination, but instead she gave a heavy sigh and nodded. "I don't want to live with him in Highland Park, no matter how lovely the setting. Not if it means I can't be a part of your life." She got up slowly, smoothed out her skirt, and smiled. "I will always love you as my own, Denali. When Chrys and I found ourselves responsible for you, we made a pact. We would always be there for you. We would never desert you as your mother and father had. And we never will. In spite of Father's ire, he knows he stands defeated in this one place. And he can't afford to lose Chrys and me. He counts on our love and affection as the only portion he has in his life."

"He could have had mine," Denali said sadly. "He only had to ask." Then she shook her head and added, "No, he only had to take it. It was there all along."

Two

Nearing eighty, Richard Devereaux was lean and statuesque. While many men his age were settling into retirement, Deveraux was running his business at full speed. He thrived on competition and aggressive business practices, and he'd convinced himself that it was these things that kept him young.

Staring down the long conference table at the Dallas headquarters of Fun, Inc., Deveraux had just about reached his limits with the newest of his clients. The group called themselves Omni Missions, but the matriarch of the group was an infuriating woman named Hazel Garrison. Younger than him by maybe half a dozen years, Mrs. Garrison was a force to be reckoned with. Her tight gray curls, stern blue eyes, and conservative business suit suggested to Richard and his people that this was a no-nonsense kind of woman with a mission of her own that no one would—or could—take from her.

Two months earlier the representatives of Omni Missions had approached the Fun, Inc. team to request designs for a Christian-owned theme park and resort. It was the group's desire to create something in the area southwest of Dallas that would cater to families in a conservative manner. Richard hadn't perceived this as a problem. After all, in his years of experience, he had learned that one theme park was pretty much like another. The terrain changed, the size and focus changed, but the driving force behind the park always remained the same: money. Theme parks—really good theme parks—were big money makers. They always employed hundreds from the community and usually drew in thousands, and in many cases millions, per season. With the cost of tickets ranging from twenty to one hundred dollars, it didn't take long to make a park very profitable. Of course, there were the downsides. Insurance was outrageous, and every inch of the park was a lawsuit waiting to happen. But it didn't stop people from building them, and it didn't stop people from going to them. Because of this, Richard Deveraux had managed to take a moderate family fortune and become a very rich man.

As of late, however, the economy had tightened, and even though he'd diversified his investments many times over, Richard Deveraux knew the signs well enough to smell trouble. If he was going to make it into the new century, he was going to have to run a tight ship with streamlined economic features. That's why he'd closed the Kansas City office and cut staff. It was also why he desperately wanted the contract with Omni Missions.

"I suppose, Mrs. Garrison," Deveraux began, "you might make more clear what it is you find offensive about my staff's proposals for your park."

Hazel Garrison put down the spiral-bound document she'd been handed by Deveraux only ten minutes earlier. She fixed him with a stare of complete disgust and leaned back in her chair. "It would be easier to point out what isn't wrong with the design." She waited a moment, as if hoping to make him uneasy. "Obviously we didn't make ourselves clear. Although I was certain that at our initial meeting we were very specific about the plans we had in mind for our park."

"You told me, as well as the staff," Deveraux replied, "that you wanted a conservative family theme park. You told us it was to be supportive of family values to better appeal to the Christian community. You made suggestions such as the need for on-site hotel accommodations, water-event-based entertainment, and areas for concert and theatrical presentations. As far as I can see, we've given you that. We even implemented a focus on the Bible. I fail to see where we strayed from your ideas."

Hazel Garrison stared at Deveraux as if considering whether he was capable of understanding. Richard knew the woman to be clearly disturbed, and while he'd like nothing better than to throw her off the premises for her pretentious, smug expression, he couldn't scoff at the millions that Omni Missions was prepared to spend on their tourist attraction.

"You aren't a Christian, are you, Mr. Deveraux?"

Richard's eyes narrowed. "In this day and age, questions like that are grounds for a discrimination suit. I have my faith and beliefs, but to discuss them here would be totally out of line."

"I suppose you think that a clever way of avoiding my question," Hazel replied, still not intimidated by Richard's harsh expression.

"I'm not trying to avoid anything. I'm simply stating what my lawyers have made clear is the only way to handle these issues. I can hardly draw clients into my office and proselytize about my convictions. You want a theme park that maintains an air of Christian values. That, Mrs. Garrison, will be up to your people after the designs are put into place. Who you choose to run your park, what company you choose to purchase your merchandise from, and so forth, are entirely up to you and your committee."

"I am well aware of how to run the business after the park is completed," Hazel said in a voice clearly registering irritation. "Mr. Deveraux, let's get down to the nitty-gritty, so to speak."

"Gladly," Richard replied and picked up his own copy of the theme park suggestions. "Simply direct me to a page."

"Twenty-seven," Hazel said, picking up her own copy and turning the pages. "Here you start the detailed explanations for theme park rides. Now, granted, it is very possible that you got the wrong idea when I suggested a Bible-based theme park, but I find most all of your suggestions offensive. We weren't looking for rides that alluded to Bible stories—"she pointed at the page contemptuously—"such as the 'Jonah and the Whale Water Ride' or the 'Chariots of Elijah Aerial Extravaganza.' " She lowered the paper. "I fully expected to keep turning pages and find a horror house complete with a room for the beheading of John the Baptist and the stoning of Stephen. We aren't looking at ways to mock Christianity, sir. God knows there are plenty of people out there who are more than happy to do that for us. We simply wish to provide a family-oriented theme park with a strong Christian foundation. Much like the park you created near the Branson area in Missouri."

Richard's face remained fixed, but his mind churned through the memories to recall precisely which theme park Hazel Garrison was referring to. "That would have been handled by our Kansas City branch," he said, remembering the park she was speaking of. "I presume you are referencing the Maranatha Park and Campgrounds just south of Branson."

"Yes, that's the one. We found this park to be exactly in keeping with our interests, only our park would be on a larger scale. We'd very much hoped to work with the person responsible." She kept her pale blue eyes focused on his face, refusing to back down or yield in the least. "Is that person available, and if so, might we expect to have him or her redraw these plans and make a more acceptable proposal?"

"Well, you see," Richard began, for the first time feeling the effects of Hazel's strength, "we are, in fact, in the process of closing the Kansas City office and consolidating everything to this location."

"And will the person or persons responsible for Maranatha be re-locating to Dallas, as well?"

Richard looked down the conference table as if seeing everyone for the first time. He quickly assessed the situation, then smiled. "Of course she'll be joining. She happens to be my granddaughter, Denali. She has headed up the Kansas City location for the last year and is scheduled to be in Dallas within the month."

"Will she be available to work on this project?" a balding man in a cheap navy blue suit asked.

Richard shared a quick glance with his right-hand man, George Al-bright. It had been George's work that Hazel Garrison found so objec-tionable, and it seemed only fitting that the project be taken from him and given to someone younger, more capable. That it had to be his granddaughter caused Richard Deveraux to nearly rethink the entire matter. He couldn't imagine having to face the girl every day of his life, yet it seemed the only way. Perhaps he could find some reason to be away from Dallas while plans were finalized between Denali and Omni Missions. He could see that they were still awaiting his confirmation and cleared his throat.

"Ah . . . if you are completely convinced that Denali's work is what will bring this project to life for you, then of course she'll head up the design. I'll put her to work on it right away. You only have to say the word."

Hazel asked for a few moments of privacy in which to discuss the matter with her people. Richard had no other choice but to graciously lead his own team from the room. When they were well out of hearing distance, Richard turned on the team of five like they had committed some sort of heinous crime.

"What in the world was that all about?" he asked, barely keeping his temper in check. "Is it too much to expect a group of qualified professionals to do their jobs? You've all been here over five years. George, you've been with me for thirty-five years—which is the only reason you've made it to the position of being my executive designer. I can't believe you didn't at least ask some questions or shoot some ideas past that old broad before dragging her down here to see your proposal." George grimaced, but Richard wasn't through with him.

"You know, George, the telephone is a fairly uncomplicated piece of machinery. And there's one in every office. Sometimes two." His sarcasm was thick, and George was now reduced to staring at the floor, red-faced. Two other men shifted nervously, while their female counterparts tried not to look as though they had any concern in George's comeuppance. "Would it have been too difficult to at least have had Janice or Rita dial up Mrs. Garrison?"

"Of course not, Richard. I apologize, but I thought—"

"No, you didn't think," Richard countered irritably. "You didn't think, and now a multi-million-dollar account is lying dead on the table unless that old battle-ax decides to accept my granddaughter's direction in the project. I don't think you have any idea just how much you may have damaged this contract. Given the facts, George, I see no reason to keep you on any longer."

George looked up, his red face now paling rather quickly. "But, Richard, it was an honest error. I went by the book. I followed the plans and ideas given at the last meeting. I consulted each of my team members and took their ideas."

"Honestly, Richard," Rita Schultz said, lowering her glasses, "we followed every detail to the letter. How were we to know that Omni Missions would find the Jonah and the Whale Water Ride offensive? After all, you yourself looked over the specs and approved all suggestions before this meeting was called."

Richard threw Rita a hard look of contempt. Unlike George, who seemed to merely fill space at the office, Rita was an extremely capable designer. If the woman was less talented, he'd fire her in a minute. As it was, he couldn't afford to lose her, and she knew it. She'd already had half a dozen job offers from around the United States. He'd only managed to hang on to her by giving her outrageous increases in pay and prestigious-sounding title changes. Rita knew it, too. She knew she could say anything to him, and he'd have to take it. And because of that, he despised her almost as much as his talented granddaughter.

Denali.

Just thinking about her made his blood boil. She alone remained the only visible reminder of his failings. *I can't think of her now*, Richard reminded himself. There was simply too much at stake to allow himself to get caught up in memories.

Richard started to speak, but the door to the conference room opened and Mrs. Garrison came out, followed by the additional board members of Omni Missions. She couldn't have been any taller than five feet four, but her carriage and determined expression suggested that she was more than an equal match for the foot-taller Richard. He reserved his judgment for how her private meeting had concluded and awaited her decision with a nervousness he'd not felt in years. It wasn't that theme parks were Fun, Inc.'s only business, but it was the most profitable part of their corporation, and he very much wanted this project.

"Mr. Deveraux," Hazel said, stopping directly in front of him and looking up, "we have decided that we will give your granddaughter a chance at this project." Richard smiled, but before he could speak, she continued. "However, we want the entire team responsible for this draft dissolved and a new team put into place. Further, we need to have the second draft available within six weeks. Do you agree to our terms?"

Richard conceded his defeat with a smile that had once charmed and delighted the ladies. "Of course, Mrs. Garrison. I'm happy we could find a solution acceptable to both sides."

"Very well. I'll set an appointment with your secretary for a meeting six weeks from today."

Richard nodded and turned to Janice Reiker. "Janice, would you be so kind as to accompany Mrs. Garrison to Gladys's office so that they may make their appointment to return?"

"Of course, Richard. Please come with me, Mrs. Garrison."

"Good day, Mr. Deveraux," Hazel said without throwing him so much as another glance.

Richard waited until the entourage had moved down the hall before turning with disgust to his remaining team. "You heard that. You're all off the project. What could have meant sizable bonuses for quality work is now something you may only dream of. I hope you realize that because of your incompetence, I'm going to bring in a twenty-five-year-old girl to replace you. I hope every time you look at her you remember this moment of humiliation and resolve to do your jobs appropriately next time."

He left them there, staring at him in stunned consideration. He hoped they sincerely hated Denali, because with more than one person hating her, she would surely find it most unbearable to continue for long. Of course, he needed her long enough to get Omni Missions' business, but after that he would cut her to ribbons. He would see to it that she was nothing more than a long-forgotten smudge on the sordid records of the family history.

Taking the back entrance into his office so as to avoid any further confrontation with Hazel Garrison, Richard reached for the telephone and dialed his daughter's number.

"Chrys, it's me," he said, his voice still edged with anger. "Look, a problem has developed, and against my better judgment, I've agreed to put Denali on a project."

He listened as his daughter questioned him about the details, then proceeded to comment on the problems that could arise from assigning Denali a project that would keep her in Dallas on a permanent basis. She continued by suggesting he put Denali on a New Orleans-based park or even assign her to his own Los Angeles project and take Dallas for himself.

"Look, I didn't call for your opinion. I simply want you to get in touch with Azalea and get the girl down here. It seems some highfalutin group of Christians have decided that only Denali can handle their concerns with the proper amount of spiritual finesse." Pause. "No, I'm not happy about it, but there isn't much I can do about it unless I let a multi-million-dollar contract go by the wayside—and I think you know me better than to imagine I'd allow that to happen."

He drew a deep breath and finally sat down behind his desk. "Chrys, just get her down here, and I mean immediately. We have a six-week deadline, and in that time period she'll have to be in touch with the client and learn whatever it is the rest of us missed."

He started to hang up the telephone, then added, "Oh, and Chrys, just one more thing. I want a good amount of warning before she shows up here at the office. I don't want to have to worry about running into her in the halls by accident."

Three

*D*enali reread the final paragraph of a letter she'd just received that morning. It had come from a locally-based amusement park, and they were offering her a tidy sum to join them as their new administrative design manager. The job entailed helping the park to stay up-to-date with new ideas and attractions while looking for ways to recycle the various entertainments already in place. It would allow her to remain in Kansas City, but it wasn't so lucrative an offer that she'd be able to buy Cambry.

Sitting down at her desk, Denali began to pray about it. It wasn't the first time she'd offered up a prayer regarding the matter. She was so confused and frustrated by the entire moving issue, and that, coupled with the fact that most of her staff was now unemployed or working at lower-paying jobs, meant Denali found the only place of comfort to be one that included prayer.

Her heart told her to steer clear of Dallas, but her mind told her it might be her only chance to confront Richard Deveraux. But was it really necessary to confront him? After all, in the years that Denali had existed on the earth, her grandfather had never offered her so much as a letter of explanation for their estrangement. She'd never been given anything but the lame excuses of her aunts.

"Your grandfather can't deal with having lost Rose," one would say. Or, "Your grandfather can't be expected to concern himself with a child when there's a business to run. That's why we're here for you."

As Denali got older, the excuses began to change. Especially after that day not long before her tenth birthday when she'd gone into the forbidden room. Her mother's bedroom. It was while desperately seeking for some connection to the woman she'd never known that Denali ran across her mother's suicide letter. She could still remember the horror of realizing that her mother had not died in childbirth, as her aunts had so often told her, but had killed herself rather than deal with some unspeakable horror. The letter was addressed to Denali's grandfather, but whether he'd ever read it or not was something Denali couldn't prove. She'd found the letter under what had been Rose's bed, and from the thick layer of dust on it, there was little doubt the letter had been there for years. She could still see the stunned expressions on Chrys's and Azalea's faces when she'd appeared teary-eyed, letter in hand, begging for some explanation. It seemed all of her life she'd been seeking answers to questions she was forbidden to ask.

"I just don't know what to do," Denali said again, as if by some chance God hadn't heard the other half a million times she'd moaned out the same words.

"Denali?" Azalea's voice called from the hallway.

"Come in," Denali called, fervently hoping Azalea would pass on the idea. But it was not to be. Azalea not only came in but had a look of determination and purpose that Denali seldom saw.

"I've just received a phone call from Chrys," she stated as she came to stand beside Denali's writing desk. "It seems there is a local Dallas group that found your theme park designs in southern Missouri to be just what they are looking for. It's my understanding that Father wishes to put you on the project, and Chrys says you must go to Dallas immediately."

"Mr. High-and-Mighty is summoning me to Dallas early? How very tolerant of him," Denali said sarcastically. "Well, I don't think I'll go. Look at this," she said, holding up the letter. "I've had another job offer."

Azalea's already pasty complexion turned even paler. "You've accepted another position?"

"I haven't accepted it yet, but I am seriously considering it."

"But you can't. You have to go to Dallas."

Denali frowned and looked at her aunt quite critically. "And why should I jump just because he says to jump? I'm not a child anymore, as you so aptly pointed out. I don't think I've ever really thought about it before this consolidation thing came up. But in truth, I've grown quite complacent living here. You and Aunt Chrys have always been my world—outside of Fun, Inc.—and I guess I just put out of my mind that the day would come when I would fly the nest. It's funny," Denali said, turning inward for strength to break lifelong ties, "but I've come to realize some very important things."

"Such as?" Azalea asked.

"Such as if I'm to truly let go of the past, then I have to immerse myself in the future. Don't get me wrong. I still want answers. I want them desperately, and I intend to try one last time to get them. But if I fail, then I'm determined to find a way to put it behind me for good. Either way, I think it's time I grew up and moved on. I've been giving a lot of thought to what we've discussed these past few weeks, and now that there's a solid offer on the house and I have another job offer, there's really no reason for me to stick around. It's just a matter of where I should go. So when God gives me the word—"

"But the word has been given," Azalea interrupted. "Father wants you in Dallas immediately. Chrys has already put your plane ticket in the works. You're to be on a 6:15 flight out of Kansas City in the morning."

"In the morning?" Denali replied in disbelief. "I couldn't be ready that fast even if I wanted to be."

"But you're already living out of boxes," Azalea protested, waving to the room of properly organized moving boxes. "You can't possibly say you aren't packed."

"Yes, but there are some things you can't box up and pack away. I haven't put in a change of address or told any of my friends good-bye. I can't just walk out of everyone's life here in Kansas City and not say something."

"But they've known all along that you were going to Dallas."

"No, they've known all along that *you* were going to Dallas. I've made it quite clear that I hadn't made up my mind on the matter. And now that I have a good job offer, there's really no reason to be at his beck and call."

Azalea looked as though she might be sick at any moment, and Denali felt instantly sorry that she'd taken out her anger on her frail aunt. Getting up, she insisted Azalea sit for a moment.

"You don't look well. What did the doctor say about your fainting last week?"

Azalea smiled. "I didn't tell him. I figured, why bother? I'm moving to Dallas. There's no sense in having a whole assortment of tests run here, only to turn around and have them repeated in Dallas." She sobered and turned pleading eyes to Denali. "Please, just come to Dallas and handle this one last project. Surely if the park in that letter wants you all that badly, they'll be willing to wait a few weeks. If not, maybe God has something even better in store for you."

"I hate being summoned by a man who can't even bother to otherwise acknowledge my existence. Is he planning on working with me on this project?" Azalea looked at the floor. "I thought not," Denali added, without her aunt having to say a word. "How does he plan to work this out? Isn't he worried about having to run into me in the hall? Or does he expect me to work out of another building?"

"I don't honestly know what the arrangement is to be," Azalea quickly replied. "But I do know that things will go much better for Chrys and me if you'll just do this one last thing."

"That's hardly fair," Denali said, turning to walk to one of the large bedroom windows where she could see a portion of the well-manicured grounds that surrounded Cambry. "If I say no, then I'm being heartless toward you and Chrys. If I say yes, then he gets his way and—"

"Denali, there's no easy answer. I'm just asking you to do this as a favor. If you see that the project is more than you can handle, then tell him so and resign."

"More than I can handle?" Denali felt suddenly indignant and turned. "There hasn't yet been a project that's been too much for me to handle. Do you suppose that's what this is all about? Has Grandfather simply cooked up some elaborate scheme to publicly humiliate me?" She felt completely incensed to imagine Richard Deveraux plotting her demise.

"I honestly don't know," Azalea replied, her color appearing a little better. "I've tried all these years to figure that man out, and I still don't have an answer for most of the things he does. I suppose this could be a challenge from him to you. Perhaps it is a project that he feels certain you will fail at. I just don't know."

Denali shook her head. "I don't believe I'm about to do this, but I'll go. I can't figure out what he's up to, but tomorrow morning bright and early I'll be on that plane for Dallas."

"Good. I feel much better knowing that," Azalea admitted.

"I hate leaving you here, though," Denali said, her voice softer now. Most of her anger abated with a single glance at her aunt's face.

Azalea reached out a hand and allowed Denali to help her to her feet. "I should be able to follow you down in a short time. I'll arrange for the movers to put everything we intend to keep into storage—until we know for sure whether you're staying in Dallas or coming back to

Kansas City. The remaining things in the house will be catalogued for the estate sale and should be taken care of easily without my being on the premises. I'm personal friends with the mother of the young man whose auction house will handle the sale, and I have the utmost confidence in his integrity. I might find myself able to join you and Chrys within a week or so."

"I hope so. I don't like to think of you wandering through Cambry without someone to help look after you," Denali said, tucking her aunt's arm around her own. "I suggest we finish discussing this over dinner. If I'm not mistaken, I smell the most enticing aroma of lamb and new potatoes. The cook must know I'm leaving tomorrow."

"I might have mentioned something along those lines," Azalea admitted, appearing almost embarrassed at having taken Denali's answer for granted.

Denali only laughed. "You know me pretty well."

Azalea beamed. Her relief at Denali's acceptance of the matter was quite obvious in her countenance. "I thought maybe with your favorite dinner on the table you would forgive me for being so presumptuous."

"Of course," Denali said, giving the older woman's arm a slight squeeze. "But in turn, you must forgive me for being so stubborn and temperamental. One of these days I'll learn not to fly off the handle when I get angry, but I'm not very good when things come at me from out of nowhere."

"Maybe you should pray and ask God to help you learn to control your temper," Azalea said quite seriously. Then she added with an amused glint in her pale eyes, "But be ready to take what comes. I once prayed for patience, and just look at my life."

Denali nodded soberly. "Richard Deveraux would test the patience of Job himself. But you are right. God is my only hope for getting past the point where my temper controls me. I have no real self-control unless I keep my temper in check."

"It will come in time," Azalea replied, her loving tone warming Denali's heart. "Just you wait and see. God has a plan for even that, my dear Denali. And He always knows just when to act and what to do."

Denali laughed. "My only question is, will I know what to do when God acts?"

That night as Denali lay in bed, a million questions rushed at her like a tidal wave, threatening to destroy her fragile facade of strength. Could she really face her grandfather and win?

Throwing back the goose-down comforter, Denali sat up in bed and stared at the shaft of moonlight that fell across the end of her bed. Sometimes her life seemed to be a search for light in darkness. It was as if her conception and birth lay swathed in a black veil with the strictest orders that no one disturb its shielding purpose. Maybe her family sought to keep her from the pain of knowing who her father really was. Maybe they thought that if she knew the man's name and where he'd gone, Denali would seek him out to exact revenge for his desertion of her mother and of herself. Worse yet, maybe they were afraid that should Denali find him, she'd form some sort of bond with him.

Hugging her knees to her chest, Denali rocked back and forth as she tried to imagine what she would say to the man if she ever came face-to-face with him.

Would she play it cool and greet him with a nonchalant "Hello, Father—how nice to meet you," or would she be harsh and unyielding? Would she seek to punish him for the pain he'd inflicted on her all these years, or would she be so happy to finally know him that the past would be unimportant?

She'd played out the scene in her mind so many times. Over the years it had become a strange form of entertainment for her. After all, she knew her mother was dead and gone, but she didn't have any idea who her father was. He might live just down the street, or he might live a continent away—or he might not live at all. It was the not knowing that ate at her emotional peace. Who was he? Why had he left without accepting his responsibility for her?

Then, as always, Denali's thoughts shifted to Rose. She knew herself to be the spitting image of her mother. It was often told to her by her aunts that her uncanny resemblance to Rose Deveraux was enough to take them back in time to their youth. And she had seen the resemblance for herself. When she'd turned eighteen, Azalea, against the wishes of Chrys, had indulged Denali with the gift of a photograph album. The album itself looked to be nearly a hundred years old. The photos inside were not quite so ancient.

Denali still treasured the album with its odd snapshots of beach and mountain vacations, laughing children, and a handsome man and dainty woman who were said to be her grandparents. Her great-grandparents, another couple she never had a chance to know, were also featured in several of the photographs. Her great-grandmother was a no-nonsense kind of woman, her hair tied back in a neat and orderly bun. Her dresses were nondescript and looked to always be some shade of black, although with the black-and-white photos it was impossible to guess what color they might have been.

Great-grandfather Deveraux had been a tall, proud-looking man with a hawklike face. His dark eyes, although rather beady, were deep set and thoughtful looking. His image reminded Denali of Mark Twain with a pipe.

But it was her mother's high school graduation picture that held a special fascination for her. Denali had placed her own graduation photo beside that of her mother's, almost for reference. It was as if in seeing the two pictures side by side, Denali could reassure herself that she really did belong in the Deveraux family. The proof was in her mother's cinnamon-colored hair and chocolate brown eyes; in the high cheekbones and oval face; in the elfish smile that suggested a mischievous prank was just about to occur.

The photograph had been taken the summer before Rose's senior year. It was a time that apparently held much happiness for Rose, and Denali knew it couldn't have been long afterward that she found herself with child and facing a life of shame for her indiscretions.

A tear slid down her cheek as Denali wondered about this vivacious woman who had died so young. Why had life been so overwhelming that she couldn't bear the thought of going on? Was it because of the illegitimate child she'd given birth to? Was her grandfather right—was Rose's death all Denali's fault?

"Oh, Mother," Denali said, whispering the name in reverence, "why did you leave me? Wasn't I enough of a reason to go on living? Didn't you see how I could need you—how much I'd love you?"

The grandfather clock in the hallway chimed twelve, and it was only then that Denali realized the lateness of the hour. She'd have to be up by four-thirty in order to ready herself for the flight to Dallas. Four and a half hours of sleep certainly wasn't going to be enough to face the day, but it would have to do. Sinking back down into the protective warmth of her bed, Denali dried her eyes and prayed. Surely God would see her through this crisis as He had all of the others. She might never know her earthly father, but she knew her heavenly one. God was there for her, and He always would be.

Four

Chrysanthemum Deveraux, Chrys to all who knew her on a daily basis, was the eldest of the three Deveraux children. And as such, upon Chrys fell the responsibility of dealing person-to-person with their father. Chrys had always been her father's favorite until Rose's surprise birth. Chrys had been fifteen when Rose came into the world. She found it easy to hand over the title of favored daughter because everyone loved Rose. Besides, by fifteen, Chrys was already consumed with the family business, and the idea of being her father's "little princess" was quickly being set aside in order to become something infinitely more important. Chrys became her father's right-hand man—or in this case, "woman."

From her father, Chrys inherited a great deal in the areas of personality and development of character. She had watched her father like a hawk, always afraid to lose track of him for too long a period. She had come into this world when her father was away serving his country in World War II, and because of his absence in the first four years of her life, Chrys had clung most possessively to the man when he'd returned home a war hero.

Of course, Richard Deveraux found this most satisfying and, in light of Chrys's devotion, had forgiven his wife the fact that she'd not given him a son. With the war behind them and business shaping up to post-war prosperity, Chrys's mother, Shirley, had again devoted herself to giving her husband an heir. Daughter number two had been born nearly a year to the day after the war had ended and was christened with the name Azalea because Shirley said daughters were like little flowers in a mother's garden.

After that came two miscarriages and a stillborn son, and just when everyone had given up hope of Shirley ever conceiving again, she announced her pregnancy. By this time, their father had plunged himself into the world of business and was gone nearly as much as he was home. Chrys missed him terribly during these absences, but it made her all the more determined to find a way to work at his side. She adored him for his strength and shrewd business acumen, and she loved him for his loyalty to her. With Shirley pregnant, Richard regained a sense of family. He began sending others, including his business partner, off to deal with out-of-town projects. He welcomed Chrys's interest in the business and heralded her ability to catch on quickly.

Rose had been born during one of the worst blizzards in Kansas City history, and while fifteen-year-old Chrys had worried that her father would be outrageously disappointed with yet another daughter, she was secretly glad that no boy had come to the Deveraux household. A boy would have taken her place as protégé to her father. A boy would have meant a male heir and successor to Richard Deveraux—the coveted position that Chrys held for herself.

When the doctor had arrived to give them the details of Rose's birth, he had also shared the sad news that he suspected uterine cancer in Shirley Deveraux. Tests were run and cancer confirmed, with an immediate hysterectomy being the end result. There would be no male heir to the Deveraux fortune. There would be no more children.

Chrys had both mourned and rejoiced. Her mother was gravely ill, and baby Rose was desperately in need of attention and love. While Shirley waned, Rose thrived under the care of Chrys and the nearly ten-year-old Azalea. Their father was devastated by the news, and for once, Chrys wrongly assumed that his sorrow was over the lack of a son. But as her mother's health faded and it was learned that the cancer had spread to other parts of the body, Chrys knew that her father was mourning the dying of his wife.

The battle raged for four years, but Shirley Fowler Deveraux finally gave up her fight and died on a rainy May night. Rose found it impossible to understand what was happening, but Richard, in infinite patience and kindness, had explained that Mommy was now in heaven.

Chrys had scarcely even noticed that Rose had taken her place as favorite daughter. Richard had come to rely heavily on Chrys, and both she and Azalea stepped in to help run Cambry and care for their little sister. That their father found comfort in Rose was not surprising or even troubling, and Chrys hardly had time to worry about this development even if she'd wanted to. But in truth, she loved Rose every bit as much as her father did, and Azalea felt the same. It was as if Rose was the gift left behind when God had taken their mother to heaven. Rose became a symbol of the good that could come out of bad. And when Rose died, the good died, too.

The ringing of the telephone jarred Chrys from her introspection. Putting aside her morning juice, she suppressed a yawn and answered the phone.

"Hello?"

"Chrys, it's Azalea. We've got a problem."

"Oh, good morning to you, too."

"Chrys, I'm serious. I barely talked Denali into making the morning flight, and—"

"She did get on that plane this morning, didn't she?" Chrys took new interest in the call.

"Yes, of course she did. But not very happily. She's filled with questions, as usual, and she's none too content to take orders this time around. One of the last things she said before boarding the plane was that it was time for Father to answer her questions or deal with the consequences."

"Great," Chrys said, reaching over to start the automatic coffee maker. With this new development she was going to need something stronger than orange juice to boost her energy level.

"I'm really afraid that this time things may get out of hand. Denali is a grown woman with a future she's mapped out for herself," Azalea continued. "She was ready to accept a job offer here just so she could stay in Kansas City. It's tearing her apart that Cambry is being sold out from under her, and she's angry that Father is treating her like a servant, expecting her to come when he calls."

Chrys laughed. "He treats everyone that way."

"This is no joking matter, Chrys. You've got to talk some sense into the girl. I thought we had this all worked out last night, but this morning she woke up in one of those moods, and I swear her temper did our Irish ancestors justice."

"I'll meet her at the airport and calm her down a bit before allowing her to go to the office. But you really don't have anything to worry about. Father has already decided to spend most of his time out of the office while she's here. I talked to him at length before calling you yesterday. He has this all figured out. There's a potential client in L.A. that he's hoping to win over with wining and dining, so he'll be out of town completely for several days. And Denali will learn right from the start that the Highland Park house won't be open to her. I'll try to ease the telling in order to keep her from being hurt any more than she has to be, but that's just the plain truth of the way things will be."

"But don't you think you should warn Father?"

"I will, Azalea. I have to call him this morning anyway." She glanced at her watch. "By my estimation, Denali's flight will be arriving in about half an hour. I'd better hurry up if I'm going to meet her."

"Well, all right. If you're sure. I just wanted you to know so there could be as little conflict as possible."

"Where those two are concerned, I don't know that it is possible to reduce the conflict. But I intend to do my part. Please don't worry, Azalea. Denali is a good girl, but we've raised her to be an independent thinker. Why should her actions surprise us so much?"

"I suppose they shouldn't, but I just can't bear to think of her getting hurt."

"I know. Me neither. Look, I'll call later and let you know how it all went. Just pray about it, okay?"

"Okay."

Chrys hung up, only to redial. "Kevin, would you have my car brought around to the front? Thanks." She knew that by the time she emerged from the apartment and journeyed by elevator from the twenty-first floor to the lobby, her black Mercedes would be awaiting her arrival under the canopied drive of LaTour. She found living in this manner infinitely more attractive than rambling about the huge stone mansion of Cambry. She enjoyed being waited upon and given respect and service when desired. But she also liked the privacy that the smaller apartment afforded her. Here there was no bevy of servants to overhear conversations or snoop through your rooms on the pretense of cleaning. Here she simply hired a woman to come in twice a week to do the dirtiest work—and all under Chrys's own supervision. When Azalea arrived, even that would no longer be needed.

A quick glance at her watch gave her the realization that there would be no chance to call her father from the apartment. She hurried downstairs, greeted the front desk staff with a warm smile and a rushed hello, then slid into the driver's seat of the Mercedes and headed down McKinney Avenue.

At the first red light, she picked up her cellular phone and dialed her father's office.

"Gladys, it's Chrys. I need to talk to my father." She waited while the woman made the announcement and connection.

"Chrys, I'm rather busy. What's the problem?" Richard's voice boomed out from the other end.

"Look, I know you're busy, but this couldn't wait. I'm on my way out to the airport to pick up Denali. Azalea called, and she was pretty upset. It seems that Denali is spouting off about getting answers to her questions and so forth. She gave up a good job offer there in K.C., and I think she feels you owe her big for this concession."

Deveraux harumphed. "That'll be the day."

"Father, I know this isn't what you want to hear," Chrys said, shifting the phone to her other ear while making a sharp turn onto the freeway, "but the fact of the matter is, one of these days Denali is going to find her answers. She's a lot like you in that respect, like it or not, and she's not going to leave any stone unturned, even if it means a gravestone."

"I don't want to hear this," Deveraux replied gruffly.

"You haven't wanted to hear this for twenty-five years. But frankly, Azalea and I think it's time."

"You and your sister would learn well to keep your mouths shut. You stand to inherit my entire fortune. I'd hate to see us have a parting of the ways and all of this money go to someone else."

"Like Denali?"

"Over my dead body."

"Well, that's the way inheritances are usually given out. Have you forgotten she owns Rose's shares of Fun, Inc.?"

"I haven't forgotten anything," her father replied ominously. "Look, just keep her away from me, and things will be fine."

"She's going to need some form of contact there at the office, and you know it won't be me because I'm too busy with that New Orleans deal. You'd better find someone who knows the business and can act as your representative. Preferably someone with the finesse and energy to keep two steps ahead of her. She's a dynamo, and she knows how to get what she wants. She's more like you than you'd like to imagine."

"Well, she hasn't gotten the answers she wants, nor will she, if I have anything to say about it. Just keep your mouth shut on this, and we'll all be much better off."

Chrys changed lanes, narrowly missing the back end of an ancient Buick. The bumper sticker read *Honk If You Love Jesus,* but Chrys wasn't inclined to share in the revelry at just that moment.

"Father, you know she's done a lot for Fun, Inc. You have to know that, or you wouldn't be asking her down here like this. You'd be a lot happier if you made your peace with her and utilized her skills to the fullest. I mean, she is who she is, and there's nothing that will ever change that. But because of who she is, she's a part of you that you should hold to tightly. If you don't, someone else will find out about her and snatch her out from under you."

"And once they do, they'll realize exactly what kind of person she is, and it won't be long until the high-and-mighty Denali Deveraux is nothing more than a bitter memory."

Chrys shook her head, and static compromised their clarity. "Don't count on it, Father," she said, knowing that she was losing her connection. "Don't count on it."

Five

At thirty-five, Michael Copeland's life was a far cry from how he'd envisioned himself at this age—a prominent architect with his own successful firm and happy little family. What he had instead were the skeletal remains of such a dream. To say that he was a bitter, angry man was to say that the Statue of Liberty was just some sculpture. His was a deeply implanted hatred that was given rebirth every time he opened the drawer of his desk and found the newspaper clipping he'd preserved for the last three years.

AIRLINER CRASHES KILLING 284 the headline blazed.

What it didn't say was that Michael felt the count might as well have been 285 because his life ended that day, as well.

Always considered rather dashing, Michael's black hair and smoky blue eyes were the most prominent features of his stern, almost harsh-looking face. He was handsome in a brutal sort of way, and his mystique seemed to draw women like bees to honey. He was tall, well-muscled, athletic, and tanned. But he was also cynical, suspicious, and at times rather inhuman. Or so he'd heard people say. He frankly had stopped caring somewhere along the way. No, he'd stopped caring at the point of the airline crash and the ensuing aftermath.

He tried to will himself to forget about the crash. Forget that his entire life had changed with that one act of fate. But he couldn't. He thought instead about how he had once believed in the love and guidance of God, how his Christian faith had collapsed with a few simple acts of betrayal. A good friend had told him that he probably wasn't really "saved" in the first place if he turned away from God just because things didn't go his way.

Losing everything wasn't just a matter of not having one's way,

Michael had told him. Losing everything was confirmation that God didn't care—couldn't possibly care and still allow such things to happen. It didn't matter that he saw bad things happen to other people. It didn't matter that he knew he'd disappointed a great many people when he walked away from his participation in Christian activities and fellowship. It only mattered that the pain he felt inside was camouflaged with anger and bitterness. The steel-hard wall he'd built for himself sheltered not only his heart but his soul, as well, and that was just as he wanted it. Let everyone else exist on their platitudes and spiritual notions, but let them leave him alone.

"Copeland," Richard Deveraux barked out as he strode into the room unannounced. "We need to talk." He took the seat opposite Michael's desk and waited for his undivided attention.

Michael quickly replaced the newspaper clipping in the drawer and offered Richard what he hoped was his fiercest-looking scowl. "I don't suppose the boss of the company has to knock, but it would be nice." He resented the man's overbearing attitude and constant reminder that Michael's position was one of employee, not of employer.

Deveraux smiled tolerantly, apparently not at all taken aback by Michael's attitude. It was clear to Michael that there was something of major proportion about to be dumped in his lap. Under normal circumstances, Deveraux would never accept a subordinate's challenge without a firm reminder of that person's position and why such a greeting was totally uncalled for and unacceptable. That Deveraux simply smiled left little doubt that he was focused on something more important than putting an employee in his place.

"Michael, my boy, we've been long overdue for a talk." He didn't wait for Michael to acknowledge this. "I know you've long desired to work on a project that would bring you the attention and focus that you deserve. I've studied your job history and background information, and I have to say I'm very impressed. You owned your own architectural firm for over ten years," he said, as if this would be news to Michael. "A firm, I might add, that maintained a tremendous reputation right up until the end."

Michael felt his patience wearing thin. He knew Deveraux's reputation as a big-game hunter, and this, coupled with Deveraux's words, made Michael feel as though the older man was stalking him for the kill.

"What's your point?" Michael asked, suddenly feeling a great deal of discomfort.

"My point is, after considering your abilities, I've come to realize that your talents are being wasted. You need a big project to prove yourself on. A project that will set you up, bring you back in the foreground of the architectural community. That's why I've determined that the Omni Missions project is right up your alley."

Michael felt beads of sweat form at his temples. The Omni Missions theme park was a coveted project he'd give his right hand to be a part of. But if Deveraux was offering it, there had to be a reason. Rumor had it that the old man's granddaughter had been personally requested by the Omni Missions board. If that was true, why was Deveraux offering the position to him?

"I thought the board members asked for your granddaughter to head that up," Michael said, leaning back to study the older man. Deveraux had probably two inches in height on him, but Michael outweighed him by thirty well-muscled pounds. Even so, they were more than equally matched in determination and business savvy. They knew what it took to make management decisions, and they knew how to get what they wanted. But where Michael had placed his trust in the people he loved, Deveraux knew better. And because of that, Deveraux still owned his own company, while Michael held only the memories of what once had been.

" . . . and so she'll need someone like you to keep her in line."

"I beg your pardon," Michael said, catching only the last line of Deveraux's answer.

Richard's eyes narrowed. "I said, while it is true that the Omni Missions board asked for Denali to head up the project, I know my granddaughter well enough to realize she's going to need someone of your caliber to guide her."

Michael kept his face fixed stoically on Deveraux. "Guide her?"

"Denali is a strong-willed young woman, and while I respect the job she's done in Kansas City, she is inexperienced in many areas. After all, the girl is only twenty-five years old. She's lived a sheltered life with her aunts, and she has no idea what it'll mean to head up this deal. Because of this, I'm assigning you to partner her on the Omni Missions project."

"Excuse me if I don't just jump at the opportunity, but I'd like to know more about this partnership." Michael tried to organize his thoughts in order to express exactly what was on his mind. "I've heard about your granddaughter's work in Kansas City. I know she's capable of heading up this project because she's taken on contracts of this size before."

"Not quite. Not exactly," Deveraux retorted. "She's headed up the Kansas City group, that much is true. But like any organization, Michael, you hire your family out of obligation. The girl has talent, but it needs direction. You have ten years of experience to offer her. Ten years of working knowledge to show her how things should be done."

The words rang false, and Michael couldn't help saying so. "Why do I get the distinct impression you're playing me for some kind of fool? Rumors of your granddaughter's abilities aren't the only ones flying around Fun, Inc."

"Keeping up with the gossip grapevine isn't a part of your job description," Deveraux said, finally sounding as peeved as Michael knew he must feel at the challenge to his edicts. "Look, the Omni Missions project will mean a big bonus for you if you can help complete plans that will satisfy that old battle-ax, Hazel Garrison. It'll mean an even bigger bonus if you keep my granddaughter occupied and out of my hair."

Michael looked away from Deveraux and studied the cuffs of his white dress shirt. "And exactly what do you mean by 'keeping her occupied'?"

"I don't want the woman to have a spare moment in which to torment me," Deveraux answered flatly. "It's true enough that there's a bit of family history between us. Problems that no doubt the office has speculated on; however, you don't need to concern yourself with it. What you need to focus on is that this project means big money for our firm. Other than this, suffice it to say I want nothing to do with my granddaughter."

"But you employ her? You bring her here to Dallas for a special project, yet you can't stand her?" Now Michael was truly intrigued.

"It wasn't my idea," Richard replied irritably. "I can't turn away profitable business, and Hazel Garrison wants Denali."

"Denali? What kind of name is that?"

Richard shook his head impatiently. "Her mother loved Denali

National Park in Alaska. So she called her Denali. Is that acceptable to you?"

Michael held up his hands. "Hey, I just asked. You can't tell me that you hear women called by that name every day, so you don't need to take up arms just because I questioned you."

"Look, I want to get this thing settled. Will you do it or not?"

"Well, taking orders from you is my job," Michael replied, beginning to feel rather heated by the entire matter. He knew he was risking his position by taking on an attitude with Deveraux, but he was feeling more and more like the patsy. No doubt Denali Deveraux was every bit as obnoxious as her grandfather, and whether they liked each other or not, she'd no doubt run to Richard, demanding her own way every time Michael dared to counter her suggestions. *Why take on that kind of grief?* Michael thought.

But he knew why.

Deveraux was offering a big bonus, and a big bonus meant he would be that much closer to his goal of leaving Fun, Inc. and starting his own business again. Money was the key to his freedom, and he knew that at this point there wasn't much he wouldn't do in order to get plenty of it.

When Deveraux said nothing, Michael eyed him sternly and asked, "All right, what exactly do I have to do?"

Richard smiled. "What does any man do with a young woman?"

"In this day and age, just about anything he wants. But because this is your granddaughter, I'd like to know what my limitations are and what entails your idea of keeping her occupied and out of your hair."

"Do with her what you will," Richard said, a suggestive leer crossing his face. "You seem quite the ladies' man around here. Women are constantly parading themselves past your office or vying for positions beside you at office meetings. It is my opinion that you probably know very well what to do with a woman. How far you take it will be up to you. I frankly don't care if you break her heart in a million pieces as long as I'm not expected to pick even one of them up."

Michael would have never guessed that Deveraux had known of the way the female employees of Fun, Inc. tormented him. He knew he was considered handsome, and he was well aware of the attention given him by women both in and out of the office, but he had no interest in their shallow-minded come-ons. Nor did he have the desire to baby-sit Deveraux's granddaughter, but at least that could prove to be profitable. His employer's lack of concern for her welfare was shocking, but Michael had long heard the rumors of Deveraux's dislike for his granddaughter. No one knew what it was about, but it was said that she was a poisonous thorn in Deveraux's side. She probably was an abomination to look at, as well, and Michael instantly imagined himself squiring some heinous-looking creature from one event to another.

"What's in it for me?" he asked, suppressing a shudder.

"As I said, a hefty bonus."

"How hefty?" Michael asked flatly.

"Fifty thousand."

"Make it seventy." Michael didn't know what had possessed him to throw out that number. Mostly he wanted to see how badly Deveraux needed the favor, but he also wanted to get as much out of the deal as possible.

"Done," Deveraux answered without batting an eye.

"What about my expenses?" Michael pressed. It was obvious Deveraux would give in to whatever he demanded so long as Denali was taken care of.

Richard scowled. "What expenses?"

"To wine and dine your granddaughter, of course. Restaurants aren't free, neither is any other form of entertainment. You can't possibly expect me to shell out my own money on a woman in whom I have no interest."

Deveraux seemed to consider this a moment before leaning forward. "I'll cover your expenses. Take her anywhere you like—even The Mansion," he said, mentioning one of the most expensive restaurants in the city. "Take her there every night for all I care, and I'll foot the bill. But," the older man said, getting to his feet, "the minute she becomes a nuisance to me, all deals are off. I keep the bonus, and you pay your own expenses and look for a new job. Understood?"

"Sure," Michael replied. "No problem. Ms. Deveraux will find herself much too busy to bother you."

"Just make sure she is." Richard paused at the door and added, "Denali isn't stupid. In fact, she's much too smart for her own good. If she suspects any of this, you won't stand a chance of making it work. For your own sake, I'd suggest you make as if you've fallen hopelessly in love with her."

Michael laughed, and the sound was bitter and harsh. "Short of marriage, I'll do what I have to for the money."

"That's the spirit!" Deveraux exclaimed, leaving Michael to contemplate the matter.

Six

Denali came down the departure ramp with the two allotted carry-on bags thrown over her shoulders. She hadn't really considered transportation to her aunt's apartment, but now that she was here, it was evident she would need to figure out a plan. Glancing around, she noticed the arrows pointing her to ground transportation and started off in that direction.

"Denali!" a voice called to her, and instantly she recognized it as that of her aunt Chrys.

Turning to search the sea of people for a familiar face, Denali was pleasantly surprised when Chrys slid through the crowd to join her. "I didn't know you were planning to meet me. Thanks for coming."

Chrys smiled. "I figured we had a lot to discuss before you went up to the office. I wanted to help you get settled in, then we can go over what Father has in mind for you." She kissed Denali on the cheek and gave her a brief hug. "Come on. My car's parked close by, so we won't have that long of a walk."

Denali was momentarily overwhelmed. Kansas City's airport was completely modern and fairly well organized, but Dallas-Fort Worth International was a world unto itself. Not only had it taken twenty minutes just to taxi to the terminal, but once inside, the traffic of hundreds and hundreds of people made Denali feel swallowed up. The crowd didn't seem to faze Chrys at all, and she quickly took Denali in hand and half shoved, half directed her forward into the flow of things.

"You can't just stand there like that," Chrys said, laughing. "Around here you have to keep moving or you'll get run over."

"Does that go for all of Dallas or just the airport?" Denali asked with a smile.

"Oh, it goes for everything here," her aunt assured her. "You have to think fast and keep ahead of the crowd. It's the truth of the matter in business or picking up groceries or merging into traffic. He who hesitates isn't usually just lost, he's oftentimes completely mowed over." Just as Chrys said this, a group of suit-clad businessmen rushed past them, cutting across their walk space in order to congregate at the pay phones.

"See what I mean?" Chrys's tone was casual and lighthearted, but Denali read something more in her expression. There was a worry in her eyes that suggested to Denali that Chrys's arrival was based on more than mere kindness to see her properly escorted into the city.

They managed to successfully execute a series of maneuvers that soon had them standing relatively unscathed at the rear of Chrys's car. She opened the trunk for Denali to deposit her bags, then motioned her niece to get in.

"It's a lot warmer down here than in Kansas City," Denali commented offhandedly. "Things are barely starting to green at home." She choked on the last word, thinking herself probably the biggest of fools to pine away for something she was certain to lose. She wanted so much for things to just go on the way they had been. In the past, if she couldn't have answers, she'd had Cambry and Azalea and Chrys. She'd had her thin thread of a connection to Rose, and she had an entire lifetime of memories. Dallas represented nothing but the future.

Chrys had started the car but sat motionless, staring at Denali. When Denali finally realized what her aunt was doing, she offered a sheepish grin. "This isn't the easiest transition I've ever made."

Chrys nodded. "I know. But you have to accept what is going to be. Maybe once you're a little more familiar with things around here, you won't feel so overwhelmed. Dallas is a great city. There's always so much to do." Chrys backed the Mercedes up and headed out of the parking lot. "There's the symphony, museums, operas, theatre, you name it. There are enough restaurants, shopping malls, and specialty stores to positively delight the heart of any female."

Denali tried to smile, but in truth she couldn't care less. She kept thinking of what she was losing, and although she had promised herself to be forward in thought, she longed for the comforts of home.

They remained silent until after Chrys had paid the parking attendant and pulled out onto the busy interstate. The flatlands that surrounded them with car dealerships and strip malls seemed less than enticing to Denali. She tried not to let herself become judgmental about the place before having a real chance to experience it, but it was hard.

"We have to talk, you know." Chrys's voice was edged with concern.

"Yes." Denali knew what was coming without Chrys offering a single word of explanation.

"Azalea tells me that you have some contrived notion of approaching Father. Is that true?"

"I think he owes me, don't you?"

"It doesn't matter what I think, Denali. What matters is that he refuses to see you. He wants that to be clear, and he wants you to understand that this is the way it will be."

"Then why did he bring me here? Why did he close the Kansas City office and leave my people without work? He offered me a job here before this local group requested me for their project. Why did he do that if he didn't want me here?"

"I suppose he was trying to be fair about things. After all, you are family."

"I might just as well not be," Denali countered. "I know his plans. I figured them out for myself. Either way, he wins. He manages to inflict the punishment of running my career, all in order to pay me back for some imagined wrongdoing. Well, frankly, Chrys, I've had as much of this as I'm going to take. He's my grandfather whether he likes it or not. He's going to see me, and he's going to answer some very big questions. Then, and only then, will I decide whether or not I'm taking on this project."

Chrys remained completely in control, unlike Azalea, who would have been fretting at this point. Denali admired her ability to remain calm and collected in the face of crisis. Chrys allowed the silence to settle around them before simply replying, "No. You can't do things that way."

Denali wanted to counter with her own insistence, but Chrys was already holding up a hand to still any protest. "Hear me out."

"All right."

"I don't know why you have to insist on confronting Father with this obsession of yours. Rose is dead and that's that. There is no great mystery. No movie of the week. No skeletons to jump out from the closet. She's dead and you're here. Father has never forgiven Rose for dying, or you for living. That's it, Denali. Those are the cold, hard facts of life. You know he would have traded you a million times over if it would have brought Rose back to life. You have to accept that it has nothing whatsoever to do with you personally. It's the death of his child he can't bear. Accept it, Denali. We can't go through life expecting everyone to love us."

Denali fought to keep her emotions under control. She didn't want to cry, not like this, anyway. "I know he doesn't love me. But I don't understand why, in the absence of love, Richard Deveraux deems it necessary to hate me."

"I just told you why he feels the way he does. Rose was everything to him, Denali. She represented his last link to your grandmother, and when Mother died, Rose became everything to all of us. She was spoiled and pampered and adored. All the things that you should have had by a mother and father of your own. Azalea and I tried to give you that, even knowing as we did that it would never be enough. It would never be a proper substitute for the mother and father you were denied."

Denali stared out the window, not even seeing the buildings and traffic that flashed by. She saw, instead, the stone walls of Cambry. She saw herself as a little girl, wandering the grounds, wondering why other children had mothers and fathers while she only had her two aunts. "But maybe he can tell me—"

"He won't tell you anything," Chrys interrupted. "Not even if he is keeping something from you. He'll walk away from you before ever speaking a single word of acknowledgment. You know it's true, so why continue to torment yourself? Do the job he sent for you to do. When that's finished, go from there. Just leave him out of it. Please, Denali, for Azalea's and my sakes, let it go."

Denali hadn't even noticed that they had turned off the interstate. Parkways evolved into busy city streets that wound their way past a myriad of businesses and ever-extending high-rise buildings toward the center of town. Denali tried to focus on what Chrys demanded she do, but her heart was protesting the idea of letting Richard Deveraux off the hook. This had almost become a crusade to Denali, and to put it behind her now was to lose a part of herself.

Chrys pulled up under the canopy of a high-rise and stopped. "Well, we're here," she said rather hesitantly. She looked at Denali, her face fixed with an expression of expectation.

Denali grew uncomfortable. She knew the situation demanded some form of truce or compromise, but in her heart she wanted things done her way for once. She wanted Richard Deveraux to answer for the pain he'd given her over the years. Instead, her aunt was quietly telling her that she couldn't even have that small satisfaction. Unfastening her seat belt, Denali took a deep breath. "I'll do my best, okay? That's all I have to give you. I won't make promises I can't keep, so take it or leave it."

Chrys smiled. "At least you didn't refuse me." She patted Denali's hand. "It's going to work out. You'll see."

"I suppose it has to," Denali replied. "You've been telling me that for the last twenty years or so. Surely by the odds alone, sooner or later you'll have to be right."

Denali's first impression of LaTour was that she was entering a very stately hotel. In the latter part of the previous decade, McKinney Avenue had become a favorite with the trendy set of Dallas. Expensive restaurants, antique stores, and art galleries had popped up to appeal to the new-money crowds. LaTour, once the playground of the elite, found itself made over and reestablished as a stopping-over place for the next generation of prosperous social climbers. The lobby, tastefully decorated in Italian modern with Donghia chairs and tables of highly polished yew wood, gave an instant air of quality and prestige.

Glancing over to the concierge's desk, Denali had the impression she should check in. She looked to her aunt as if to question the situation, but Chrys took charge and quickly introduced her to the staff.

"Kevin, Charles, I'd like you to meet my niece, Denali Deveraux. Denali will reside with me for a time." Then, turning to Denali, she smiled and added, "These are two of the most competent young men around. No matter what I need, they always seem quite capable of assisting me."

Denali smiled at the two men. They appeared to be around her age and were attired in dress slacks, shirts, and ties. "It's nice to meet you."

They exchanged complimentary greetings before Chrys announced she'd be back for her car directly after seeing to Denali. As Chrys led the way through the lobby doors and down a short corridor, she explained to Denali how to find her way around.

"If you get lost, just go back to the front desk and ask directions. They're happy to help you here, and they get paid plenty to make themselves available to help you."

Denali nodded, still not certain how she felt about her new surroundings. Everything seemed designed to keep her from having to concern herself with anything—large or small. It was much the same way her entire life had been lived, and Denali wasn't at all convinced that this was a good way to do things.

They entered the elevator and shared their ride in silence. Denali watched the floors click by and was suddenly reminded that they were heading for the twenty-first floor. Azalea had told her about the apartment's lofty perch, but up until now Denali had never really considered living so far off the ground.

"Don't you ever worry about fires?" she asked without thinking.

"What?"

"Fires. Storms. Don't you ever worry about being up on the twenty-first floor of a building? I mean, you do get tornadoes in Texas, just like we get them in Kansas."

Chrys laughed. "There are so many other things in life to worry about, I guess it was easy to trust God with this one. Being up high also has its benefits. We're removed from the rest of the world. Standing out on the balcony, you can peer down on the world below and somehow feel separated from the noise and strife. You can look out across the city, and it's pure pleasure to behold the variety of architectural stylings. You'll appreciate the artistry of it, just as I did. Ah, here we are."

From the elevator, they stepped out into a carpeted hallway that boasted a black marble table. Atop the table was an orchid plant with its lovely lavender and white flowers in full bloom. They were reflected in the mirror that graced the wall behind them, further adding to the atmosphere of elegance and beauty.

"Nice," Denali said, captivated by the newness of it all.

"I hope you'll like your new home. We don't have yards and yards of space, but we tried to utilize what we do have to our best advantage."

Denali knew that her aunt was quite masterful in this area. Chrys seemed to have an inherent capability to turn even the tiniest of nooks into a cozy resting place and had proven her abilities many times over at Cambry. Remembering the hominess of that turn-of-the-century home, Denali found herself actually quite eager to see what her aunt had managed to do with the LaTour apartment. When Chrys opened the door, revealing black-and-white Italian marble tile on the floor, Denali smiled knowingly. What else should a proper foyer have?

"Welcome home," Chrys said in a rather proud way that instantly made Denali feel glad she'd come.

"It's beautiful," Denali declared, following her aunt through the door.

"Why don't you just drop your bags there," Chrys said, pointing to the floor beside an antique receiving table. "I'll give you the tour of the place first, and then you can settle in while I run a few errands."

"All right," Denali replied, looking around her, eager to absorb everything at once.

"This is the main living area. You'll recognize many of the pieces as ones we had up in Cambry," Chrys began. "Of course, the sofa is new. I handpicked the fabric for it and nearly went mad before finding just the right thing."

"It's beautiful," Denali replied, running a hand gently over the gold-colored raw silk. The sofa was covered with a variety of throw pillows, and Denali could easily imagine herself curled up there with a good book.

"The Lalique crystal vase is new," Chrys announced, pointing at the coffee table. "But you'll recognize the other vases." Indeed, Denali did recognize the Sevres porcelain, which dated back to the mid–1800s. Azalea had shipped them down only days before Denali's departure.

"I like the way you've given the room a feeling of elegance while at the same time managing to make it look so comfortable."

"Well, we have to live here," Chrys said, unbuttoning the jacket of her pale pink suit coat. "You know Azalea and I have always said it's one thing to have beauty around you but another to leave it standing as a useless artifact."

Denali glanced around, taking in the Aubusson and Biedermier chairs. They played off nicely with the gold-colored sofa, while delicately carved tables of walnut contrasted the effect.

"This is beautiful," Denali commented, gingerly touching the inlaid porcelain work of a small walnut writing desk. Touching had always been quite imporant to Denali. It somehow connected her to the piece and even to the artist responsible.

"I found that little treasure during my lunch hour one day. Isn't it a great piece?" Chrys said, obviously pleased that Denali had noticed. Without waiting for comment, Chrys continued. "Here's the balcony." She slid back the glass door and breathed deeply of the fresh air. "Feel free to enjoy yourself for a bit of sun and solitude. Summer won't offer you as much of a desire to linger here, especially on the very humid days, but nighttime can be magnificent."

Denali walked out through the sliding glass door and marveled at the city skyline. "I feel as though we're on top of the world looking down." The city didn't seem quite so intimidating from twenty-one stories up.

"In here," Chrys said, quickly resuming the tour, "we have the dining room. You'll remember this table from Cambry's breakfast room."

And indeed Denali did remember it. Remembered, too, her sorrow when the antique English refractory table had been loaded up and taken to Dallas. It was the first time she had realized the seriousness of her grandfather's intent.

"I found a beautiful sideboard to go along with it. The store will deliver it Saturday—thus the empty spot," Chrys said, motioning to the corner.

Denali nodded and tried to take it all in. They passed through the kitchen and into the hallway where the first of two bathrooms was pointed out.

"And in here is Azalea's and my bedroom," Chrys announced.

Denali noted the matching twin beds with their ornate gothic designs. "Wow!" she exclaimed, running a hand along the peaks and valleys of the footboard. "These are very impressive."

"Aren't they?" Chrys replied. "I got them for a song. I'll show you where. I simply love to shop for antiques in this town. Now come back this way and I'll show you to your room. Then I positively must run. I know you'll probably want to acquaint yourself with the place and with your new project. I have the dossier in the other room. It should show you what they want and what they don't want," Chrys announced, taking Denali by the arm and leading her back down the hall. "Here we are."

Denali stepped through the door and felt the perfection of the room engulf her. A highly polished walnut sleigh bed casually graced one wall, while a writing table accompanied by matching bookcases decorated the opposite side of the room. The real attraction was the huge window that faced out to greet the city. Denali was enchanted. "It's wonderful."

"I hoped you'd like it. The bed only arrived last week, and as you've probably figured out, I've developed a real passion for walnut wood. The bedspread is Chinese petit point."

Once again, Denali found herself needing to touch the object in question. The reds and golds of the graceful spread appealed to her artistic sense of color, especially when coordinated against the dark wood and matching draperies. Denali found great satisfaction in her aunt's decorating taste.

"I'm still working on the place, so don't necessarily expect things to stay the same way for long. Once Azalea gets down here and starts in on things, we may find the entire apartment redone."

Denali laughed and shook her head. "Well, neither one of you need to change anything about this room. It's perfect." She glanced around to find that even the paintings on the wall met with her approval.

"I'm glad you like it." Chrys glanced at her watch, rebuttoned her jacket, and motioned Denali to follow. "On the desk in the living room is the Omni Missions project dossier. You'll find everything you need there. Go over it and read the notes from the meeting. I'm sure you'll see for yourself where the last team went wrong. Monday you'll go to the office and meet with your new team."

"But I thought I'd get right down there—"

"No," Chrys said flatly. "Not today. There's nothing to be gained by going in on a Friday. I'll set up a meeting between you and the client for Monday morning."

Denali decided that rather than argue, she'd let it drop. "Whatever you say, Aunt Chrys."

Chrys smiled and nodded. "That's my girl."

The day passed quietly from morning to afternoon. Denali pored over the details of the Omni Missions project and instantly saw the tragic mistakes made by the other team. Obviously no one had bothered to really work with the board members. There were no notes of conversations made prior to the disastrous meeting, and what few comments were scribbled from team members during the design creation were sketchy and useless. By three-thirty, Denali had had enough. She also realized that she was quite hungry.

Getting up, she went to the kitchen and snooped around. Her efforts were soon rewarded with the makings of a ham and cheese sandwich. She threw this together, grabbed a can of cola from its hiding place in the bottom drawer of the frig, and walked out onto the balcony.

The afternoon sun was warm, almost too warm, but Denali forced herself to take a seat on the wicker settee and watch the world beyond. She ate in silence, wondering if she'd be able to perform the miracle of saving the Omni Missions project. It crossed her mind that maybe she wasn't intended to save the project, and the prospect of this consumed her thoughts while she tried to enjoy her lunch.

"If he wants me to fall flat," she mused, "he certainly picked one doozy of a project to accomplish the task with."

She ravenously ate the sandwich and gave serious thought to making another one, but, upon rising from the settee, she caught sight of a lovely park directly across the street from LaTour. Closer inspection proved that it wasn't a park at all, but a cemetery. Denali had always loved to wander through cemeteries, perhaps because her mother was dead, and visiting her headstone always seemed to give Denali some moderate feeling of comfort. Maybe it was because in the solitude and quiet of such places, Denali could let down her guard and be herself. Forgetting about the second sandwich, Denali decided instead to take a short walk through the grounds and see if this place might offer her a haven in the future.

Realizing she had no key, Denali left the door unlocked. Surely in a place as well guarded and maintained as LaTour, she could manage to leave for a short time without locking the place. She memorized her path on the way to the elevator and found herself in the lobby before she knew it.

Spying Kevin at the front desk, Denali hesitantly stopped to make sure of her directions. "I saw a cemetery from the balcony. I wondered if you'd tell me how I could get there from here?"

Kevin smiled. "Just walk right around to your left. You can't miss the gates."

"Thanks," Denali answered and turned to leave. "Oh, if my aunt Chrys returns, would you tell her I'll be right back?"

"Sure thing."

Denali smiled and left the building with a deep sense of satisfaction. She was taking herself out and about, ignoring the fears she might have assigned a city as big as Dallas, disregarding her own protected past. She was nearly ready to burst into song at the pure pleasure of enjoying the moment when she rounded the corner without looking and was instantly knocked to the ground.

Seven

Denali hit the ground bottom first. The impact so startled her that she was momentarily frozen. It took only seconds, however, to discover that she was hopelessly entangled with another human being, as well as a face-licking cocker spaniel. It was the sudden friendliness of the dog that made Denali laugh.

Her jean-clad legs were wrapped together with the binding red nylon of the cocker's leash, and, while the dog seemed perfectly content to jump up and down on Denali, the dog's owner was already growling impatiently to be rid of this inconvenient nuisance.

"I'm so sorry," Denali said, trying to pet the dog and free her feet at the same time.

"Yeah, whatever," the man muttered, already on his feet and seeking to find a way to untangle his animal. He roughly pushed Denali's hands away and pulled at the leash.

As it tightened on her ankle, Denali let out a yelp of protest. "That hurts," she said, this time pushing his hands aside. "Let me do it." She reached for the leash as the cocker danced around her. "It's okay, boy, I've almost got it."

"Look, I haven't got time to play around all day. Forget about the dog and just get that leash straightened out."

Denali's hand refused to move. She looked up slowly to find a harshly handsome face staring down at her. Letting her gaze travel back down to the man's feet, Denali had to swallow hard to steady her nerves and keep feelings of both anger and awe from showing in her voice or expression. The man was gorgeous. Built like a dark-headed Adonis, he stood tanned and lean in his jogging shorts and tank top.

"I am sorry," she said again and managed to make her hands finally work at untangling the leash. She freed herself and got to her feet, no thanks to Adonis. Rubbing her sore backside, Denali waited for the man to say something less hostile. Maybe even apologetic. Instead, he yanked on the friendly cocker's leash and growled out a command to heel.

"Maybe if you weren't quite so—" Denali began, but the words stuck in her throat as the man threw her an intimidating, clearly irritated look.

"If you'd been watching where you were going," he began, "this never would have happened. Now the dog is excited and completely out of control, and I won't have you stand here and tell me what to do in order to rectify the situation."

"Maybe if you weren't so rude," Denali countered, knowing that she was losing control of her temper, "the dog would be more inclined to toe the line."

"I have little reason to suspect or care that my rudeness either meets with or goes against Dusty's standards. He's not even my dog. I'm just giving him a run for a friend who's out of town. Now, if you'll excuse me—"

"Not hardly," Denali countered. She found Dusty jumping at her feet and turned her attentions to the dog. "You don't deserve excusing, but Dusty, who was the truly injured party in this whole affair, deserves my sincere apologies. Don't you, boy?" she questioned in a softened voice.

The man reined the dog back. "Look, lady, I haven't got time for this. You've already done your utmost to disrupt my day. Now, if you don't mind, I've got places to be."

"Well, la-di-da," Denali said, straightening up. With hands on hips, she eyed the stranger critically. She found herself notably fearful of the steely blue eyes and the expression of rage that seemed to emanate from them, but nevertheless she managed to stand her ground. "You're just as much to blame for this as I am," she said, feeling her own eyes begin to narrow in anger. "If you had bothered to watch where you were going or to slow down when rounding that corner, neither one of us would have been waylaid for more than a moment in passing. I've apologized for my indiscretion and lack of attention, and while I don't expect someone of your caliber to understand the manner in which one makes an apology, I intend for you to know that I think you're easily the rudest man in all of Dallas. You'd do well to learn some manners from the dog."

"I'd rather deal with dogs any day than have my character wrongly assessed by a disgruntled female. At least the dog usually minds." With that, he gave a sharp pull on the leash and yanked the cocker behind him as he resumed his run.

"Well, of all the nerve," Denali said, watching the man as he jogged away.

She was still shaking her head as she crossed the street and entered the wrought iron gates of the cemetery. *Who did he think he was, anyway? He acted as though I had set out to ruin his day.* Denali tried to put it behind her, but her mind kept reliving the scene over and over. He certainly was a handsome man. Too bad his personality wasn't as nice to consider. She gave a sigh and decided to let it drop.

The cemetery drive beckoned her forward with lovely shade trees and a welcoming stillness that Denali found herself craving. Still rattled by her encounter, Denali took several long, slow breaths and forced herself to relax.

"Lord," she said, looking skyward, "what am I doing here?"

She turned back around to gaze at the high-rise she'd just come from. Denali was uncertain she could ever love this modern magnificence of stone and glass looming above her like a watchful sentry. Where Cambry welcomed her with open arms that seemed to envelop her with protective sanctuary, LaTour looked cold and indifferent to her plight. *Still,* she thought, looking back around her, *this is a wonderful cemetery, and I can walk here just like I could at Cambry.* It wasn't the same, but in some ways it was almost better. She didn't feel so alone here, whereas wandering around Cambry only served to remind her that although she might be striding where her mother had once walked, there was nothing left to cling to. No memory would rise up to fill her head with splendor of days long gone by. She had no personal memories of her mother. She lived solely on other people's memories.

Turning to walk down the shaded lane, Denali wondered at the people buried in the cemetery. Some of the stones were quite old, while others were fairly new. *Life insists on closure,* she thought and gently, almost lovingly touched a marble obelisk marked HAYES. All around her stood proof that she was not the only one to suffer loss in her young life. Here stood the graves of soldiers, mothers, fathers, sons, and daughters. Lonely reminders of lives once lived and now silenced.

The day was perfect, and the afternoon sun filtered down through the trees to warm her. Finding a marble bench, Denali sat down and relished the silence. "What should I do?" she questioned, her gaze searching out across the headstones.

She thought of the Omni Missions project and wondered what her grandfather was up to. She wondered, too, why Chrys had been so insistent that she remain here. There was a great deal of work to be done, and Denali hated having her plans delayed.

"It wasn't like they didn't know I was coming," Denali protested aloud. Somehow talking to herself in a cemetery didn't seem at all out of place. "I mean, they were the ones who sent for me. Maybe Grandfather didn't think I would come. Maybe Chrys had to go tell him that I'd truly made the journey."

She shook her head and, placing her hands on the cold marble, leaned back and crossed her legs at the ankles. "I'm twenty-five, almost twenty-six," she told the utter stillness. The cemetery was set in the middle of the busy uptown district, yet within the confines of those iron gates, quiet prevailed against the onslaught of daily life.

"Twenty-six isn't so very old," she assured herself. "But then again, it's only four more years until I'm thirty." This seemed to dampen her spirits. She thought of Anne Gilbert, her former assistant in Kansas City. Anne was thirty and had three beautiful children and a husband whom she adored. Gary, Anne's husband, practically worshiped the ground his wife walked on. He was constantly sending her notes and flowers or just showing up at the office to take her to lunch. And it wasn't as if Gary wasn't busy in his own right; he was, after all, a very successful real estate agent. Denali envied Anne and had confessed as much on more than one occasion.

"You should find someone, Denali," Anne had told her.

But Denali only shrugged off the advice. She was afraid to love anyone. Afraid to be rejected and left behind again. First it was her father, then her mother, then Grandfather. Soon, even though they would never admit it, her list would also include her aunts. Keeping those feelings within her, Denali found it a simple matter to refrain from finding that one special man. It was easier to guard her heart and never fall in love than to think about dealing with yet another desertion.

Still, Anne had the life that Denali would have chosen for herself had things been different. Had she known a mother and father's love, maybe she wouldn't have been so shy of becoming a parent herself. Had she at least had her grandfather's love, maybe she wouldn't be so terrified of men and what they represented to her.

This is foolish, she thought and got to her feet. She smoothed her hands down her jean-clad legs and looked around her. She had several choices of which way to go. Go right, and she would wind back around to the gates from which she'd entered the cemetery. To the left, she would walk into even deeper seclusion. Behind her and just to the right was yet another roadway that made its journey winding around several sections of headstones. It appeared to weave around and come back up to join the entrance road, so Denali chose this one in order to have some more moments of solitude.

She thought of the project again and smiled. She could already tell she was going to like this Hazel Garrison woman. She found a letter in the file, written by Hazel the day after the disastrous meeting with Richard Deveraux. The woman was unconcerned with impressing Denali's grandfather and made it clear that should Denali be unable to come up with reasonable plans for the park, she would not hesitate to take her business elsewhere. Denali could only imagine that this had irritated the old man to no end.

Shoving her hands deep into her pockets, Denali pondered the park for a moment. She considered the work she'd done in Missouri and realized that keeping matters simple seemed best in these situations. If Hazel Garrison liked the work done there, then Denali had no doubt in her mind that she could reach an agreeable solution for the Omni Missions project. However, if this was all just a setup . . .

She frowned and kicked at a rock. "Even if this is just a setup," she murmured, "I still have very little choice in the matter."

She tried not to believe that Hazel would purposefully deceive her. After all, she didn't even know the woman. It hardly seemed fair to judge her character on Richard Deveraux's merits.

"I suppose the best thing to do is call her," Denali told herself. "I've always been good at telling when people are lying to me, and I've always been a fairly good judge of character."

This made her reconsider the man she'd run into earlier. She had been instantly taken in by his looks, but his eyes were so cold, his expression so harsh. Here was a man who'd been through something very painful, something life-changing. Her aunts might have laughed at her surmising such a thing. After all, they'd merely had a momentary collision, not a real conversation or even a proper introduction. But Denali knew pain. Knew the look without having to be introduced. *That man was hurting,* she thought, *and I did nothing but snap at him and accuse him of rudeness.* Her pride had gotten the better of her, and she knew it.

Instantly she wished she could seek the man out and ask his forgiveness. It might not have mattered to him, and in all honesty, he'd probably not give her a second thought. Nevertheless, Denali wished she'd conducted herself with more kindness.

"I know what it is to be in pain," she whispered. "I know how it alters your perspective on life." Glancing back up at the building that was to be her home, Denali felt an aching inside her. "I've lost so much, Lord," she said in a barely audible voice. "Please help me to be content with what remains."

Eight

On Monday it poured rain from a thick wall of black clouds that seemed to settle down over the city like a dome. Denali tried not to think of it as a bad omen, but it couldn't help but dampen her spirits a little. She dressed carefully in one of her more conservative suits. The navy blue jacket was trimmed with a wide band of white on the lapel, and white buttons accented the front. It was just enough white to offset the sleek navy blue skirt and allow Denali to wear a gorgeous pair of navy-and-white pumps she'd acquired shortly before her move.

She slipped into the pumps and went to her aunt's bedroom to catch a quick view of herself in the full-length mirror. Satisfied that she looked professional but not too stuffy, Denali then shifted her attention to her hair.

"I think I'm going to cut it," she told Chrys after wrestling it into a French braid. "I mean, I'm almost twenty-six years old. Somehow, waist-length hair seems to be a sign of my long-lost youth."

Chrys laughed as she secured earrings to her ears. "You aren't that far from youth, my dear. Tell me how inappropriate long hair is when you're in your fifties or sixties."

Denali smiled. "Well, it's too hot for Dallas temperatures."

"I'll give you that. I wouldn't want to carry that mane around come August."

"Then that settles it. Set me up with your hair stylist as soon as possible, and we will remedy the problem."

Chrys nodded. "I'll call her from the office. Say, have you seen my briefcase?"

"It's by the front door. I put it there with my own." Denali grabbed a waiting glass of orange juice from the counter and raised it in a toast

66

to the day. "Well, here's to us and Omni Missions and an agreeable compromise."

"Here, here," Chrys agreed.

In spite of the heavy downpour outside, Denali felt confident of the project and of her position. What she wasn't confident about was the idea of meeting her grandfather. Downing the orange juice, she looked to Chrys.

"Will I get to meet him today?"

"Who?" Chrys asked, as though she hadn't any idea what Denali was talking about.

"You know very well who. Grandfather."

Chrys shook her head. "I told you before. He has a great many projects, and most of them will keep him busy and away from the office. He's in Los Angeles right now. Or at least he will be until Friday. Friday night there's an important client party that he's throwing—that is, if all goes well in California."

"Can I meet him then?" Denali asked hopefully.

"Absolutely not," Chrys said emphatically. "You aren't invited. But don't worry. There'll be plenty of other things to keep you busy."

"But I don't want to be busy with other things. I want to talk to my grandfather."

Chrys paused, her hand midway to the telephone. "Look, Denali, just play this one by the rules. Father has a great deal on his mind. Prove yourself with this new project, and *then* worry about getting in to talk to him about the past."

"It isn't just the past I want to talk about," Denali protested. "I want to talk to him about the future, as well. I even want to talk about the present."

Chrys shook her head and dialed the concierge. "You aren't invited, and that's that. Don't take it so personally. These aren't clients you will be dealing with anyway, so it isn't important that you be there."

Denali's feelings were still smarting by the time they'd driven through the rain to the heart of downtown Dallas. Fountain Place, home to multiple businesses including Fun, Inc., was located at the corner of Ross and Field. The green glass skyscraper seemed dull and dingy because of the rainstorm, but Chrys assured Denali it was generally a lovely sight.

They passed into the building from the underground parking and rode the elevator to the forty-third floor, where Denali would begin her new job.

"We have offices on the floor below, as well," Chrys was telling her, "but the forty-third is devoted to Fun, Inc."

Denali tried to take it all in as a rush of people moved in and out of the elevator. Some smiled and nodded; most just got on in a preoccupied daze and looked up at the numbers in anticipation of their floor.

"Here we are," Chrys said, escorting Denali off the elevator.

Just ahead of them, stenciled glass doors welcomed Denali to Fun, Inc. *Pity that Grandfather couldn't do the same*, she thought. She tried to put such thoughts from her mind, but it wasn't easy. Especially considering that she was here by his order—not because he wanted her, but because someone else did.

The office looked very rich and very masculine. A perfect fit for her grandfather. She knew him to be a no-nonsense, all-work-and-no-pleasure kind of man, at least from what Chrys and Azalea had told her. This office seemed testimony to support that fact, with its ash paneling and ebony trim. There were lovely buffed brass sconces on the walls, as well as a variety of beautifully framed art.

"Father believes in supporting the artistic community," Chrys said, as if noticing where Denali's gaze had led her. "He plays patron to many a struggling young artist."

"How good of him," Denali said sarcastically, but Chrys paid her little attention.

"Good morning, Chrys," the receptionist said to Chrys. "I have your plane tickets ready and your itinerary typed."

"Plane tickets?" Denali questioned her aunt.

"Yes. I have to fly to New Orleans this afternoon. I'll be gone for two, maybe three days. Oh, and before I forget," she said, reaching into her purse, "here's the key to the apartment."

Denali took the key and stared at it for a moment. She couldn't help but be confused by her aunt's sudden declaration of departure. "I can't believe you're going to leave me alone," she finally said as Chrys surveyed the articles handed her by the receptionist.

"I won't be leaving you alone," Chrys said, stuffing the papers into her briefcase. "You've been assigned a very competent partner. He's going to be available to you day and night. In fact, Father told me to encourage the two of you to get to know each other very well. It will help you in your work on the project. Believe me, it's much easier to plot and plan when you feel comfortable with your partner."

"But I don't want a partner. Well, that isn't necessarily what I mean," Denali replied. "It's just that no one here knows what took place on the Maranatha project, and to take up working with a stranger—"

"Don't worry about it," Chrys interrupted. "Just wait and see what happens. Oh, by the way, this is Sharon. Sharon handles all our incoming visitors and directs calls. She's also doubling as my secretary this week because my assistant's out on vacation until next Monday. Sharon, this is Denali Deveraux, my niece."

"I'll be taking your telephone messages," Sharon told her and added with a conspiratorial wink, "They still haven't seen fit to equip this office with voice mail, but we get by."

Denali smiled. "It's nice to meet you, Sharon."

"Come along, Denali," Chrys said, already moving down the office corridor with quick, determined strides. "Your office is down this hall and to the left. This is the secretarial pool, or whatever politically correct name you want to call it by."

Denali noticed that the area maintained the same Italian Renaissance flavor as the reception area. She also noted additional offices beyond her own but decided to investigate the details about their occupants at a later time. She followed Chrys into the wood-paneled office and immediately liked it. It was small, with an expensive-looking desk of ebony trimmed in yew wood. She liked the way it played contrast to the walls, and the buffed brass desk lamp carried on the theme of the hall sconces. In the corner a drafting table and an ebony and yew armoire stood ready to receive her attention. Denali pulled open one of the armoire's doors and found it filled with the necessary drawing supplies and drafting equipment.

"You'll note that the size is rather small and that there's only one other chair besides your desk chair. You can work privately with one of the associates in here, but we don't meet clients in our offices. We always conduct business in one of the four conference rooms. This way we have recording equipment in place, and Sharon has an intercom to the room—it's just our procedure for doing business. Your staff meetings will also be held there. Your grandfather deplores having people in his private offices, and therefore that's the rule for the entire office."

"Of course," Denali said with undisguised sarcasm. "Where does that door lead?" she questioned, suddenly seeing the door just off to the left of her desk.

"That adjoins to your partner's office. Father put you in here on purpose, knowing that the closer you were to each other, the easier it would be to complete this project. You have to understand, Denali, time is of the utmost importance."

"I do understand. I just wish I didn't have to work with a stranger. At least let me call on one of my people from Kansas City. They know how the Maranatha project went and—"

"It's out of my hands, Denali. And out of yours. You need to forget about doing things your way and just adhere to what your grandfather has mapped out for you." Acquiescing to the painful reminder, Denali nodded. "Good. Now, the conference rooms are in the other direction, with the exception of Father's main conference room, which seldom gets used by anyone but him. Just bring your things and I'll take you around, and then"—she glanced at her watch—"it'll be time for your meeting."

"You won't be there?" Denali questioned, following her aunt into the hall.

"No. I'll make your introductions to the rest of the staff, but after that I have to get going. I know you just got here, but if you want, I'll leave you the Mercedes so you have something to get around in while I'm away."

"No," Denali said, knowing that Dallas driving would be too much to take in all at once. "I'll just take cabs."

"Suit yourself. I suppose we really should make some arrangement to get your car down here. After all, you're going to have to experience city driving sooner or later. You'll go broke taking taxis. Of course, there's always the buses."

Denali smiled at the people she passed and made note of their re-actions. She couldn't help but wonder what, if anything, her grandfather had said to his staff about her arrival. Nervously, she began to worry that perhaps he'd spoken ill of her. Perhaps he wouldn't care how it affected the workings of the office. But even as this thought came to her, Denali shrugged it off. Her grandfather was all business. He might hate her, but he loved Fun, Inc. He wouldn't risk losing business over her.

"Here we are," Chrys said as they entered a large conference room. "Everyone, I'd like you to meet my niece, Denali Deveraux."

Denali glanced at the four people who were already seated at the table. The men quickly rose in greeting, and Denali swallowed back her fears and smiled.

"This is Jim Cannon. He has the office across from yours. Jim is our executive engineer. He handles a staff on the floor below and deals as an engineering and contracting consultant."

Denali nodded. "It's nice to meet you, Mr. Cannon."

"Call him Jim," Chrys told her before the man could speak. "We're all on a first-name basis here."

"Nice to meet you, Denali. If I can help you in any way, just let me know."

"Thank you," she told the older man. She estimated his age to be somewhere in the late forties and immediately looked to his hand to detect whether or not he was married. A thin gold band marked his ring finger, and Denali smiled. "I see you're married."

Jim nodded. "Twenty-nine years."

"Impressive."

"Especially given that Jim's involved," a cute, pixieish woman said. They all laughed, and then the same woman beamed Denali a smile. "I'm Phoebe Myers, your assistant. I'm not married, but I am making plans in that direction. I'll be your right hand here at Fun, Inc. I'll keep you posted on the really important things—like when someone brings treats for their birthday or if Nieman's is having a really great sale."

Denali instantly like Phoebe. She was outgoing and bubbly with an obvious openness that Denali looked for in people. "Phoebe, it's definitely good to meet you. But I thought my partner was going to be a man."

"Phoebe is your secretary," Chrys said simply. "Or office assistant, as she prefers."

"Phoebe really doesn't care what she's called as long as she's paid," the only other man in the room chimed in. He extended his arm to shake hands. "I'm Dean Davis, married, one child—a boy. I'm one of the many architects on staff."

Denali smiled and shook hands. She was glad to find the staff so easygoing. "Nice to meet you. Are you my partner?"

He laughed. "Don't I wish. I'll bet you're infinitely easier to work with than my partner, Bob Kreiger. Oh, by the way, this is my secretary."

The middle-aged woman gave a tight-lipped smile to acknowledge Denali. "Carla Warner," the woman said.

"Glad to meet you, Carla."

"Well, now that that's taken care of," Chrys said, "I need to be on my way."

Denali turned sharply. "But what about my partner?"

Phoebe's nose wrinkled up. "Michael's been delayed, but he'll be here as soon as he can."

"Michael?" Denali questioned.

Chrys nodded. "Michael Copeland. He's one of our best."

Just then the phone beside Phoebe buzzed. She pressed the intercom button. "Yes?"

"The Omni Missions board is here," Sharon's voice announced.

"Oh, send them right in," Phoebe replied and switched off the phone. "I guess it's show time."

Denali felt her palms grow sweaty. She glanced around for the best vantage point and felt a small amount of relief when Phoebe gave Jim a nudge.

"Go sit over there with Dean so Denali can sit by me. I am her assistant, after all." Jim looked as if he might make some smart comeback, but already they could hear their clients coming down the hall. Quickly he jumped up and offered his chair to Denali before joining Dean on the opposite side of the table.

"Thanks," Denali said, slipping into the warm leather chair.

She'd no sooner sat down, however, than she found herself standing again in order to welcome the Omni Missions board members. "I'm glad you all braved the rain to make our meeting," she announced, meeting the gaze of an older woman who was unmistakably Hazel Garrison.

The woman smiled, and there was an instant, unspoken rapport between the two of them. "I'm Hazel Garrison."

"It's nice to meet you," Denali said, feeling as though that's all she'd said all day long. "I'm Denali Deveraux."

"I'm glad to finally meet you. I've heard many good things about you, and I've witnessed your work in Missouri. I was very impressed."

"Thank you."

There was a brief round of introductions before they all seated themselves at the oval conference table and began their meeting. Denali spread her papers out and took up a yellow legal pad and pen. "I've looked over the entire file, including the proposal that my grandfather offered you. I'm sorry I wasn't called in on the project earlier in order to save you some time, but now that I'm here, I'd like to fully understand what you're looking for in a theme park and resort."

Hazel opened her mouth to speak, but just then there was a commotion at the conference room door.

"Sorry I'm late," the newcomer announced in a gruff voice that sounded insincere.

Denali held her breath and looked in stunned surprise at the man. "You!" Denali barely breathed. It was Adonis. Her brutally handsome, very rude jogger. She was unwillingly taken back to that moment when they'd collided on the pavement outside of LaTour. For a moment the man appeared just as stunned as she was, but he quickly covered up any discomfort with a self-assured nod.

The Omni board members were clearly nonplussed, and Denali immediately realized she'd have to make introductions and act as though nothing was amiss. To do otherwise would make her appear incompetent and rude.

"Mrs. Garrison, this is—" she paused and looked to Michael to finish the introduction.

He closed the conference room door, then moved forward to take the chair beside Denali. "Michael Copeland. I'm working with Ms. Deveraux on your project."

His expression was stern, yet there was something very charming and so totally in control that it stunned Denali. She took a deep breath to steady her nerves. "Mrs. Garrison was just about to explain what the board has in mind for their theme park."

Michael met her gaze and nodded. His steely blue eyes pierced her facade of cool indifference, demanding from her something she wasn't yet ready to give. She resented the fact that he'd taken the seat beside hers. Resented that he was close enough for her to smell the deep, musky scent of his cologne. She found herself annoyingly captivated by long, tanned fingers that reached out to take up a copy of the old proposal.

"Please continue, Mrs. Garrison. I certainly didn't mean to interrupt."

Hazel nodded. "As I've tried to explain before, we're looking for a tasteful, respectful, Christian-based resort. We want to appeal to clientele from all over the world, to offer a spiritual haven and resting place for those who might desire a less secular setting."

"In other words, no beer, no rock concerts, no scantily dressed park attendants?" Michael asked, perfectly serious.

"To say the least," Hazel countered.

"And your targeted age group?" Denali questioned, struggling hard to regain her focus.

"We'd like to appeal to everyone. All age groups," Hazel replied. "I want an area for young children and their road-weary parents. I want attractions for boisterous teens and their endless energy. I want it to be inviting to the romantic young couple as well as the senior citizen. This park should have a balance of something for everyone."

Denali nodded. "Do you prefer it sectioned off, or should it blend together? In other words, should the park strive for an atmosphere that brings folks together as one big happy family?"

"I think some separation will be necessary. Obviously teenagers aren't going to appreciate rides designed for the very young child. However, I want a feeling of openness to it all. As I stated, we do want the regular theme park attractions, but we also want water events where folks can just swim and water slide, as well as a shaded resting place where people can sit back and enjoy doing nothing at all. Just like the park you designed in Missouri."

Denali was more confident now. Michael had had no part in her park for Maranatha, and she felt her courage bolstered by the fact that Hazel kept it as a ready reference. "Exactly like it?"

"In content, but not necessarily design," Hazel replied. "I suppose design would be better based on the landscape and the area we've chosen for the site. Oh, and as you can see for yourself, it encompasses a great deal more acreage."

"Yes," Denali agreed.

"I've just been brought in on this project," Michael announced, as though it were news to the Omni board. "But can you tell me what you didn't like in the old proposal?"

Hazel fixed her stare on him. "As I've said in the past, it would be easier to say what I did like, which wasn't much. I think the variety of rides was on target, but outside of that, I was sorely disappointed in this firm's lack of understanding. A Christian-owned-and-operated resort park does not need rides where the water parts or flowery sanctuaries called The Garden of Eden. I think if you spend time with Ms. Deveraux, you'll understand perfectly what we're about."

Denali felt almost smug in this praise. That is, until Michael looked her full in the face. His eyes narrowed, and the edges of his lips turned up in a hard, emotionless smile. "I'll be sure to spend time discussing it extensively."

Denali felt a flush of embarrassment wash over her. He was very nearly leering at her in the middle of a business meeting. Desperate to put his indescretion to an end, Denali turned to the rest of her team. "I'd welcome any questions you'd like to ask," she told them.

Several additional issues were discussed before Hazel and the rest of the board rose to make their exit. "I look forward to talking to you later this week," Hazel told Denali as they parted company at the door. "I'm sure this is going to work out just fine."

Denali waited until they were out of sight to close the door and return to the table. "I'd say that went pretty well," she told her team.

"From what I heard about the last time," Dean offered, "I'd say you very nearly had that old woman eating out of your hand."

"It's a matter of understanding her heart in this," Denali replied and took her seat. "It's difficult to explain if you aren't looking to understand the board's motives and desires."

"Which you perceive to be what?" Michael questioned.

"Isn't it obvious?" Denali stated, forcing herself to look him in the eyes. She knew that only by constantly exposing herself to his features and making him as familiar as possible would she be able to relax and treat him just like anyone else. He wasn't going to have the upper hand in this, nor was he going to unnerve her every time they met.

"You tell me," he said rather sarcastically. "I hear Christian-based, tasteful, and respectful, but The Garden of Eden is out."

Denali frowned and bit at her lower lip. She wanted to choose exactly the right words. "The park I designed in Missouri is the pattern from which they want to work. I have copies of the plans already available for each of you. There are theatres and outdoor stages for Christian performing artists. There are also shops that offer tasteful memorabilia from the region. The rides needn't be named after Bible characters or stories, but anything lewd or suggestive is way off base. You know as well as I do that oftentimes things get out of line in these places, and innuendo serves to attract less-desirable people."

"By less desirable, do you mean non-Christian?" Michael asked.

"Are you going to stand at the gate and ask if they're a card-carrying member of a Christian church or organization? Sounds like the 1950s all over again, only this time it's a Christian hunt instead of a Communist one."

Denali felt her ire rise. "Not at all, Mr. Copeland. However, I believe the thought was that this park would offer a respite from the routine ways of the world."

"Sort of a heaven away from heaven?" he asked with a laugh. "Maybe someone else could create the 'hell park' just across the street."

Denali had taken as much as she could. "I can't work with this man!" she said, reaching for her briefcase. She slammed it down on the table, gathered up her papers, and, much to everyone's surprise, got to her feet. "I can't work with you, Mr. Copeland!"

She headed for the door and into the hallway and immediately realized that in her anger she had no idea which way to go. She headed down the hall, only to find that she needed to go in the other direction. As she turned abruptly to retrace her steps, she managed to once again plow right into Michael Copeland.

Nine

D enali, wait," Michael commanded in a low, stern voice. His strong hands steadied her to keep her from falling.

Jerking away, she turned back around as if to find a way of escape, but Michael quickly acted. Seeing her plans, he grabbed her and pulled her into one of the empty conference rooms. Stunned, she stared up at him with huge, chocolate brown eyes and dark black lashes that showed the barest touch of makeup.

"Let go of me," she said, trying desperately to back away from him.

"I will, but I want you to hear me out," Michael said. Seeing her so angry, he had instantly realized that she was no wallflower to be pushed around the dance floor. Dealing with strong-willed, self-determined women had never been his forte. His charm and wit, when excercised, could usually serve to get him out of trouble. Of course, she hadn't witnessed his charm, he thought, and gave her a smile that he knew melted most women in their tracks. "Please," he said softly and released her.

"Why?" she asked, the anger in her voice quite evident.

"Because we need to better understand each other, and I need to apologize."

"Yes, you do," Denali said, eyeing him suspiciously. "But it won't change a thing. I can't work with someone like you."

Michael felt an uncomfortable panic rise inside him. He had to work with Denali—had to win her over and keep her occupied. Otherwise, there'd be no bonus and no way of getting his own business back up and running. And he wasn't about to jeopardize that—even if he had to eat his own pride to accomplish the task.

"Look, I know we got off to a bad start. Friday, well—" he paused, trying desperately to think of some excuse. "Friday was a bad day for me. Nothing went right from start to finish." She appeared unimpressed, so he continued. "I had bad news," he lied and waited for her reaction. Sure enough, he saw her face relax a bit. He had figured her like her grandfather but had hoped she might have some tenderness of heart. Apparently his hope was not misplaced. "I am sorry for the way I acted," he said, pouring on the charm. "I acted, as you put it, like the rudest man in Dallas. I was angry and hurt and well . . . I just didn't watch where I was going."

Denali continued to stare at him from where he'd backed her up against the conference table. He couldn't help but wonder what she was thinking. Somehow he had to endear himself to her. Or if not endear, at least make himself more acceptable to her than he was right now.

"I know this might sound hard to believe, but I went back looking for you," he lied again. This seemed to do the trick.

"You did?" she asked softly.

"Yes. I felt really bad. I still do. And whether or not you believe it," he continued, "I feel bad about upsetting you in there just now."

Denali shook her head. "It's just that this project seems important to my grandfather. He's never appointed me to work on one thing in particular, yet this time he did. All the projects I managed in Kansas City were of my own choosing. But this time my grandfather has requested me to take a project. I don't want to make a mess of this project and fail him."

He nodded. "Nor do I," he said, knowing his reasons were far less altruistic than hers. He could just see that seventy thousand flying right out the window if she rejected him as a partner. Not only that, but she was incredibly good-looking, and the thought of wining and dining her suddenly didn't seem so unappealing. No strings attached. No entanglement of the heart to worry about, and all the while someone else picked up the tab. Who could ask for anything more?

She seemed to be relaxing, so he tried a new maneuver. "Look, could we sit down and talk this through? I mean, this project is important to me, as well. I can't say that I totally understand it, but I want to make this work. You seem like a very reasonable, very good-natured person."

She tensed, and he wondered why. Why, when he'd complimented her, had she put up another wall? She allowed him to pull out a high-backed leather chair for her and, with great reluctance showing through her facade of indifference, sat down to hear him out.

"I think you misunderstood me in there," Michael began.

"I don't think I misunderstood you at all," Denali countered, her voice sounding stressed. "You obviously have a disregard for spiritual matters, or you would not have acted that way."

Michael shrugged. "I think spiritual matters are better left on an individual level, not a corporate one."

Denali crossed her arms and glared at him. "They can work together."

"I doubt that very seriously," he said flatly. "You can't discriminate and hire only born-again Christians. Besides, people can tell you until the sun goes down that they are Christians, and it doesn't mean a thing." His words were laced with bitterness, but he didn't care.

"You don't respect my feelings on this matter, and neither did the previous team respect Hazel Garrison's feelings. You don't know anything about building your life on the foundation of Christian beliefs, or you wouldn't act the way you are now."

"My, my," he said, forgetting momentarily about wooing her. "You certainly sound the prideful authority on Christendom. For your information, I know plenty about the foundations of the belief. I'm less impressed by the living actions of its followers."

"So you aren't a Christian," Denali said in an accusing manner.

Michael detested feeling as though he were on the witness stand. It was immaterial to him whether Denali and her client were Christians or Buddhists or Muslims. Such nonsense no longer interested him. He'd trusted God once, believed in all the things they said to believe in, but nevertheless his life had fallen apart.

"I don't believe it's any of your business, Ms. Deveraux, and that is exactly my point."

"My point, too," Denali said, starting to get to her feet. "And exactly why I plan to remove you from this project."

"You're firing me on the grounds of religious beliefs?" Michael questioned rather snidely. "Do you know how big of a lawsuit this might well constitute? Imagine my keeping this place tied up in litigation for, say, two or three years—maybe even more—and then ending up with a multi-million-dollar settlement. Talk about failing your grandfather."

Denali paled and sat back down. It was exactly the response he'd hoped for. Once again, he felt like he had gained some minor portion of territory in their battle. She looked up at him, her expression teetering between anger and what he could only surmise was hurt.

"Why are you doing this to me?" she finally asked. "You don't even know me, and you certainly don't know this project. I only want to do my job and be done with it, but your rudeness and lack of ability to play fair is really starting to grate on my nerves." As she spoke, her voice seemed to strengthen, and Michael took a step back when she got to her feet and stared at him with a hard, determined look. "If you insist on remaining on this project, I will expect you to take your directions from me. Mrs. Garrison has already expressed her expectations, and I have the know-how to create the park she desires.

"I did not demand that you take on my religious beliefs, nor would I fire you because you aren't a Christian," Denali continued. "However, neither will I brook insult from you for the fact that my life has been built on a firm Christian foundation. I hold those truths to be dear and valuable. Believe what you will, but it would indeed help matters in this case if you at least understood the thinking, beliefs, and considerations of this particular group of Christians."

She walked toward the door and threw him one last angry look. "I still plan to speak to my grandfather on this matter. He doesn't return until Friday, however, so I suppose I'll have to endure your presence on this project until I can make the request to have you removed. Oh," she added, almost as an afterthought, "don't think you can turn on your charm and use your good looks to impress me. I don't think much of you right now, especially having witnessed your demeaning attitude. You won't gloss this over with a few slick words, no matter how well thought-out and placed those words are. I don't intend to have to put up with this for any reason."

She walked through the door and slammed it shut behind her, leaving Michael to wonder what his next move should be. He was stunned that she hadn't fallen at his feet like most of the women he worked with. He knew he was attractive, and therefore it wasn't even encouraging to him that she had mentioned his good looks. At least she hadn't said he was repulsive, but he had a feeling she probably felt repulsed by him. No, she was only stating the obvious and, even at that, wasn't doing so to impress or smooth talk him. She was merely laying the groundwork for the game. Setting up the rules and telling him what she would and would not accept as a wild card.

Frowning, Michael realized that one way or another he had to reach her. Had to make her see that he was worthy of her time and attention. Otherwise, when Richard returned on Friday, he wouldn't just dismiss Michael from the project. He'd fire him from Fun, Inc., and that simply couldn't happen.

Ten

Denali arrived by taxi at the Beverly Drive address of her grand-father's home. Paying the driver, she was surprised when a smartly-dressed valet opened the door of the cab and offered to assist her from the vehicle. He was dressed in a style that seemed nearly as fashionable as the guests around him. Starched white linen shirt, black silk bow tie, and red brocade vest topping off black trousers and highly polished black shoes. Denali tried not to be overly impressed, but in truth she was. She might have always known wealth, but she wasn't used to parties of this caliber, and for a moment she wondered if she could hold her own.

"Thank you," she said, trying not to give off any hint of her un-invited status. Remembering the company being honored here tonight, Denali swallowed back her nervousness and said, "I'm here for the Talupa Corporation party."

The valet nodded and pointed the way to the entry court where several other people were greeting each other and passing into the house. She had purposefully arrived nearly a half hour into the party in order to be able to just mingle in with others. It looked as though that plan had worked.

"Thank you again."

She let out a breath and bolstered her courage. The first hurdle was past her. Not that she'd really expected the valet to give her an escort off the property. Still, she felt strengthened by his congeniality. Moving toward the house, Denali gazed up in appreciation of the well-lit Tudor home. Her aunt had called it "Tex-English" and said it was a lovely home, although only half the size of Cambry. The door was opened to her after a single knock, and a uniformed man, obviously in charge of ushering in the guests, merely nodded in welcome and extended a gloved hand to point the way.

She smiled and settled her nerves. Hurdle number two was now behind her. *I guess it pays to dress the part*, she thought, catching a quick glance of her profile as she passed a gilded mirror in the huge, open foyer. Her dress, sleek and black, was straight out of a New York fashion house. The matte satin felt good against her skin, and the draped neckline and form-fitting lines of the gown accented her figure in the best possible ways. This, coupled with her wonderful new layered hairstyle—cut just below the shoulders and now curled and artfully pinned atop her head—gave Denali the confidence of being a force to be reckoned with. She felt good and knew herself to be on equal footing with the others in the room. Keeping this in mind, Denali pressed forward in her search for Richard Deveraux.

"Good evening," a tuxedo-clad man said as she passed by. He gave her a thorough once-over before allowing his gaze to rest on her face.

"Good evening," Denali replied, giving a curt nod. She recognized immediate interest in his eyes, and although he was quite a dashing figure with his gold hair and winning smile, Denali wanted no further delays in reaching her grandfather. "Can you tell me where I might find our host?"

The man nodded. "He's in there somewhere. I saw him once, so I know he made it back. Are you with Fun, Inc.?"

Nodding, Denali ignored his obvious desire to continue the conversation and excused herself. Directly ahead, an ornately carved staircase graced the foyer. Although it had been roped off with a red velvet braid, Denali felt herself drawn to the grandeur and beauty. Reaching out, she ran her fingers across the scrolling trim of the bannister post and sighed. Her grandfather lived in this house. The interior furnishings and designs were all a part of his world. A world she knew nothing about. She knew him only through his daughters' accounts and her own vague memories. She could clearly remember him ordering Azalea and Chrys around, but there was no face associated with the voice. And while she'd seen plenty of pictures of the man, Denali found it impossible to put the two together. Now, glancing around the room, she couldn't help but wonder if she'd recognize him when she saw him.

The foyer spilled into two other rooms, both quite large and magnificent. Denali could see that most of the people had gathered in the room to the left, while only a handful mingled and conversed in the room to the right. Peering to the left, Denali could clearly see that this was the trophy room. The perfectly preserved heads of her grandfather's kills lined the walls, causing a chill to go up Denali's back.

Telling herself that it was only because of the crowded conditions of the room and not the reminder of death, Denali turned to her right and chose the room with fewer people. Stepping through the arched portal, she found herself in a warmly lit library. The furniture had been removed, with the exception of a few chairs and one rather whimsical wooden bench with horses' heads carved up and out of the frame at each of the four corners.

"It's by McKie," the golden-haired man told her, reappearing at her side.

"How interesting," Denali murmured.

"Isn't it, though? Say, I don't think we've been properly introduced. I'm Tyler Kent."

Denali stopped him before he could go any further. "I'm sorry, Mr. Kent, but I must find my grandfather. If you'll excuse me."

She brushed past him and hurriedly surveyed the people around her. Several women in flashy cocktail dresses gave her a look of contempt before she managed to work her way around them and into yet another room. This room looked to be a small, comfortable parlor setting where people were lounging about on overstuffed chairs and sofas.

Denali paid little attention to the approving looks she received from the men. In fact, she paid little attention to anything outside of the certainty that her grandfather was also not in this room. She started to turn around and go back when she spied Tyler Kent trying to make his way to her once again. A woman in a bright red mini dress of beaded silk proved to be Denali's salvation, however, when she squealed in greeting at the man and practically fell into his arms.

Taking the opportunity to escape, Denali noted that open French doors leading outside were her only real choice of exit. Too many people were gathered near the double oak doors that led deeper into the house, and Tyler and his new friend blocked the other entry. Slipping through the crowd, Denali made her way outside and took a deep breath of the heavenly scent that greeted her.

A lighted path enchanted Denali and drew her forward into the well-groomed garden. There were very few people out here, and in spite of the fact that Denali felt certain her grandfather was elsewhere, she chose to stay a moment and enjoy the pleasant atmosphere. It was difficult to see exactly what variety of flowers and vegetation graced this particular garden, but with the rich velvet blackness of the night sky overhead and the glittering of a million stars, Denali thought she'd very nearly walked into heaven.

Strolling aimlessly along the walkway, Denali lost herself in thought. *Somewhere in this house lies the key to my past. If only he will talk to me,* she reasoned. *I just know we can put this all behind us and work through whatever he has against me. He's never even tried to know me, and I can show him that he needn't fear anything from me—that I only want to know about my mother and father—then surely we can make a new start. Be a real family.*

"You look incredibly beautiful," a low voice called out behind her.

Denali turned, nearly catching her heel in the cobblestones of the walk. "Mr. Copeland," she murmured.

He came toward her, smiling, his dark hair combed back in popular fashion, his smoky blue-eyed gaze never leaving her for a moment. He looked extraordinarily handsome in his tailored tuxedo, and for just a moment, Denali forgot about their conflicts.

"I much prefer this look to business suits. It does a great deal more to show you off. You are truly a beautiful woman, Denali Deveraux."

Denali told herself that his flattery was insincere. Bracing herself for whatever else he might say, she tried to guard her response. "Have you seen my grandfather?"

"Yes, I have. He's quite pleased with the progress we've made this week on the Omni Missions project." Michael eyed her seriously for a moment, then added, "I'm sure he'll be surprised to find you here tonight."

Denali swallowed hard. So he knew that she'd crashed the party. Was he to be hurdle number three? "I came because I wanted to talk to him. He never showed up at the office today, as you probably already know."

"Yes. Something about a delayed flight, I think."

"Well, be that as it may, I'm here to talk to him now."

"He won't like it, you know," Michael said, his voice sounding stern.

Denali felt like a child being taken to task. "And just why not?" She couldn't help but wonder exactly what this man knew of her relationship with Richard Deveraux.

Michael smiled, and the look nearly froze her in place. Why did he have to be so good-looking? Why did he have to smile like that and make her forget everything she was going to say?

"Because, my dear Denali," he said, reaching out to take hold of her bare arm, "Richard Deveraux doesn't like to be reminded of failed projects. Things are being rebuilt on this project, but they are hardly put right. Not yet. You approach him on this matter tonight, and he'll eat you alive."

"I beg your pardon?" Denali said, mesmerized by the way Michael took charge of her. The contrast of light and shadows gave his face a masklike appearance.

He led her to another section of the garden, still farther away from the house, before pausing to speak. "I'm glad you're here, Denali. I've struggled all week long to think of how I could explain my behavior to you. I knew you were unhappy with me, but I had to try one more time to explain."

Denali glanced down to where he gripped her arm, then back up to his face. His touch felt warm, but his gaze made her feel even warmer. "Must you do that?" she questioned, unable to think clearly.

"Do what?" he asked, his expression nonplussed.

"That," she said, glancing down to where he stroked her arm with his thumb. "I mean, I understand your leading me here to talk, but now we're here, and you needn't touch me in order to explain yourself."

Michael grinned and dropped his hold. "Maybe not, but it felt nice."

Denali bit her lower lip to keep from agreeing. It had felt very nice, but she wasn't about to tell him that. "All right, now continue so that I can be done with this and find my grandfather."

Michael nodded. "I suppose the best way to explain is just to give you the facts of the matter. I haven't been myself, and, of course, that isn't your fault. But it does affect our relationship and our work." He paused, seeming to struggle for words. "Three years ago an airliner crashed back east. You might remember it. It happened in Pennsylvania—there was a freak storm, and they're still arguing about what really did and didn't happen. My wife was on that flight, and when it crashed, it killed her and nearly three hundred other people."

Denali felt as though he'd dealt her a blow. "How awful. I'm so sorry."

"So was I, but for more reasons than I can go into now. Suffice it to say, my entire life changed with that one fateful event. I lost everything." He looked away, as if unable to go on.

Denali instantly felt sorry for him and put her hand on his forearm. "I really am sorry that you had to go through something so horrible."

He looked down at her, his eyes burning with an emotion Denali couldn't quite place. He seemed angry and yet sad at the same time. "Thank you," he whispered, then cleared his throat rather nervously and stepped a few paces away.

Denali feared that she'd somehow offended him, although for the life of her she couldn't figure out how she could have done that. She had touched him, that much was true, and possibly it was this and not her words that had caused him grief. Still, he had touched her first and alluded to pleasure in the action. Confused, she struggled to focus on what he said next.

"The anniversary of that flight was just a few weeks ago. I suppose this will always be a hard time of the year for me." He stopped, turned to face her, and smiled. "I know I've been a bear to work with, and I know, too, that I've been out of line in the way I've treated you. But I'm asking you, even begging you, to overlook the past and let me stay on this project." His smile broadened. "I like you, Denali, and I like the work you do."

She felt her face grow hot and was glad for the shadowy lighting to keep from revealing her discomfort. "I didn't come here to get you thrown off the project, if that's what you think." Michael's face seemed to relax, and Denali was taken aback for a moment. "That is what you thought, isn't it?"

"Well, you said that you'd speak to Richard about it on Friday, and I know you to be a woman of your word."

"But I would hardly take time to interrupt a party for something as minor as our disagreements at work."

"They didn't seem so minor at the office," Michael said seriously. "You intended to see me fired."

Denali winced. "Well, maybe at first I felt that way. But you've been decent to work with the rest of the week, and like you said, we've accomplished quite a bit already. I guess what I'm trying to say is that I think we both need to keep a tight rein on our personal beliefs and comments, and then, just maybe, we can work together without strife."

"So you'll let me stay on the project with you?" he asked softly.

"Yes," Denali said, her breath catching in her throat. Her gaze locked on to his eyes, and she immediately realized the mistake she'd made. He looked at her with such intensity, such command, that for a moment Denali couldn't think or understand what she should do next. Finally in desperation, even fear that she or he might do something they'd both regret, Denali asked him the first thing that came to mind.

"Would you like to tell me about your wife?"

Michael's expression grew hard. Here was the harsh, angry man she'd first met. The man who had little concern or feeling for her having fallen on the sidewalk. "No," he answered curtly. "I wouldn't like that at all."

"I'm sorry," Denali said and without meaning to, took a step backward as though he might strike her.

Michael seemed to instantly understand her reaction and gave a heavy sigh. "See what I mean? I didn't intend to offend you just now, yet I know that's exactly what I did. I just can't discuss her. Okay?"

"Sure," Denali replied with a hesitant nod.

"Look, a lot happened to me when she died. Actually, it'd been coming on for a long time. I know it may be hard for you to believe, but I used to go to church and believe in a caring God, just like you do."

"What happened?"

"The crash," he stated flatly.

Denali shook her head. "But why did that change your belief in God? If anything, I would think that tragedy would just draw you closer."

"Hardly. Not when I believed it was God's way of punishing me or getting back at me for not being good enough."

"Nobody's 'good enough,' as you put it. Do you blame God for your wife's death?"

Michael grew rigid again. "No. I blame her for that."

"I don't understand. How can you blame your wife for dying? It isn't like she had a choice."

"Oh, she had a choice," Michael said, then seemed to realize what he was saying and stopped short. "Look, I don't want to talk about her. I want to talk about us."

"Us?" Denali couldn't help but wonder exactly what he meant.

"Yes, us. We need to know each other better in order to work together in a more efficient manner. What would it take for me to convince you to have lunch with me tomorrow?"

Denali was surprised by this approach. "I don't know. I suppose you could start by asking me."

"Would you have lunch with me tomorrow?" he asked without hesitation.

Denali bit her lip and tried to keep from being consumed by the intensity of his stare. "I suppose I could. What did you have in mind?"

He shrugged. "Let's play it by ear. Think on it, and I'll pick you up say, eleven-thirty. We can even make a day of it if you'd like."

Denali couldn't begin to admit to herself or to Michael Copeland that she thought she might very well like to spend the day with him. He was such an enigma to her. Such a complete contradiction of character, yet she felt unmistakably attracted to him. Maybe if she spent time with him she'd better understand her feelings, and maybe then they wouldn't be consuming.

"All right, but only for the sake of our work. This isn't a date," she replied, wondering if it was the right thing to do. "I live with my aunts on the twenty-first floor of LaTour. Do you know where that is?"

"Yes. I live one floor down. In fact, I have the apartment directly below yours."

She felt a tingling sensation run down her spine. He knew quite a bit about her, yet somehow that didn't surprise Denali. Michael Copeland had proven himself to be a very thorough man in the office. That he should know where she lived didn't shock her in the least.

"Until tomorrow, then," she said and turned to leave.

"Denali," he called her name.

She stopped and only after drawing a deep, steadying breath, turned. "Yes?"

"Be careful in dealing with Richard. It really would be better if you left here tonight and didn't make a scene."

"Better for whom?" Denali questioned matter-of-factly.

Michael shrugged. "Have it your way, but just remember that I warned you."

Denali forced herself not to shudder. His voice seemed so ominous in its warning, his expression so unyieldingly stern. She gave him a curt nod, then made her way back into the house. *One way or another*, she thought, *I will make this work.*

Eleven

Richard Deveraux smiled at his oldest child with satisfaction. The party was a success, and the Talupa Corporation executives had finally agreed to all of his terms and conditions.

"So?" Chrys questioned with the single word.

"So I talked them into it," Deveraux replied, taking a generous drink from the glass of whisky and soda in his hand. Seeing the contents nearly gone, he put his drink down on the bar and motioned the bartender to fix him another.

"And this party is your celebration?" Chrys said, glancing around the room at all of the beautifully dressed people.

"Well, it is now. If I hadn't remained in Los Angeles for those extra two hours, I doubt we'd have anything to celebrate at this point." The bartender put down a napkin and the refreshed drink before heading to the other end of the bar to serve someone else. Richard picked up the drink and smiled again. "Talupa will make us a fortune."

"I'm sure," Chrys replied.

Deveraux eyed her seriously. "You don't sound very convinced."

"We've never taken on a full shopping mall," Chrys answered flatly. "I thought we were only going to be responsible for designing the amusement park inside the mall."

"Well, at first that's all they wanted from us," Deveraux admitted. "But I convinced them otherwise. Look, I know you have your apprehensions about this, but honestly, the matter is well on its way to being resolved. Let's just have a good time tonight and not worry about it. The Talupa people are happy. I'm happy. Leave it at that, and we can discuss business on Monday morning."

Chrys nodded. "I suppose there's nothing to be done about it now."

"Exactly. Now, go enjoy—" Deveraux stopped in mid-sentence, and had he been a man of less composure, he might have dropped the drink in his hand.

"What is it?" Chrys asked, seeming to sense her father's change of mood.

"Rose." The simple name came from his mouth in an utterance of shock and pain.

"Rose?" Chrys turned. "Oh no," she muttered.

Richard Deveraux stared at the enchanting form of his granddaughter, still not entirely convinced that it was Denali and not her mother who had come to torment him. She was the exact replica of her mother. The same eyes and expression. The same full lips and delicately arched brows. He felt his heart begin to pound and his chest tighten. He wondered for a moment if he might be having a heart attack.

"I told her not to come," Chrys offered in apology. "Honest, Father. I told her."

Deveraux said nothing. He found it impossible to speak. Impossible to look away. The sight of Denali took him back twenty, even thirty years. Why did she have to look like Rose? Why did she have to come here tonight?

He watched her for several moments, weaving in and out of the crowd, her eyes searching, her face smiling in greeting from time to time. He saw, too, the way the men received her. The way they stared appreciatively at her femininely rounded form. It had been the same way with Rose. Always wearing her heart on her sleeve. Always opening herself up to disaster.

"I'll go tell her to leave," a voice said from somewhere outside his thoughts.

He turned as if to acknowledge his daughter's words, then shook his head. "Why is she here?"

"I honestly don't know," Chrys replied. "I know she wants to talk to you about her project. I know, too, as well as you do, that she wants answers about the past."

Deveraux gulped down his drink, feeling the liquid burn his throat, then fade into a comfortable warmth. He looked across the room again. She was closer now, yet her image was a mirrored reflection of her mother's. *Rose*, he thought. *My sweet Rose*. Just then Denali's gaze locked on him, and Richard felt his chest tighten even more. Maybe he would die. That would be poetic justice. Die with his last visible image being that of the daughter he had so loved and so wronged.

He shook his head. She wasn't Rose. He had to remember that. Denali came toward him with determined strides, and Richard wanted nothing more than to escape any confrontation. He'd worked too hard, too long, to have everything fall apart on him now.

"You know, Father," Chrys said, her voice nearly trembling, "sooner or later she's going to get the answers she wants. Why not just talk to her? Tell her the truth. Let the whole thing come out in the open. What could it hurt?"

He looked blankly at Chrys. She had no way of knowing what she was saying because she didn't know what that referenced truth really was. "Get rid of her," he told his daughter, his voice nearly sounding like a growl.

"If that's really what you want," Chrys answered, defeat ringing clear in her tone.

"It is. Do it now," he said and watched as Chrys moved out to intercept Denali.

He planned to take that moment to slip off into another part of the house, but it wasn't to be. Denali simply sidestepped her aunt and refused to hear anything the woman had to say. To see the stunned expression on his daughter's face told Deveraux all he needed to know. Denali had come with a purpose, and she wasn't about to be turned away without some form of confrontation.

Glancing around the room, Richard realized that the last thing he wanted was a public display. He headed off in the direction of a long, narrow corridor. It led to the back of the house where another hall intercepted the first and created a four-way crossroads. Deveraux turned left and made his way to the end of the hall where he unlocked the door to his private study and, without bothering to shut the door behind him, went in to await his granddaughter.

He knew she would come. Knew she would follow and demand her answers. He steadied himself, grateful for the liquor he'd just consumed. He had faced bigger obstacles than this little slip of a girl. He bolstered his courage with anger. How dare she defy him and come here tonight? How dare she confront him about anything?

And then, all at once, she was there, staring at him with huge brown eyes so reminiscent of her mother's that for a moment he was tempted to rush into her arms and beg her forgiveness.

"Grandfather," Denali spoke, breaking the image in his mind.

"What do you want?" he asked harshly. "Your aunt told you that you aren't welcome here. Why did you go against our orders?"

Denali clasped her hands in front of her just as a breathless Chrys entered the room and stopped at her side. "Denali, come with me," she said and reached out to take hold of her niece.

"No," Deveraux said flatly. "If she wants to defy me, she can learn the consequences."

At this, Denali laughed, and it so surprised him that Richard could only stare at her for several moments. How dare she laugh at him?

"As if I haven't suffered your consequences all of my life," Denali said haughtily. "I'm your own flesh and blood, yet you deny me the right to be a part of this family. You hide me away in Kansas City. You refuse to speak to me or even see me. You hold me responsible for some sort of imagined wrong, but I'm not allowed to defend myself or face my accuser. What can you possibly do to make my life any more miserable?"

Deveraux narrowed his eyes and dug deep into his hatred. "There is a great deal you cannot even imagine," he said in a low, ominous tone. "You think you know misery now, but you haven't even tasted what I'm capable of."

"Father, please," Chrys said, coming to his side. Reaching out to take hold of his arm, she added, "We shouldn't do this here. Not now. What if someone overhears?"

Deveraux shook her off. "She started this; now I'm going to finish it."

"Not hardly," Denali replied, meeting his temper with her own. "You started this when I was born. I'm just here to get some answers and put the past behind me. I have a right—"

"You have a right to nothing!" Deveraux interjected. "Your generation thinks the world owes them something. A good living. A beautiful home. Better pay than their parents. You don't stop there, either. You demand answers for questions that you have no right to ask. You demand your way, with blatant disregard for my authority. And you have somehow convinced yourself that you are entitled to meddle in the lives of others. Well, I'm here to tell you that you are greatly mistaken. I don't have to answer to you, Denali." He said the name in as hateful a manner as he could muster. He hoped she read disgust and total rejection in his expression. He wanted to crush her. Defeat her now before she could rise up to destroy him.

"It's my life, too," Denali said, seeming to falter only momentarily.

"I do have a right to know the truth. I am a Deveraux, and I have a right to know who my mother and father were."

"If that had been important to them—if *you* had been important to them," Richard said snidely, "they would have stuck around."

"That's not fair."

"Maybe not, but I certainly don't care," Deveraux said matter-of-factly. He could read by her expression that he was gaining ground. Just plunge the knife in a little deeper. Turn it a little harder. He would destroy her, and then he would finally have peace.

"You killed your mother as surely as if you'd put a loaded gun to her head. You killed her because she couldn't live with the shame. You stand here demanding your rights when as far as I'm concerned, you should be put away from good society for the pain you've caused."

He saw tears in her eyes and smiled. "You think to soften me by crying?" He laughed, then moved around behind his desk and took a seat in the black leather executive chair. In truth, he'd seen Rose look the same way, and it was taking a toll on him that he would never, ever admit. A part of him wanted to scream out for her to stop crying, while another part of him wanted to run as far away from this room and the confrontation of this woman as he possibly could. And for those feelings he despised her even more. No one made Richard Deveraux feel this way. No one.

"You are heartless," Denali said, tears running down her cheeks.

"Yes. You're absolutely right on that point. My heart died when you killed your mother."

"Stop saying that!" Denali protested. "I didn't kill her. I was an innocent baby."

"Nobody is innocent, Denali. Especially not you."

"I'll have the truth," she murmured, her voice ragged with emotion. "I will have the truth." She turned to leave, then paused at the door. "You think you can push me around and order me here and there like you do Chrys and Azalea. But you're wrong, Grandfather."

Her eyes narrowed at him, and her face took on a hardness that for once reminded him of someone other than Rose. It reminded him of himself.

"I've tolerated doing things your way for long enough. If I have to hire a team of investigators to give me the information I want, then that's what I'll do. I'm not stupid, and while you may have controlling interest of Fun, Inc., you certainly don't have control of me. Fire me if you like. Get someone else for the Omni Missions project, but don't fool yourself. I will find the truth."

With that, she stormed out of the room, leaving Chrys to stare in silence at her father. Deveraux eyed his daughter contemptuously for a moment, then began to laugh. "Well, that was quite the act."

"I don't think it was an act," Chrys said, moving toward her father's desk. "I think Denali meant business."

"Who cares? She's not going to find anything out, even if she hires a hundred private investigators. PIs are only as good as the available information. And there is nothing for them to find this time. Let her blow her money on such stupidity, but when it's gone and she has nothing to show for it, then I will stand back the victor."

"But this is your own granddaughter," Chrys replied and hesitated for a second before continuing. "When I was a little girl, you always told me that family was the most important thing."

Richard slammed down his fists on the desk. "That was before your mother died. Before Rose died. Before . . ." He let the words trail off, then shrugged as if it had all been an insignificant misunderstanding. "She'll get over it. If not, she'll realize the consequences and then change her ways. If she's as smart as you like to believe, she'll soon tire of her excercises in futility and toe the line. If not, I can take care of myself."

Chrys squared her shoulders. "You never have before," she said evenly. "What makes you think you can now?"

Richard knew the truth in her words. Knew that she realized how dependent he was upon her and Azalea. It was one of the deciding factors in closing the Kansas City office and bringing Chrys and Azalea to Dallas. He had to rid himself of Denali in order to reinstate his precious daughters in his home. He needed them, although he would never admit that to anyone. But at nearly eighty, death seemed a very real destination at the end of the journey. And, unlike his ability to put off such thinking when he was forty and fifty, this age made him only too aware of his own mortality. The thought of being left to the care of strangers was something that Richard Deveraux feared like nothing else.

He calmed a bit and glanced up at Chrys. "You know how important you are to me. I won't lie about it. But that child is not important to me in the least, and I resent her presence in my life."

"Well, she's important to Azalea and me," Chrys said, smoothing down the lines of her silk pantsuit. "You can't just hurt her like that and not expect some of those consequences you're so quick to speak about. You'd like to ignore it, but as much as she looks like Rose, she's more like you in spirit and determination. Why not capitalize on that and realize the ally you could have in her."

Richard tensed. Even the idea of bringing Denali close to him caused great pain. "I won't stand by and let her destroy everything I've worked for. I won't tolerate her drudging up memories that are better off forgotten."

Chrys shook her head. "Like you could ever get those memories out of your mind. Has her absence helped you to do that, Father? Has hiding Denali away in Kansas City given you the peace of mind you'd hoped for?"

"Enough," Deveraux said, getting to his feet. He wasn't about to endure this pyschological feast on his thoughts and emotions. "I have guests, and so do you. I suggest we put this entire matter behind us and forget it ever happened. Denali may be strong willed, but she isn't even playing ball in the same league with me. If you and Copeland don't keep her out of my way, I'll run her over faster than you can blink your eyes."

Twelve

Michael had managed to hear the entire conversation from the hall-way. He was stunned at the bitter hatred displayed by Deveraux. Denali had been crushed by her grandfather's cruelty, and with good reason. Michael stood for several moments after Denali had rushed from the room before making up his mind to go after her. Standing there, he found that a part of him wanted to march into Deveraux's study and punch the guy squarely in the face. It wasn't something he really understood, and it frightened him. He wasn't used to caring how anyone else felt. Not after three years of turning off his emotions.

Forcing himself to leave Deveraux and go after Denali, Michael tried to imagine what he could say or do that would help her. He, too, knew what it was to be betrayed by those he loved. Those who should have loved him. He knew what it was to need answers to questions that no one would even acknowledge. But would she listen to anything he had to say? Would she care that he understood her plight and felt concerned about her well-being? *Then again,* he thought, *do I really care? Or is this just one more way I can get close enough to Denali to keep my bonus?*

He found himself outside in the garden again, and for a brief moment he nearly turned around and went back inside. *Don't do this to yourself, Copeland. Don't worry about how she feels. Just play the game and get the cash. Then get out.* He couldn't help but remember the way Denali had looked at him earlier in the evening. She was completely unaware of the intentions he had toward her. Michael actually suffered a momentary twinge of guilt. She seemed like a nice enough woman, and now that he knew her story, he wasn't sure he wanted to play into Deveraux's hand and hurt her even more.

Michael stopped near a wrought iron gate and considered his

situation for a moment. He had agreed to this game because of the money involved. But it wasn't like he didn't have money. In fact, he made a good salary at Fun, Inc., and he was living in grand style. He had the LaTour apartment, paid for free and clear, and he still drove a fairly new Mercedes. But it wasn't enough. Not if he wanted to get his business back up and running. His reasons for agreeing to Deveraux's proposition shouldn't matter. But for once in a long, long time, his motives suddenly seemed important. He was used to women's attention. Used to them fawning and pawing him, all in order to worm their way into his life. He wanted nothing of them, and they knew it. And in turn, it drove them crazy. Denali wanted nothing of him, and because of this, Michael found himself almost driven to connect with her.

Still confused, he resumed his search for her. Then, as if they had agreed to meet in the same spot, Michael came upon Denali where she'd left him earlier in the evening. This time, however, she was sitting on one of the stone garden benches. Her face was buried in her hands, and she was sobbing. He stiffened at the sound, uncertain what he could do. It made him uncomfortable to hear a woman cry. Renea had used tears to control him when they were married. Of course, he hadn't realized that fact early on, and by the time he had known what she was doing—it was too late. Maybe if he had paid less attention to his business and more attention to his wife, he could have saved them both. He felt himself tense even more, and his hands automatically balled into fists.

Get ahold of yourself, Copeland. You can't think about that right now. There's too much at stake here.

He drew a deep breath and forced his facade of control into place. Moving toward Denali, he tried to figure out what to say. He had to be careful, and he knew beyond all doubt that this would be the situation to make or break their business relationship.

"I heard what happened," he finally said softly. "I'm sorry." He sat down beside her, not even waiting for her to acknowledge him.

For a moment Denali did nothing. Even her tears seemed to have halted in the face of being discovered. Then slowly, like a flower opening up, she raised her head to meet his gaze. "This isn't your affair," she said, trying to wipe her tears with her fingers.

Michael reached in and pulled out his handkerchief. He thought to just hand it to her, but instead reached up and gently wiped away the smudges of makeup. "I know it's none of my business," he told her, finally handing her the cloth, "but I wanted to help."

"Just go away," she said, pushing the handkerchief back in his hands. "I don't need anyone to help me."

"Do you think if you tell yourself that long enough, you'll finally believe it?" he asked matter-of-factly. He watched her expression contort as if in pain, and then once again she was perfectly under control. "Look," he continued, "I'm not trying to make a nuisance of myself. I just heard the fight and wondered if you were okay. Deveraux seemed a bit out of line."

"He's always out of line, but he's powerful and rich and doesn't care who he hurts or how he hurts them."

Michael thought of himself and his own actions. Hadn't he taken on that same mentality for his own life? People had hurt him; therefore, he now had a free and clear license to hurt back. "It's how he protects himself," Michael said, never having intended to speak the words aloud.

"That may be the case," Denali replied, "but I still intend to have the truth."

"About your mother and father?"

She nodded. "I guess if you listened to the whole conversation, then you know my grandfather blames me for my mother's death."

Michael nodded. "Do you want to talk about it?"

"No," Denali said flatly and got to her feet. "I don't want to talk about it."

"What about her?" he asked softly, gazing up at her with what he hoped was a sincere look of sympathetic understanding.

"I especially don't want to talk about her." At this, Denali turned and started down the garden path.

Michael's only choices were to let her go or follow after her, and since the latter seemed the wiser choice for getting at the heart of his own desires, Michael followed Denali deeper into the garden.

"Don't bother me anymore," Denali said. She came to a complete stop, almost as if she were waiting for him to join her. "I can't talk to you about all of this. It's nothing personal, and yet it is. You don't know the details, and I don't feel like acquainting a complete stranger with all the skeletons in my closet."

"I guess I can understand that," Michael replied. "But I'm not a complete stranger."

"As far as this matter goes," she said, looking him square in the eye, "you are."

"So you think burying your anger inside is going to give you the fuel and energy for the fight to come? Is that it?" he asked. She narrowed her eyes, and he could see that he'd angered her further.

"Look, if you really want to be helpful, just go tell my aunt Chrys that I'm taking a cab home. I don't want her wandering around here looking for me."

"Why don't you wait, and I'll take you back to LaTour. We can go to my place and talk," he said.

"I don't think so."

"Look, I'm a good listener, and my place is just one floor down. We can have some drinks—"

"I don't drink," she interrupted.

"I didn't necessarily mean liquor. I just meant we could kick back and relax and . . . well . . . come what may." He said the words, not intending for them to be a come-on but quickly realizing that they sounded to be exactly that.

"I'm not in the habit of indulging in 'come what may.' I don't frequent men's apartments, and that you should offer up such a thing tells me that you are exactly what the office gossip suggests you to be."

"Now, wait just a minute," Michael protested. He wasn't about to let her get by with insulting him that way. "I was only offering friendship, and if you'd stop acting like a prude, you might realize the truth in this matter."

"I don't have to act like a prude," Denali countered, "I am one. Proudly so. I count sexual purity as a merit instead of a liability. When I marry, my husband will know that he's the only one. Therefore, Mr. Copeland, I stay out of men's apartments, and I don't set myself up for temptations that might get the better of me."

With that, she left him, and Michael found himself sorely taken to task. He hadn't meant to cause such a reaction in her, and that she found herself defending her desires for sexual purity almost made him feel like some sort of monster.

As her heels clicked in staccato rhythm down the cobblestone walkway, Michael couldn't help but wonder what he could do to reach her. She was clearly in pain, but there was also a great deal of anger inside her. He knew it to be true because he recognized it from that which was inside of his own heart. *Like knows like*, he thought. And this time was no exception. Denali Deveraux had been crushed and wounded by those around her, but instead of merely being hurt, she was enraged by their actions. Enraged enough to go head-to-head with her grandfather, a man few others would have felt strong enough to battle.

That she hadn't been with a man didn't really surprise him, but instead struck him as a sharp contrast to the woman he'd once loved. Denali prided herself on going into marriage pure and clean, while Renea had thought experience made things better. Even the women he'd dated since Renea's death were more of a mind to have a good time enjoying anything that developed, rather than concern themselves with the consequences.

Michael felt very dirty and very inadequate in the light of Denali's statement. It wasn't that he'd gone out of his way to throw off his old beliefs, but he certainly had put them aside in order to do things his own way whenever the old beliefs interfered with his new life. She gave him reason to reconsider, and he didn't like that. He didn't like it one bit. *I've mapped out my life, and I won't have Denali Deveraux tell me my course is all wrong.*

Thirteen

*I*nstead of meeting Michael for lunch on Saturday, Denali had Chrys tell him that she needed time alone. Cancelling the lunch date seemed the only way to save face, and Denali knew that in her present state of mind, Michael Copeland was the last person in the world she could deal with.

Chrys had approached her more than once over the weekend. First to chide her for going to her grandfather's party in the first place, then to offer comfort for his cruel behavior. She had told Denali of Richard's reaction when he'd first spotted her in the crowd.

"He thought you were Rose, at least for a moment," Chrys had said, and the words stayed with Denali all weekend.

Monday morning, Denali knew she would have to face Michael again, and she tried to think of what she would say to him. He was difficult to peg. In the beginning she thought she understood him perfectly. He was a corporate climber without feelings for anyone or anything. Then she learned about his wife's death, which changed her opinion.

Dressed carefully in a cream-colored linen suit, Denali entered Fun, Inc. in an almost hesitant manner. She greeted Sharon, took her messages, and made her way through the maze to her office.

"Hey, don't you look great," Phoebe called in greeting. "Wish I had your figure."

Denali laughed, and for the first time since her grandfather's party, she felt like maybe things weren't as bad as they seemed. "I should keep you around me all the time," Denali told Phoebe. "I ran late this morning and was just thinking of how hungry I was, but since you made that comment, maybe I'll just wait until lunch to eat."

"Oh, but you can't. Michael brought cinnamon rolls for us."

Denali tried not to react to the name. She still had to face the man after her childish display on Friday night. "What's the occasion?"

"His birthday. I figured you'd know that; after all, you worked with him all last week. I figured he'd be talking about how old he felt and how thirty-six was nearly over the hill. In fact," Phoebe said, lowering her voice conspiratorially, "it's the first time he's brought treats. I think you've had a good effect on him. He's not nearly so grumpy and mean since he began working with you."

"I can't imagine that," Denali said, feeling guilty. "I've done little but berate him since we first met."

"Well, you have to have one of these cinnamon rolls. They're the best in all of Dallas and just oozing with fat and calories."

"I figured that much. Okay, where do I land one of these delicacies?"

Phoebe jumped up from behind her desk. "I'll bring you one. You just settle in, and I'll have it and some coffee on your desk before you can whistle 'Happy Birthday.' "

Denali laughed and took off for her office. *Phoebe always seems to know the right thing to say*, she mused. *I was really dreading this day, but now it doesn't seem so bad.* She had just managed to flip on the lights when a knock sounded from the adjoining office door, and Michael popped in.

"Ready to get to work?" he asked casually.

Denali nodded. "As soon as I get my cinnamon roll. I understand congratulations are in order."

Michael shrugged and replied dryly, "I didn't do anything but endure another year."

Denali took a seat behind her desk and pretended to busy herself with the papers she'd left strewn on top. "Well, happy birthday anyway." She nearly added that her own birthday was in two weeks, then decided against it.

"Thank you. I was hoping to take the occasion to solicit a gift from you."

"What?" Denali's head snapped up, and she met his amused grin. "What are you talking about?"

"Well, you reneged on our lunch Saturday, and I thought maybe you'd take pity on me because of my birthday and have lunch with me today."

Denali nearly said no but realized she might just as well deal with Michael head on. "All right. Lunch it is."

"Thank you. You won't be sorry."

At that, Phoebe entered with the coffee and roll. "Here it is!"

"Wow, how come I didn't rate that kind of service this morning?" Michael asked.

"Because you scare people, and they don't want to bring you things for fear you'll throw them," Phoebe said matter-of-factly.

Michael seemed taken aback for a moment, and Denali wondered if it would jeopardize his seemingly good mood. She started to say something on his behalf but realized that Phoebe had perfectly pegged the way she herself felt about Copeland. He was something of a puzzle. A frightening yet alluring puzzle that she couldn't seem to fit together.

"I suppose I had that coming," Michael said, his expression quite serious.

"Yes, you did, and you know it. If you'd stop trying to be the big, tough man all the time and just be human, we'd all like you a whole lot better," Phoebe said and turned to leave. "But I like you anyway, Michael. You remind me of my brother Kevin. He always thought he was real tough, too."

"You make him sound past tense," Michael replied.

Phoebe stopped at the door. "Kevin is past tense. He died."

Denali cast a quick glance at Michael and then Phoebe. "I'm sorry, Phoebe. Has it been a long time?"

"About ten years," she said without a hint of emotion.

"What happened?" Michael asked her softly.

"Cancer is what the doctor labeled it. But if you ask me, he was consumed by his bitterness and hatred. He saw what he'd done to himself, but by then it was too late. The big, tough man wasn't tough enough to beat the odds."

She left them then, and Denali couldn't help but feel sad for her co-worker. There was a look in Phoebe's eyes that suggested her pain was still very real. It amazed Denali that she could have something like that in her past, especially when she was such a bubbly, upbeat kind of person.

"Well, I suppose I should return this call to Hazel Garrison,"

Denali said, trying to move past Phoebe's declaration.

Michael remained fixed in place, however. He seemed genuinely disturbed by Phoebe's words, and only then did Denali remember that Phoebe had come down hard on Michael for his harsh
facade.

"Michael?"

He glanced down at her. "I'll be in my office. Let me know what
Garrison has to say."

"Look, I'm sorry if Phoebe upset you. I don't think that was her
intention," Denali offered.

"It's not a problem. Make your call. Christians are waiting to have
fun—not that I thought they ever did, given their serious demeanors
and inability to laugh."

Denali frowned and shook her head. "Where is this coming from?
I honestly don't know why you insist on being offensive to me, but
I think Phoebe's right. You probably do it to keep people at arm's
length. Well, insult away and feel better, but you won't change my
mind and you won't change this project. Christians have a great deal
of fun, and they do know how to laugh. But if it makes you feel better
to think of us all miserable and pious sitting in our sackcloth and
ashes, then by all means think what you like."

Denali had rather surprised herself by taking this line. She had
thought to counter his words with her own anger, but instead this
do-what-you-will attitude came out and she found herself feeling
quite good about it. In fact, she felt like the weight of the world had
been lifted from her shoulders.

Michael, on the other hand, just stood staring at her as she
reached for the telephone. "Oh, by the way, twelve-thirty works
best for me."

"What?"

"Twelve-thirty," Denali said, punching the numbered buttons.
"Remember? Lunch? You asked me to lunch today, and twelve-thirty
will work best for me."

"Oh," he said. "Right. Twelve-thirty is fine."

He went back to his office just as Denali heard the voice of Hazel
Garrison come on the line. "Hello, Mrs. Garrison. Denali Deveraux
here."

"Are you ready?" Denali asked, walking into Michael's office un-announced.

Michael glanced up from his desk, then quickly looked away. He wasn't about to let Denali see how she was starting to affect him. But affecting him she was, and he didn't know quite what to do about it.

"Just give me a minute to wrap this up," he told her and jotted a few notes onto the paper in front of him. The notes made no sense at all, but they allowed him to focus his attention on the paper and to think of how he would deal with Denali.

"I had a great discussion with Mrs. Garrison. She thinks we're well on our way to accomplishing what her board is looking for. She was notably impressed that after only one week, we already had managed to outline a good portion of the new designs."

"Outlines aren't blueprints," he said, sounding harsher than he meant to.

The whole discussion with Phoebe and Denali had left chinks in his armor. He felt as if someone had cracked the mask he hid behind while on duty at Fun, Inc. Always before, he had his pro-tective mechanisms in place, refusing to let anyone see him as vul-nerable or softhearted. At least until Denali Deveraux came on the scene. There was something about her, however, that caused him to forget his focus. Caused him to rethink his plans. He almost threw everything away Friday night—and all because he felt sorry for her.

Deveraux had been cruel to her, and Michael knew that she'd been crushed by her grandfather's reaction. Even this morning, when Richard had called Michael into the conference room to talk about the week to come, Michael had been on the verge of telling the old man exactly what he thought. He held back just in time—shocked at the thoughts bombarding his mind.

With a deep breath, he put his pen down and looked up. She stared at him with a quizzical look, as if trying to read his mind. Michael got to his feet and grabbed his suit coat. "How about we go to Larry North's," he suggested. "They have the fattening stuff and the not-so-fattening stuff. You can have your choice of being bad or good."

Denali smiled. "After that cinnamon roll this morning, I'd better be good."

Michael followed her into the hall and down the corridor. "I doubt you're ever anything but good," he said in a low voice that he wasn't sure she could hear.

But she obviously did hear it, and instead of being offended like he worried she might, Denali laughed heartily. "That's only because you don't know me very well, Mr. Copeland."

Fourteen

Richard Deveraux remained hidden away at his desk until he was certain Denali would be away for lunch. But much to his surprise, when he stepped into the corridor outside his office, he saw Michael with his hand to the small of Denali's back, guiding her through the reception area. Denali laughed at something, and Michael grinned. It made quite an impression on Richard, and stepping back inside his own office, he smiled. It was the first time he'd smiled since Denali crashed his party.

Just thinking about the party caused Deveraux to suppress a shudder. He felt out of control, like everything around him was spinning in different directions. It seemed his plan was going ahead full speed, but how could he be sure?

He went to his desk and picked up the receiver. Then, after checking Chrys's itinerary, he dialed her cell phone, hoping to catch her in a free moment.

"Chrys Deveraux," the voice at the other end responded.

"Chrys, it's me."

"Problems?" Chrys asked.

"No, in fact, things are going rather well. I am curious about something, however."

"What?"

Richard tried to think how he might verbalize his question without appearing too interested in Denali. "I wondered how she acted after the party."

"Denali?"

"Yes."

Silence filled the other end of the line for several moments. Then Chrys answered, "Hurt, of course. But she always has been. She moped around the apartment all weekend and wouldn't even go with me to church." There was a long pause, as if Chrys expected him to say something, but Richard was too lost in thought.

"I suppose the biggest problem is that she feels guilty for caring so much. She wants to understand the past and know who she really is, but on the other hand, she knows it won't do anything but bring destruction to those she loves.

"She honestly tries to maintain a balance, and I think in her own way she really loves you and wants to tear down the wall between the two of you."

"Rose always acted that way," Richard said without thought.

"Maybe so, but we're not talking about Rose," Chrys countered. "This is her daughter, and the sooner you find some way to deal with this and put it to rest, the happier all of us will be. Look, I've got to run, but I thought you would like to know that Azalea will be joining us soon. Everything has been wrapped up in Kansas City, and I know she's very anxious to be among family again."

"Good," Richard replied, still lost in his thoughts. "Keep me posted."

He hung up the phone, then leaned back in his chair. His mind refused to stop dwelling on the matter. Rose had meant so much to him. She had easily become his focal point after the death of his wife. He could still picture her as a little child. Dependent and loyal. Needy.

"Oh, Rose," he whispered.

A light knock at his office door brought Richard out of his stupor. "Yes?"

"Oh, good, you're still here," his plump, matronly secretary told him. "Here's the file you asked for. I didn't want to just leave it out where someone else could get their hands on it." Gladys came in wearing an obnoxious orange-and-raspberry dress she liked to wear every summer. "I'm on my way out. A few of the other secretaries are joining me for lunch. Want me to pick you up something?"

Richard shook his head. "No. I'll probably leave early. Maybe even after checking this file."

Gladys nodded. "I suppose I should cancel your three o'clock, then?"

Richard frowned. "Who do I have a three o'clock with?"

"The last of the engineering applicants."

"Let Jim decide. I've seen enough, and he knows what I think of the lot."

"I'll tell him," Gladys said without registering the slightest bit of surprise at this change of events.

"Good," Richard replied. "Oh, and Gladys, don't ever let me catch you leaving this file unattended. If I had gone to lunch and returned to find this on my desk, you'd be dealing with the unemployment office instead of a lunch date." His voice was cold and unemotional. Gladys paled and nodded. "Good," Richard said, seeing she fully understood the seriousness of the situation. "Now go ahead to lunch. I'll return this to the safe when I'm finished. If I'm not here when you get back, just plan on seeing me in the morning."

"Don't forget your Talupa meeting at 8:30."

"Noted."

Richard waited until Gladys had closed the door behind her before opening up the folder she'd brought him. Within, the contents lay secured in a sealed evelope. Richard had purposefully done this to assure himself that no one else had access to the documents enclosed.

Carefully, he broke the seal and reached inside to pull out the half-inch-thick stack. The details of his business were written upon these pages. Details that could cause him more than one headache if given over to the wrong hands. That's why he kept it inside the safe. That's why the papers could never be left unattended. The only other person who knew the combination to the safe was Gladys. And she wasn't going to cause him any problems. Of that, he was more than confident. Gladys made too much money to be anything but loyal, and besides that, her husband was ill and dependent upon her health insurance benefits. Richard could tell by the fear he'd seen in her eyes that Gladys wouldn't be a problem. She needed this job, and the generous salary Richard paid her ensured her complete devotion.

Looking over the papers one by one, Richard noted the conditions of his business. The stock had never been opened to anyone outside of family, with the exception of his business partner. In fact, in the beginning it was just his seventy percent and Bill's thirty.

He tensed. He hadn't thought of Bill in years. Of course, he owed Fun, Inc. to this man. After coming out of the war, Richard still had plenty of family money, but little else. For some time he puttered around, dabbling in this and that, not finding satisfaction in anything. He wanted a skill and a scheme that he could grow into a full-blown corporation, and after years of searching, he found the man with the solution.

Although several years Richard's junior, Bill had architectural training, and not only that, his father had owned and operated an amusement park in California. There wasn't any aspect of amusement parks that Bill didn't understand, and when he came to Richard with the idea of specializing in these mechanized playgrounds, Richard saw the merit. After all, the war to end all wars was behind them now, and life was good. Even the Korean conflict couldn't put a damper on their plans.

No, the country was ready for fun and entertainment. Amusement parks were doing banner business, and Richard could only view the potential as the pot of gold at the end of the rainbow. After hearing Bill's plans, Richard readily agreed to put up all of the capital in return for seventy percent of the stock. Bill would retain thirty percent and provide the know-how. And because Bill knew he had few other options, he agreed to the arrangement.

Richard casually scrutinized the papers, turning one page after another until he came to what he'd been looking for. After the death of his wife, Richard had found it necessary to set up a trust for each of their daughters. Shirley had left them each a small fortune—money given her by her own family. Richard hadn't minded that Shirley wanted to earmark the money for their daughters. After all, he'd never intended that Shirley's money should be used for anything but gaining interest. He wasn't about to let his wife support him. To live off even a portion of her money would have made him feel like less of a man. So he'd allowed her to set up the trust, and after her death he followed a similar pattern in dividing his Fun, Inc. stock with his daughters. For tax purposes, it made it much easier to assign them each ten percent of the company. It still allowed him forty percent, and that in turn gave him controlling interest over Bill's thirty—and there was never any question about how his daughters' shares would be voted. They would do whatever Richard wanted them to do. At least he had planned it to be that way.

The paper he now held showed the cursory trust information. Chrys and Azalea had already been given their trusts and had used the money for additional investments. Rose's money sat in the bank building interest, but Richard couldn't touch it—all because of the past and Denali's and Rose's selfishness.

He'd never allowed Chrys or Azalea to tell Denali about the trust.

He didn't care if she died a pauper. He'd never let her have that money. Furthermore, if he'd have had his way, she'd have never known about the stock, either. But Chrys had let it slip one day that Rose had left Denali her ten percent of the company and with that simple announcement, had let several rather ugly worms out of the can.

"Well, you don't know the truth by half," Deveraux said and pulled the papers back in order. "And you never will. Not about the trust or anything else."

He pulled out another confidential envelope, inserted the pages, and sealed it against intrusion. No one need ever know the truth, he assured himself, slipping the envelope back into its original folder. Without any regard for his actions, Richard left his desk and went into the outer office where Gladys's desk sat in pristine organization. Behind her desk and beneath an oil painting provided by one of his favorite Texas artists, Richard dialed the numbers to his safe and opened the door.

He thought about merely stuffing the envelope and folder back inside, but a silver picture frame caught his gaze. His heart pounded furiously at this. He knew what the photo meant. Knew the face beneath the glass. He reached for it hesitantly, like a small child reaching for a gift from a stranger.

Pulling it out, he shoved the folder in and closed the door to the safe. He refused to look at the photo until he'd returned everything to order and sat once again in the stillness of his office. Then slowly, almost reverently, he turned the frame over and met the image of his youngest child.

He remembered the photo well. Remembered Rose's reaction when he'd taken it. She was a lovely young woman—happy, healthy, and so very vibrant. She stood beside her new car, a birthday gift from Richard. The red convertible had seemed just the thing for his favorite child. It was sporty and fun and promised adventure. So, too, did Rose.

How he missed her. How he wished she could be back at least long enough for him to explain himself. He hated that she died thinking him an ogre. Thinking him some sort of hideous monster for the actions he'd taken on her behalf.

In the photograph the young, auburn-haired woman stood casually in jeans and a poet's blouse, which had been cinched at the waist with a silver concho belt. Her hair was blowing in the breeze, and Richard could almost smell the freshness of that summer day so long ago.

But as he studied the photo, Richard locked his gaze on Rose's eyes. Instead of laughing and joyous, they seemed almost accusing, as if she had risen from the grave to haunt him through this picture.

"I was happy, Daddy," she had told him shortly before her death. *"And now I'm not, and you're to blame. How could you?"*

Richard tightened his grip on the photograph. "Leave me be, Rose," he muttered.

"It's all your fault. You live with the consequences, because I won't."

They were the last words she spoke to him. In a rage at the memory, Richard hurled the photograph across the room—the spell of his misery breaking with the tinkling sound of glass.

"I did what I had to do. Just like I'm doing what I have to do now," Richard said, nearly growling the words. "You left her behind, and now I have to deal with her; but I won't, and that is my perfect revenge. Denali is not a part of my life, nor will she ever be."

He stared at the broken glass and the twisted photograph. "Not now. Not ever. Not even for you, Rose."

Fifteen

Michael and Denali found the days pass in amicable order. Together they were repiecing the broken Omni Missions project, and together they were accepting an unspoken truce regarding values and beliefs.

"We really should go out to the site this week," Michael suggested as they pored over design details for one of the gift shops.

Denali pushed her hair back over her shoulder, and Michael admired the way the auburn layers caught the light. He found himself actually wishing he could touch the silky strands and pulled himself up short of doing exactly that.

"I know you've been to the site with Phoebe and Hazel, but I think it's time you included your partner in the matter." He smiled, hoping to appeal to her. He had yet to feel as though she ever willingly included him on anything related to this project.

Denali straightened up and stretched. "I'm ready to go whenever you give the word." She stifled a yawn and leaned back over the drawings.

"You look tired," Michael said, hoping she wouldn't take offense. Denali Deveraux took offense at the strangest things, at least in Michael's opinion. He was never quite sure how to react or respond to her moods, and now was no exception.

"I suppose I haven't been sleeping all that well. It's kind of startling to lie in bed and gaze out the window and see airliners heading straight for the building," she replied.

Michael laughed. "I know what you mean. The first year we lived there, Renea thought we were doomed for sure. I kept assuring her that the flight pattern into the airport allowed for such things as skyscrapers, but she wasn't convinced."

At this, Denali put down her pencil and straightened again. "How come you never talk about her? I mean like this. This is the first time I've ever heard you say anything about the woman when it wasn't laced with bitterness and anger."

Michael stiffened. She was right, of course, but he didn't want to discuss it. "How come you never talk about your mother?"

Denali's defenses went up in a most visible way. She squared her shoulders, tilted her chin ever so slightly, and fixed a stoic expression on her face. "There's not much to talk about. I never knew her. You, however, knew your own wife."

"Not well enough," Michael muttered before turning to his desk. He made a pretense at downing the cold, stale coffee in his mug before turning back to face her. "Why does your grandfather blame you for your mother's death?"

Denali paled at this. "I don't want to talk about it." She pushed aside the drawing she'd been working on and pulled out a huge rolled map. "Here, you might want to look this over before we make a site visit. I've marked the areas where Hazel suggested we put particular features."

Michael realized her game and moved closer. He wondered what it would take to get her to stop talking about the site. He leaned down, balancing with one hand on the table and the other on the chair behind Denali's back. It made for a very close, very intimate moment, and Michael was suddenly caught up in the sweet scent of her perfume.

Apparently Denali found the moment disturbing, as well, for in a matter of moments she had stopped talking altogether and instead merely stared at the map in front of her.

Michael thought about his agreement with Deveraux and of the attractive young woman beside him. He was supposed to keep her occupied, even seduce her, in order to earn a bonus that could help him regain his business. He wanted that money in the worst possible way, and by playing false with Denali, he could have it all. He didn't want to hurt her. In fact, ever since the party, Michael had the strangest desire to protect Denali. Even help her find the truth. There had to be something more to her circumstance. Something that Deveraux wasn't saying. Something that would change everything.

All of this was running through Michael's head when Denali began to speak. "I don't need to explain to you what happened in regards to my mother. You heard my grandfather at the party. You know very nearly as much as I do." She didn't move, didn't look up to see if he'd heard her but continued in a voice that sounded desperately close to breaking. "I . . . when I . . . was ten years old, I was playing in her room. I wasn't suppose to be there, but I would sneak in there whenever I got the chance. The room was supposed to be off limits for everyone but Grandfather, but I thought if I could just be there . . . touch her things . . ." She fell silent for a moment, then looked up at Michael. "Touching has always been important to me."

Michael leaned closer. "Me too." His voice was low and seductive. Treading on this dangerous ground, Michael felt his own heart start to race.

Denali lowered her gaze again. "I suppose it's partly because of the artist in me, but it also connects me to the things around me. I always got in trouble when we went to the Nelson Art Gallery in Kansas City because I would inevitably touch something. They had this room set up in period style, and you could look inside and see how it would have been in the seventeen- or eighteen-hundreds. When our class tour moved on, I fell behind and crossed the roped boundary and entered that room. I just had to touch those things and connect to the past." She shook her head and looked back up. "Does that sound insane?"

"No," Michael whispered, losing himself in the depths of her brown eyes. "Touching is very important."

"Do you really understand?" she questioned, as if no one had ever taken the time to listen before now.

Michael felt an aching to show her exactly how much he believed in touching. He wanted to hold her in a way that he never thought he'd ever want to hold a woman again. He straightened up at this thought and looked at her. "I'd like to think I understand," he said, his voice sounding foreign in his ears. He was sweating and his heart pounded rapidly, almost as if he'd just taken his daily run.

"I found my mother's suicide note," Denali said softly. Apparently she didn't see Michael's discomfort. "She said she couldn't live with the ugly truth. Grandfather has always maintained that I was that ugly truth." Tears formed in her eyes. "He said I killed my mother because she couldn't live with the shame of having an illegitimate child."

Michael barely held himself in check. "You can't blame a child for something like that. There has to be more. What of your father?"

The tears broke free and slid down her cheeks. She shrugged and looked away. "I've never known him. Grandfather won't tell me who he is," she said. "No one will. My aunts claim not to know, although I think they know more than they're saying." She sniffed, and as if realizing for the first time that she was crying, she wiped at her tears and tried to regain her composure. "Sorry."

"Don't be," he said, reaching out to touch her face. He felt her tremble and wondered if she was scared of him like Phoebe suggested most of the office was. "You don't need to be afraid of me," he whispered but knew it was a lie. She had a great deal to fear from him. Not only was there the deal he'd made with Richard, but his own feelings were rapidly raging out of control.

"I'm not afraid," she said, never taking her gaze from his face. "I'm not afraid of anything."

He smiled at this and, as if to prove her wrong, leaned down to kiss her. Denali instantly stiffened, her eyes growing wide. "All right, you win. I am afraid." She pushed away from him and got up to leave.

Michael reached out to take hold of her, and without missing a beat he swung her into his powerful arms and kissed her soundly on the mouth. She didn't fight him. Not really, and so he let his lips linger on hers for a moment longer. When he felt her relax against him, he pulled away and found her eyes closed tight.

"Still afraid?" he whispered.

Her eyes opened, and in them he saw the depths of raw, unhidden pain. "Especially now," she murmured and hurried from the room.

For the rest of the day, Denali found ways to avoid being alone with Michael. At first he thought it kind of amusing, almost flattering. But after trying unsuccessfully to pin her down on a date for visiting the park site, Michael grew frustrated and then angry. Rather than cause a scene, he let it slide, and when the day was over, he headed home to rethink his strategy.

Maneuvering his Mercedes into LaTour's underground parking, Michael tried to imagine how he could win Denali over. Then his conscience started to question him. Win her over for what? To meet Deveraux's desires? Did he really want to aid a man who blamed an innocent baby for the death of her mother? Of course, she wasn't a baby anymore, and maybe Deveraux had some other reason for hating her. Maybe she'd been a real terror to raise. Maybe she had caused him a great deal of pain. Maybe she was just as deceiving as Renea had been.

He recklessly slammed the car into his assigned space and turned off the engine. For several moments, all he did was sit there and contemplate what to do next. A battle raged inside him, and Michael felt torn between the two sides. For the last three years, he'd survived his own pain only by making himself hard and unyielding. It was only in refusing to care about the feelings and pain of others that he could forget about his own misery. But that was before Denali Deveraux had come to town.

He closed his eyes. He could still feel her in his arms. Still feel her soft lips pressed against his. She had aroused in him feelings that he'd thought were dead. Killed with his adulterous wife.

He pounded his fists against the steering wheel, wincing at the pain. Jerking open the door, he gathered up his things and started out across the garage. He refused to allow Renea any control over him, yet even as he thought about it he realized she had always controlled him and the circumstances of their life together. Maybe that was why he felt such anger now. He'd given her everything she'd wanted, but it had never been enough.

He buzzed the front desk in order to be let into the building, and after retrieving his mail, he waited at the elevators.

I don't know what to do, he thought, giving his mail a cursory examination. *I don't know which way to go. She wants nothing to do with me, yet in order to get that bonus, I have to keep her occupied and out of Deveraux's life. She's attracted to me, but she won't admit it. And pressing her further may see me off the project.*

The elevator door opened, and Michael stepped inside. He reached out to press the number twenty, then changed his mind and pressed twenty-one. *Denali would be home by now*, he reasoned. *I have to get her to accept me in her life.* But even as he wondered how to make it happen, Michael knew that the biggest wall he had to break through was Denali's prejudices against him. She told him she couldn't date a man who felt so contradictory to her belief in God. She was sorry Michael had been hurt in the past, and even though she didn't know the depth of his pain nor the details of Renea's betrayal, he was certain that she meant every word. She felt sorry for him, but she drew the line there.

The elevator doors opened to the twenty-first floor, and Michael hesitated only a moment before stepping out. He slipped his mail into his briefcase, then went to the Deveraux apartment. Knocking loudly, Michael stepped back and waited for Denali to answer the door. Instead, Chrys Deveraux pulled open the door and stared at him in total surprise.

"Michael?"

"I need to talk to Denali. Is she home?"

Chrys shook her head. "No, I'm sorry. She was here for a few minutes—just long enough to change her clothes and ask to borrow the car. I'm afraid you just missed her."

"Where was she headed?" he asked, wondering if he could catch her out somewhere.

"I really don't know. She mentioned shopping but didn't say which mall."

Michael tried to sound nonchalant. "I guess that's what women do when they're upset."

Chrys frowned. "Why would Denali be upset?"

Michael saw this as the perfect opportunity to get more information on Denali. "Chrys, may I come in for a moment? There's something I'd like to ask you about Denali."

"I don't know if that's a good idea," Chrys said, stepping back. "But I suppose if you insist."

Michael tried to appear humbled by her allowance. He knew he could be very intimidating when he wanted to be, but right now didn't seem the time to try a power play. He waited with his head bowed until Chrys closed the door.

"What's this all about, Michael?"

He looked up. "Denali is very upset about the past. She told me Richard blames her for the death of her mother. I thought you could give me a better understanding of the matter." Chrys looked so taken aback that Michael instantly questioned her. "Are you all right?"

"What . . . what did she tell you?"

Michael tried to appear as though the matter wasn't all that important to him. "She said she found a suicide note when she was ten. The note implied that Rose couldn't bear the ugly truth, and that Richard said *she* was that ugly truth."

Chrys began to shake. "You must never repeat any of this ever again."

"But why? I don't understand. How can anyone blame a child, especially an infant, for the death of a parent? Besides that, where's Denali's father in all of this? Why didn't he protect her from Richard's harshness and blame?"

"Michael, you must stop," Chrys said sternly. She seemed to regain a tiny bit of control.

Michael had never worked much with Chrys, but he'd heard she could be just as hard-nosed as her old man. He suddenly began to wonder if she'd have him fired for some strange form of insubordination.

"Look," Michael said, "I'm just worried about her. That's all."

"You must never bring it up again. My father has never recovered from Rose—I mean Denali's mother's death. It was tragic, and she was very young, and that's all. Denali needs to put her search to an end. If you can convince her of that, you will have our undying gratitude."

"So why is this such a big deal?" Michael questioned. "If there's nothing to hide, why all the secrecy?"

Chrys opened the door, signaling it was time for Michael to go. "I didn't say there wasn't something to hide. But I will say this: You are an employee of Fun, Inc. If you intend to stay that way, you'll do as you're instructed. Understand?"

"Sure, Chrys," Michael said, trying to smooth his way back into her good graces. "I didn't mean anything by it."

Chrys visibly relaxed. "I'm sure you didn't. It's just that this is a very delicate subject best left to the family."

"I understand," he said, walking into the hall.

"I hope you do, Michael," Chrys said before closing the door on him.

Michael stood for a moment staring at the closed door. There was more to this than anyone was letting on, and he intended to find out what it was all about. A few well-placed phone calls to Kansas City ought to make for a good start. He pushed for the elevator, then opted for the stairs. One way or another, he'd find out what Deveraux was hiding.

Sixteen

C hrys fought the overwhelming urge to call her father. She didn't want to cause even more problems, but if Denali was discussing family business with Michael, there was a good chance she might be discussing it with other people, as well.

Pacing a path through the living room and into the dining room, Chrys wondered how she should deal with the matter. After all, Michael didn't know much more than the very basic facts. Rose had killed herself, and Richard blamed Denali. But that wasn't entirely true. Chrys knew her father blamed himself, as well. Maybe even more than Denali. In fact, Chrys was very nearly convinced that he didn't actually blame Denali at all but used the excuse to exorcise his own demons. Over the years, keeping her secrets and knowing the truth about more than she'd like, Chrys could finally stand back and say that if anything, Richard needed Denali in a way he didn't need anyone else in the world. He kept her at arm's length, refusing to speak with her or see her; but on the other hand, he always wanted to keep tabs on her—know where she was, what she was doing, who she was seeing. He might tell everyone else that he despised her, but Chrys felt strongly that in truth, he despised himself.

She reached for the telephone just as it rang. Jumping, Chrys picked up the receiver. "Hello?"

"Ms. Deveraux, this is Kevin. Your sister has arrived."

"Azalea? Already? By all means, send her up."

Chrys hung up the phone and went to open the front door. She hadn't anticipated Azalea's arrival until the next day, but it was a pleasant surprise to have her show up early. Chrys delighted in Azalea's company more than anyone else. It was more than the fact that they were sisters. They shared the bond of blood, but they also shared a bond of tragedy and secrecy. For the most part, Chrys could be honest with Azalea, and in light of Michael's revelation, she was suddenly very relieved to have Azalea's companionship. Maybe her sister would have some new insight on how to deal with the problem. After all, she had spent the last six months alone with Denali in Kansas City. Surely that would give her some sort of fresh knowledge about the girl. Something they might have missed during their twenty-five years of raising her.

Azalea came around the hall corner, and behind her came Kevin pushing a baggage cart. She smiled and met her sister's loving gaze. They fell into each other's arms and embraced.

"I've missed you so much," Chrys admitted. "I didn't think I had because we talked nearly every day on the phone, but I've been miserable without you."

Azalea pulled away and smiled. "Me too."

"Come on inside. Kevin, just set those things inside the door," Chrys instructed. Azalea handed the man a five-dollar bill and thanked him for the help.

"I wish you would have called. I'd have met you at the airport," Chrys said as she directed Azalea to the living room couch. She waited until Kevin had exited the apartment before adding, "You couldn't have come at a better time."

"Oh?"

Chrys looked at Azalea for a moment. She looked tired. Even though she'd just turned fifty-one a few months earlier, Azalea looked as though she were ten years Chrys's senior instead of six years her junior. Gray liberally sprinkled her once-auburn hair, and her face was lined with wrinkles, suggesting that worry and concern filled much of her thoughts.

"There are some problems."

"Didn't we know there would be?" Azalea asked, easing back against the couch with a sigh.

Chrys nodded and took a seat beside her sister. "Denali will never let this drop, will she?"

"No," Azalea answered simply.

Chrys eyed her seriously. "You're that confident?"

"Absolutely. She's like a volcano that has lain dormant for as long as it will. She's blowing off warning signs of smoke and steam, and one of these days she's going to release the full force of her power upon us, and then . . . God help us all."

"Maybe we should tell her about the trust fund. Maybe that will change her attitude and keep her from desiring to destroy her family."

"It won't stop at the trust, and you know it," Azalea said softly. "But I'm of a mind now that perhaps it shouldn't stop there."

"What are you saying?"

Azalea got up and went to where her suitcases had been placed in the foyer. She retrieved a small square bag and brought it back with her to the living room. Opening it, she revealed a small white box.

Chrys gasped and recoiled. "Why, Azalea? Why did you bring that here?"

"Perhaps because I've been doing a great deal of soul-searching," Azalea said, growing thoughtful. "We both know there's a lot Father has never confided in us. Who knows where this thing will end? We may not be able to tell her much about her father, but Denali has a right to know her mother. This will help her to know Rose a little better—maybe even give her insight into her father. Perhaps it will also bring Denali peace of mind regarding her own existence."

"But are you ready to accept the consequences?" Chrys asked. "This will change the rest of our lives."

Azalea's expression reflected bittersweet pain. "I suppose I'm selfish in this matter. You see, the rest of my life won't be that much longer."

"What are you saying?" Chrys asked, fearing the answer.

"I'm dying, Chrys," she said matter-of-factly. "I know this is a shock, but there's no easier way to tell you other than to just state the facts. That was the reason I delayed coming to Dallas. I haven't been feeling good. In fact, I've had some pretty bad spells of pain. Denali wanted me to see the doctor when it first started up, but I couldn't see the sense in it. I figured I'd look into it here. But before I could leave Kansas City, I had a bad enough spell that I collapsed. The staff called for an ambulance, and I spent two days in the KU Medical Center."

"Why didn't you let me know?"

"You were in New Orleans, and you were very busy. What could you do that wasn't already being done?" Azalea reached out to take hold of her sister's hand. She patted it lovingly. "I know this is hard for you to hear, but I don't want to spend our remaining time dwelling on my death."

"I can't believe this," Chrys said, fighting back the tears. "You can't be dying."

"But I am. I have the same type of uterine cancer that killed Mom.

I waited too long to find out about it. I refused to go in for those pesky yearly check-ups. The doctor told me that had I come to him years ago, this wouldn't be the ordeal it is now."

"I refuse to accept this," Chrys said sternly. "You'll go to my doctor. You'll get a second opinion."

"If that makes you feel better, I will," Azalea replied. "But we can deal with that later. Right now I think we should deal with this." She let go of Chrys's hand and patted the white box.

"He'll be furious with us."

"Father has had his way long enough. We love Denali and we love him. Shall we compromise one over the other?" Azalea questioned.

"Do we have any other choice?"

"If that's the case," Azalea answered, "then my vote goes with Denali. We've allowed Father to dictate for too long. He's lived his life the way he wanted to. He's made his choices. Now it's time for Denali to be given the same rights. Of course he'll be furious, but we have a certain control in the knowledge we share with him. Denali has an inheritance that belongs to her."

"It's more than that and you know it," Chrys replied and got to her feet. "If you give her those things, she'll know that we purposefully kept her in the dark all these years. And she won't stop at a box of her mother's treasures. She'll want to know what else we've lied about."

"I don't know what else you've lied about," Azalea said with a shrug. "I've always assumed there were things going on between you and Father that you never clued me in on." Chrys started to protest, but Azalea held up her hand. "It's all right. I'm glad I don't know everything. I can't die in peace knowing that I've held even a portion of the answers she's sought. I've kept my tongue time and again. I've done things Father's way, and now that I'm dying, I should have the freedom to do what I feel is right. I suppose that's why I'm glad you have your secrets, Chrys. If I knew them, I'd only want to share them with her." She stopped and looked up at Chrys, her eyes pleading. "Even so, I want us to do this together. I don't want to hurt you in the process of helping Denali. You don't have to tell her everything, but the things you and I have shared together I think will do more good than harm. At least it will give her some answers. She'll see for herself that her mother never blamed her for anything." Azalea took a deep breath. "Look, it's important to me. I want to stand before God with a clear conscience."

Chrys bit at her lip and studied Azalea. No wonder she looked so tired. The signs were all there. The drawn, pale face. The sunken eyes and dark smudges beneath them. The thinness that only now was evident to Chrys. And in that moment, Chrys knew that a second opinion would only confirm the truth of the first doctor's diagnosis. Azalea was dying. A sob broke from her at this thought, and the misery sent her to her sister's side. "We can tell her whatever you like, but I can't lose you! I can't!"

They held each other, both now in tears. Chrys couldn't even begin to speak what was on her heart. At that moment, it mattered very little that her father would be enraged at their decision to help Denali. At that moment, all Chrys could think about was going through yet another painful funeral for someone she loved more than life itself.

Seventeen

D enali was overjoyed to have Azalea join them in Dallas. She came just in time to help celebrate Denali's birthday, and the day seemed suddenly more tolerable with the stalwart love of her aunts to bolster her. She said nothing at work, not wanting to have Michael make any comments or see Phoebe fuss over her. The only thing that really seemed to bother her was a kind of reservation Denali noted in Chrys and Azalea. But whenever Denali asked about it, they always assured her that everything was fine.

On the work front, Denali had to deal with the tension between herself and Michael. They had put off the site visit as long as possible, and finally Michael laid down the law and told her he would pick her up Saturday morning and she could just plan to spend the day going over the site with him.

She didn't argue. It had to be done. Nevertheless, it unnerved her. What if he started asking her questions again? What if she broke down and allowed herself to be vulnerable and weak in front of him? When Saturday arrived and she found herself belted into Michael's Mercedes, she couldn't keep the questions from her mind. *What if he gets too close? What if he wants more from me than I can give?*

The land chosen by the Omni Missions Board was a barren strip of property that lay to the southwest of Dallas. To the average eye, the land looked desolate and without merit, except that it was within close proximity to both Dallas and Fort Worth. But to Denali's artistic eye, the land was perfect. Together with Michael, she covered every inch of the site—walking through the open field, noting the lay of the land, discussing the necessary landscaping.

At one point, he smiled at her in regards to something she'd said. Denali instantly focused on his lips. Chiding herself for the mistake,

Denali wasn't prepared for the overwhelming memory of his kiss. The intimacy instantly made her uncomfortable, and she struggled to refocus her attention on the job at hand. To Denali, it remained very important that she keep herself distanced from feeling too much, but in her heart she knew what a poor job she'd done where her family was concerned. What would happen with her awakening to Michael's actions was anyone's guess.

Nervously she slid her hands into the pockets of her jeans. They'd both agreed to dress casually, since Denali had made the mistake of inspecting the land the first time in a business suit. She had ruined a favorite pair of heels trying to traipse through the brush, not to mention that they were most uncomfortable—not at all suited for hiking. So this time she'd dressed carefully, donning jeans and hiking boots and topping them with a sleeveless, olive-colored blouse that seemed to make her dark cinnamon hair look even redder.

"They could make an instant fortune here in tract housing. Of course, I'm talking tract houses that would start from $200,000 and go up," Michael said with a laugh. "I still question the soundness of putting in a theme park when Six Flags Over Texas is just miles away."

"The land has been owned by the church for over twenty years and many people have sought to buy it from them, but Hazel told me they were always certain that God had special plans for the land," Denali replied. "I think the park and resort is the perfect solution for this land. I mean, just look at the layout. I can't imagine that it was designed for anything else. It's easily accessible from several interstates, the airport is a quick drive away, and there's so much to do in Dallas and Fort Worth that if they grow bored with the resort, they can always take a day trip. And even with Six Flags so close, I doubt they'll have any trouble keeping the park up and running. After all, they are a part of a major church denomination. That, in and of itself, will appeal to groups all over the nation."

Michael, clad in blue jeans and a white button-down shirt, smiled tolerantly and kicked at the sandy soil with the toe of his boot. Denali wondered if he wanted to offer some snide remark but didn't wait to see if he would. She wanted to keep things light, and she didn't want to have to look him in the eye. If they argued, she'd no doubt have to face him, and she'd done an admirable job of avoiding that very thing.

She cast just enough of a side glance his way to add, "Hazel was told over and over that she'd never get proper zoning passed for a theme park, but it sailed through without a hitch, and here we are. I believe it was preordained." The minute the word came out of her mouth, she regretted it. She hadn't meant to just throw it out there like that. In fact, she was rapidly beginning to guard every word that came out of her mouth, rather like a person speaking a foreign language. Each word was considered and translated, and only after weighing the choice was it uttered. Not so with her last comment.

Michael continued staring at the ground for several moments, the light summer breeze playing havoc with his dark hair. "Do you believe it's also been preordained for you to be here?"

Denali looked out across the field. She knew that no matter what she said to Michael, he'd find some way to either twist it or be critical of it. She didn't want to spoil the amicable trust between them, but neither did she want to be less than true to her faith. How could she explain to him, without sounding like some sort of pompous, self-righteous Christian, that she felt confident of God's direction in her move to Dallas?

"I do believe God brought me here for a purpose. Maybe not the one I've hoped for," she admitted. "But nevertheless, a specific purpose, and right now that purpose is Omni Missions' park." She held her breath. Would he criticize or drop the subject?

"So if I read the map and the designs correctly," he said, suddenly changing the subject, "this area is marked for the children's attractions."

"Right," Denali said, letting out her breath. She took out a small photocopy of the entire layout. "The smaller children will have simple rides and attractions such as a petting zoo and puppet shows. Most of the rides are nothing more than the circle-styled ones. You know, boats, cars, carousels, that kind of thing. They won't spin or go fast like the adult rides. There will also be a little train that will take them on a slow ride through the entire children's area. Oh, and there's to be a network of tunnels and a ball room, and all of it will be large enough that parents can play with their children."

"I don't mean to sound petty, but I've noticed that this area has a definite Bible-story theme. I thought Hazel Garrison found that offensive." He mentioned this in a calculated manner, leading Denali to believe he was really trying to keep things on an even keel.

"Not at all. What she found offensive was the manner in which my grandfather went about laying things out and naming them. For the children, Bible-story themes are cute and impressive and very acceptable. The Noah's Ark Petting Zoo will have a little ark-styled entrance and a colorful display along the fences and stalls that will tell the story of Noah. The puppet shows will be reenacted Bible stories, and not only that, there will also be some simple character-building stories. Like respecting one another and how it's wrong to steal and lie."

"You don't want to teach the adults the same thing?" Michael said, finally raising his head to meet her eyes.

She didn't have time to look away and met the smoky blue gaze with apprehension. "The park isn't really designed for that purpose," Denali said. "I mean, Hazel told me that many churches will hold conferences down here and probably have wonderful workshops with a variety of speakers to teach the attendees. They want the park to be fun, but they also want it to be a haven for people who are tired of the reigning politically correct mentality. They won't cater to special interest groups, but neither will they reject them."

"But aren't they catering to a special interest group when they make this a 'Christian' park?"

"Sure. But it's their money and their park. Why can't they build exactly what they want? If no one else likes it, they don't have to spend the money to attend. I'm tired of this world telling me that I have no right to seek out what's important to me."

"And a Christian resort is important to you?" he asked, his voice tinged with sarcasm.

Denali bit back an angry retort. Her temper felt dangerously close to erupting, and she determined not to let that happen. Michael had changed a lot since she'd come to Dallas, but he still came across outspoken and very happy to put her in an uncomfortable position.

"It's important to me that I have the same rights as everyone else," she finally told him. "But most of all, it's important that I be true to my beliefs and not just pay lip service to my ideals. If that means I don't go to certain places or do certain things, then so be it. But it also means I take a stand. My aunt Chrys used to say if you don't stand for something, you'll probably fall for just about anything."

Michael didn't reply to that, so Denali started off down a narrowly cleared path. She knew he was following her, as she could hear his footsteps, but she had little desire to make a point of acknowledging him. Instead, she continued their inspection, jotting notes and suggestions, praying that she would keep her mouth under control.

By late in the afternoon they both seemed comfortable with the landscape, but Denali couldn't help but feel even more uneasy about Michael. The sun bore down in unbearable intensity, and this, coupled with the humidity of the day, created a sauna effect. Denali felt the sweat drip down the back of her neck. She longed for a cool shower, a cold drink, and a great deal of distance between her and Michael Copeland. She turned around to find Michael only a matter of inches away. Instantly the hair on the back of her neck stood up.

He looked at her with such intensity that Denali could very nearly read his mind. He knew he'd just made her uncomfortable, but it was as if he rather enjoyed the idea. His lips curled ever so slightly, and for a moment, all Denali could do was focus on them. She could still remember the way they felt against her own lips. His kiss had aroused in her a feeling that she'd never experienced. She'd left work early because of that kiss and spent the entire evening shopping in order to forget it. But forgetting was impossible, and she now knew that more than ever. The trouble was, she realized by the look in Michael's eyes that he knew it, too.

"Ah . . . the . . . ah . . ." She whirled around, putting her back to him once again, and defensively held up the paper. "The plan," she said, forcing her eyes to the paper, "shows the layout, but if you'll remember the . . ." She fell silent because he had stepped up to stand directly behind her. He looked over her shoulder to view the reduced design, and Denali could smell the musky scent of his cologne as the breeze picked it up.

He didn't touch her, and for this Denali was grateful. She knew that if he touched her, it would be her undoing. She wanted him to touch her. She desired it more than anything she could think of just then. She remembered his arms around her and the way he held her so protectively.

This has to stop! she rebuked herself. *I can't let myself go on like this.* She tried desperately not to think of his kiss and instead forced her mind to remember his arrogance and intolerance of her feelings and beliefs. It was her only defense, she told herself, and in order to keep from losing control, she walked several steps away and turned to question him.

"Why do you hate God so much?"

Denali watched his jaw clench and his eyes grow dark. "I never said I hated God."

"But you act as though you do. You act as if He's some big enemy you have to fight at every turn. Surely your feelings aren't justified just because your wife died. My guess is there's something more." She took a deep breath and immediately felt the feelings of overwhelming desire pass from her. *Good. Let us argue and fight, but don't let me desire him,* she half thought, half prayed.

"I suppose it might seem that way to you," Michael said flatly. He stared at her hard, as if to dare her to question him further.

Denali repressed a shudder. That he was angry didn't surprise her in the least. That he appeared to be challenging her unnerved Denali. *What does he want from me? Can't he see how uncomfortable this all is?* Of course she knew he could. He no doubt relied on her discomfort in order to get her to drop the subject.

Instead, Denali swallowed her fears and pressed for an answer. "Tell me I'm wrong."

"You're wrong," he stated, never dropping his gaze.

"You don't hate God?"

"No."

She shifted from one foot to the other, trying to decide what to say. "Then why the negative attitude toward this project? Why such negativity toward Christians?"

"If I answer your question honestly," he began, "will you answer one of mine?"

Denali couldn't imagine that he could ask her anything that unbearable, so she immediately nodded. "All right."

Michael stepped forward, and his voice lowered in an almost seductive manner. "Are you sure? I mean, I want an honest answer, not something contrived to avoid the truth."

Denali felt her breath catch. She remembered a time in private school when her best friend had stolen the teacher's favorite pen. She'd known all about the theft, and yet to admit it when questioned was to betray her friend. She felt that way now, but for reasons that were beyond her. Michael intended to have the truth about something, but in giving him the truth, Denali felt certain the cost would be dear. Maybe even require that she betray herself—her innermost feelings. It was one of those moments in which she could go forward with her pursuit and line of questioning or drop the entire matter. The latter seemed safer.

"Just forget it," she said and hurried past him to retrace her steps through the trees. "We need to be getting back."

She didn't think about whether he would follow, and she tried not to dwell on what he might have asked her. Still, what could he have wanted to know?

Stuffing her copy of the park layout into her back pocket, Denali caught the toe of her hiking boot on an exposed tree root. She started down face forward, only to find herself rescued by Michael's ironlike grip on her upper arm.

He swung her around and into his arms and for a moment did nothing more. Denali felt all of that unbidden passion return. Her mind raced with images and thoughts, and she longed for him to kiss her again.

"I didn't figure you to back down so easily," he said in a deliberately slow manner.

"I didn't figure you to care," Denali countered breathlessly.

He grinned at this. "I'm finding that I care a little more each time we have one of these private conversations. I'm just not sure what exactly it is I'm caring about."

That broke the spell for Denali. She pushed him away and shook her head. "Maybe that's your problem, Michael. You don't know what to care about."

With that, she hurried back to the car and climbed inside. She knew this time that she'd left him standing there to wonder at her statement. But she didn't care. Inside, the turmoil and anxiety of what had just happened was more than Denali could understand. She had actually wanted him to kiss her. In fact, she knew it would have taken very little encouragement for her to instigate the whole thing herself. But for what purpose?

Still panting, she tried to steady her breathing. She told herself the hike back to the car caused her breathlessness, but in her heart she knew better. She caught sight of movement in the trees, then Michael emerged, walking slowly, seeming to take all the time in the world.

"I'm just fooling myself," she whispered as she watched him approach. His long, measured strides gave an air of confidence, but not so his face. His expression suggested disgust, even anger, but as he came closer Denali saw that his eyes were clearly marked with pain. Had she hit some sort of nerve and not even realized it?

He got into the car and started the engine. "Want to stop for some lunch?" he questioned without bothering to look at her.

Denali realized she felt famished, but she really wanted nothing more than to be rid of Michael's company at the first possible moment. "No," she replied. "Just take me home."

He nodded and didn't say another word until they pulled up to the front door of LaTour. "I have other business, so I'll drop you off here," he muttered.

Denali nodded and grabbed her purse. "I'll work over those changes we discussed earlier and see you at work Monday."

He looked at her, opened his mouth as if to say something more, then abruptly closed it and gave her a curt nod.

Denali had barely stepped away from the car when Michael hit the gas and tore out of the drive.

"Afternoon, Ms. Deveraux," the doorman said in greeting.

"Hi, Charles," she answered, her mind still very much on Michael. "What's the weather report for this evening?" she asked, not really even thinking of the weather.

"Stormy," he told her.

She glanced up and smiled. "How appropriate."

Eighteen

*H*ow was your visit to the theme park site?" Chrys asked as Denali let herself into the apartment.

She tried to smile. "I think it went well. Michael and I made some changes, and I'll probably draw those right up after I get something to eat."

Azalea appeared from around the corner, laundry basket in hand. "Chrys is just fixing us a late lunch. Why don't you come help me fold these towels and then share lunch with us?"

Denali sniffed the air. "Mmm, smells wonderful. What are you fixing?"

Chrys laughed. "I'm just reheating Chinese food that we ordered a couple of hours ago and then got too busy to stop and eat."

"Sounds perfect." She threw her purse and notebook down on the chair, then took the basket from Azalea and went to the living room.

"So you and Michael are spending a lot of time together, eh?" Azalea questioned, taking a seat beside Denali on the couch.

"One of the hazards of my job," Denali said, trying not to think too much about the harshly handsome man. "Too bad OSHA doesn't have warnings about people like him."

Chrys had just brought in a tray of food when Denali made this statement. "I thought you liked Michael. I mean, you two seemed to be quite chummy the other day."

"It's a roller coaster ride," Denali said, carefully folding a burgundy-colored towel. "He's a very moody man, as you well know. One minute he's up and pleasant to talk to, the next minute he's growling and ranting at everyone in sight."

Chrys nodded and for Azalea's sake explained, "Michael Copeland has been with the firm for about three years. He used to own his own business, and I'm not sure what exactly happened, but it folded. There was some rumor that his partner had run off with the money and that rather than file charges or bankruptcy, Michael liquidated a great deal that he owned, with the exception of his apartment here at LaTour, and honored his obligations."

"And then closed shop?" Azalea asked.

"Something like that. It's all rather confusing. His wife died about the same time, and when he showed up at Fun, Inc., he just wanted a job. His reputation preceeded him, and Father instantly hired him. I don't know what his future plans are, but it wouldn't surprise me if Fun, Inc. is just a stopping-over place. Maybe it's like a regrouping kind of thing."

Denali took all this in, wondering at the same time about the details of his partner's actions. This news intrigued her. Michael had never once mentioned a partner cheating him out of his business. She wanted to question Chrys about it but instead changed the subject. "How soon will my car arrive from Kansas City?"

Azalea put down the folded towel and thought for a moment. "If I remember correctly, all of our things should be here by next Wednesday."

"All our things?" Chrys asked. "You've got more coming?"

Azalea laughed. "I didn't know what to bring. I didn't know the size of this apartment or what you'd actually have already in place. I just brought some of our favorite pieces, along with a few things I didn't want to do without."

"I don't know where we'll ever put it all," Chrys stated and went back to the kitchen to retrieve the drinks.

Denali thought it the perfect opportunity to voice her opinion. "If I weren't living here, you'd have an entire second room open to you. I've been thinking about it a great deal, and I'm wondering why we don't approach Grandfather about allowing me to live with him for a time. In spite of the way he's treated me, I'm determined to have some answers. If we pressed him to let me stay there, he just might relent and talk to me."

Chrys had returned by this time and very nearly dropped the tray she was carrying. "That's completely out of the question!"

"Honestly, my dear," Azalea said, looking at her with a shocked expression that left Denali cold, "you shouldn't even suggest such a thing."

"Why not? We're packed in here like sardines, and he's living in a thirteen-room house. I suppose I could try to find my own place, but you both know that I don't intend to stay here in Dallas, so leasing something seems like a real waste."

"We'll get by," Chrys told Denali firmly. "Don't even mention this idea of yours again. Father would never hear of it, and it would only cause more problems."

Denali stood up, letting the towel she'd just folded fall to the ground. "I'm sick of this!" she declared. "I'm sick and tired of being treated like a child. Don't question this—don't do that. I'm a grown woman, and it's time I took the initiative to see some things done my way."

"Having your own way isn't always what it's cracked up to be," Azalea said softly.

Denali shook her head. "You know I love you both, but honestly, if this is the way I'm to spend the rest of my life, then maybe it would be just as well if I leave right away. I mean, the Omni project is back on target, and I'm not really needed here." She tried not to think of how much it hurt to imagine separating from them. Then Michael came to mind, and she quickly dismissed any thoughts of her feelings for him.

Chrys put down the tray and came to Denali. "It won't always be like this. I promise. Once Father is gone . . ."

"I can't wait that long," Denali replied softly. "I feel like I'm slowly going insane. I want to know about my mother and father. I want to know who I am and what about me is like them. I want to find my father, if that's possible, and learn why he deserted Mom and me. Don't you see? I have to deal with this one way or another. If I can't have answers here, then I'll go somewhere else and seek them out."

"Be patient, love," Azalea offered. "Trust God's timing on this."

"I'm sick to death of everyone else's timing," Denali retorted and stormed off to the balcony.

Securing the sliding door closed, Denali felt the heat of the afternoon assault her once again. The city seemed covered in a haze of humidity that kept the skyline muted and out of focus. *That's how my life is,* she thought. *Muted and out of focus. I can see images and shapes, but I don't know what they mean or what they really represent. I hurt the people I love by demanding my own way, yet it seems entirely reasonable to want to know who you are and who your parents were.*

She leaned on the railing and stared out across the cemetery. The rich green of the lawns and trees suggested haven and comfort, but Denali couldn't bring herself to go there. All she really wanted to do was go to sleep and forget that any of this had ever happened. She wanted to fall asleep and wake up being someone else. Someone whose past was routine and normal. Someone whose future didn't seem so unclear.

Michael spent the rest of the afternoon and evening in his office at Fun, Inc. He had gone there to accomplish a few things he'd left undone on Friday, but he'd also gone there because returning to the apartment made him uncomfortable. Every time he was there, he couldn't help but think of Denali living in the apartment above him. And every time he thought of Denali, Michael felt his carefully ordered world falling apart.

What was he supposed to do now? Denali Deveraux affected him in a way that he'd just as soon ignore, but that was impossible. He tried to focus on his goals, his ambitions for the future. He had to put together enough money to start up his business again, and it had to be enough money to do it in style. Clientele who paid big bucks required the trappings of an office that suggested success and confidence.

That was all he really wanted. At least it was until Denali came into his life. Confused and frustrated, Michael felt anger creep over him. Anger at himself mostly, but also anger at her. She had unsettled him and made him see things he'd just as soon ignore. She reminded him of a faith and set of beliefs that he'd tried hard to bury away with his dead wife.

Michael finally gave up on having any peace of mind and had just about decided to return home when he heard voices coming from somewhere in the office. Since it was Saturday night, he couldn't imagine who had come in. Getting up, he slipped into the hallway and listened. Now he could distinguish the voices of a man and a woman. Cautiously maneuvering toward the point where his hall intersected with the main office thoroughfare, Michael was rather surprised to realize that the voices belonged to Chrys and Richard Deveraux.

"She wants answers, and Azalea and I think it would be best to at least give her Rose's things. We have the diary and letters and some of

Rose's memorabilia that we couldn't stand to part with, and we want Denali to have it."

"No!" Richard declared adamantly. "I won't hear of it."

"She has a right to know her mother and father."

"Did you hear me?" Richard countered. "I make the decisions for this family. I alone am responsible for the protection of its members, and I say no."

"Denali is no longer a child to be concerned about protection and your authority over this family. She doesn't even care that her job is on the line. And in truth, why should she care? She owns stock, and then there's the trust fund—"

"Don't ever speak of that again!" Richard raged. "And don't even think of telling her anything!"

Michael heard a door slam and quickly made his way back down the hall to his office. He could hear the voices now in the hallway as Chrys followed her angry father.

"It was a mistake to bring me here tonight," Deveraux declared. "I thought we were going to have a pleasant dinner. Look, just take me home."

"Please just listen to reason," she was begging him as they exited the office. "There're too many other things. . . ." Chrys's voice faded.

Michael felt his heart pounding furiously. He had barely made it out of sight before Deveraux and his daughter passed. If they'd have discovered him, there would have been no telling what the repercussions might have been.

But as he calmed, Michael became more intrigued than ever in Denali's plight. Chrys mentioned diaries and letters that would shed light on Denali's parents. They also mentioned stock and a trust fund, and Deveraux was clearly agitated that his daughter should even speak of the matter.

He had already placed one call to an old acquaintance in Kansas City. Another couldn't hurt. He would check up on what, if anything, the man had learned about Denali's birth and her mother's death, then he would check into what kind of trust fund it was that Chrys Deveraux had mentioned. Picking up the phone, he began to dial, then replaced the receiver.

An unsettling feeling washed over him. For a moment, he questioned his own motives and wondered if he was doing this for himself or for Denali. Thinking rationally where the intriguing young woman was concerned was nearly impossible. Michael remembered the look in her eyes, the way she'd tried to hide her very evident feelings for him. She always stared at him with an expression of awe and fear, almost like a child gazing into a cave of wonders—fearful to go forward, afraid to stay behind.

She'd told him she was a virgin, but she surely couldn't mean to imply that she'd never fallen in love. Still, Michael knew from the way she reacted that it was all new to her, and the idea that he was her first somehow intrigued him.

Then a shadow fell across his thoughts and cast hopelessness upon even the tiniest pleasures there. Denali had made it clear that her beliefs in God and her faith in Him were the foundations for her life. She wouldn't date him because he scoffed at her views and made it clear that he didn't share the same ideals.

I did once, he thought, but instead of comforting him, this only made him feel worse. He hated the way this revelation seemed to overpower everything else. No matter the fact that Denali felt something for him—maybe had even fallen in love with him. She'd never give in to her feelings so long as they were separated by spiritual issues.

"This is a good joke, God," Michael said, casting an upward glance. "The first time someone means something more to me than a good time, and you have to be the common ground on which we can meet." He shook his head. "Why do you want me back, when I'm so completely messed up inside? Why now, after taking everything away from me, destroying all that I had hope and faith in?"

Because that hope and faith should have been better placed, Michael thought to himself and wondered if the answer had come from God or just natural logic.

Pounding his fist on the desk top, Michael took in a deep breath and blew it out. "I'm not going to play this game. I don't need that old way of life. I don't need Denali Deveraux's innocence and complications. I don't need . . ." His words trailed off, and the misery and emptiness inside threatened to swallow him whole.

"But I do need," he whispered, wishing he didn't have to face the truth.

Turning off his desk lamp, he walked over to the window and looked out at the city lights. He felt very much alone in this mammoth city. Millions of people lived stacked on top of one another inside a fifty-mile radius, and yet he felt alone. How could that be?

Thinking of this only made him more acutely aware of his feelings for Denali. He longed to find her, to hold her and tell her that he needed her. But it was impossible, and he knew it. Until he made some sort of reconciliation with God, until he figured out how to put the pain of the past behind him, it would be hopeless to pursue a relationship with Denali.

"If I leave the past undone," Michael whispered in the darkness, "I'll never be sure what motivates my feelings for her. I'll always wonder if deep down inside I'm just using her to get the money I need or to banish the memory of Renea or to punish Deveraux for succeeding where I failed."

And with that, the truth was suddenly painfully clear, and Michael found himself once again against a solid obstacle that he couldn't simply muscle his way around.

Nineteen

Weeks passed in an onslaught of activities. The plans were coming together in short order, and Denali had made it her business to keep close tabs on Hazel Garrison's wishes. She met with Hazel regularly and found herself looking forward to their talks. They discussed more than just business, and Denali saw Hazel as a great source of spiritual strength.

Sitting across from the older woman, Denali smiled. Hazel had graciously invited her to come to her small but elegant home not far from the Highland Park house where Denali's grandfather lived. The English cottage home seemed out of place with the grander, more estatelike properties, but Denali instantly loved it and told Hazel so with great enthusiasm.

"What a charming house. I mean, it's just nestled here among these vast estates with their mammoth houses."

"I think it provides us a better setting than that stuffy office of your grandfather's," Hazel replied.

"No doubt," Denali agreed. "I think it's absolutely delightful."

"I fell in love with it the moment I first laid eyes on it," Hazel admitted. "It only has three bedrooms and the layout is quite simplistic, but it's all I need or want."

"I can see why. You've made it a wonderful home. So comfortable and charming."

"Thank you, my dear," Hazel said, offering her a cup of tea.

Denali took the cup and saucer and lowered her gaze. Hazel's searching eyes made Denali want to hide away her feelings of discomfort. After all, she wasn't uncomfortable with either Hazel or the Omni project but rather with her family and Michael Copeland. She'd tried all night—in fact, had worked feverishly at it for the past week—to drop the concern she held about both topics. But instead of feeling better, Denali felt dangerously close to falling over a precipice ledge.

"Perhaps we could postpone talking about the project," Hazel said quite seriously as she poured steaming tea into Denali's cup.

"Why would you suggest such a thing?" Denali asked, trying carefully to balance the saucer and spoon sugar into the cup at the same time.

Hazel leaned back and looked at Denali, forcing her to raise her face to meet the old woman's eyes. Something about Hazel Garrison demanded that people meet her eye to eye, and Denali realized it was no good offering pretenses with her.

"Denali, I'm most impressed with the way you've saved this project. I'm pleased with your sensitivity and understanding of our desires and vision for this resort. However, I've always sensed in you a certain spirit of distress. An unfulfilled need, perhaps. Can you talk about it with me?"

Denali shifted uncomfortably and sipped her tea. She didn't know what to say. It felt both good and frightening that someone like Hazel could read her so easily. "I suppose I have been rather preoccupied at times. But I assure you," Denali added quickly, "that the project will not suffer because of my personal life."

"I didn't think it would, child." Hazel looked at her with motherly affection. "You misunderstand my intentions if that's what you think. As one who shares your faith, I simply thought you might need a listening ear."

An all-encompassing warmth spread over Denali. "Thank you for caring so much," she murmured.

"Are we not to bear each other's burdens?" Hazel questioned.

Denali tried to refocus on the tea, but her gaze always rose to meet Hazel's sympathetic face. "Yes," she said, nodding slightly. "It's just that—"

"Speaking of it often leaves us feeling vulnerable and exposed?" Hazel interjected.

Denali laughed. "You have a very clear concept of my feelings."

"I don't wonder," Hazel replied, taking up her tea. "You remind me of myself in so many ways. I was just like you when I was young. Competent, strong, passionate about my faith. Of course, by your age I was married and already had two children, but nevertheless, we are cut from the same cloth. Your mother and father must be quite proud of you."

Denali looked away uncomfortably and wondered how she could explain her circumstance, but before she could say a word, Hazel spoke again.

"This is about them, isn't it?"

"Yes," Denali whispered and felt her throat tightening as though she might actually cry. "I'm sorry," she added, trying hard to get control of herself.

"Don't be. Please tell me what's going on."

With that, it took little else to encourage Denali. She soon poured out the entire story to Hazel, including her feelings for Michael.

"I noted that tension immediately," Hazel laughed. "But maybe you'll turn out to be good for each other. I've already seen a change in that young man."

"But he isn't happy, and he questions God."

"Well, who doesn't?"

"You question God?" Denali asked softly. "I thought that was a mark of immaturity."

"Oh, maybe it is to some. I see it more as a sign of comfort and companionship. When things happen that I don't understand, who else should I ask for an explanation? I feel comfortable in taking my questions to God because I know that He is not offended by my need to comprehend. He knows the questions in me anyway. He knows what I will seek to understand before I even know it for myself."

Denali smiled. "I've always been told that questions were invasions of privacy and that I needed to keep them to myself."

"Questions come up because things have been left undone. Whether it's a matter of a need to understand, as sometimes is the case with God and me, or because some task needs a better explanation, it's all the same."

"But we can't always know why God allows some things. Even the Bible says 'Who can know the mind of God?' Yet the whys and hows are often my biggest concern," Denali admitted.

"They are mine, as well. But you know, Denali, it's times like that when I figure I must trust God to show me what I need to know as I need to know it. It isn't a sin to ask God questions, but I think ignorance is another matter. I think when we bury our heads in the sand so we don't have to deal with an issue, or when we walk away from tough problems so that we don't have to alter our course in order to make things come together, that's when I think we err."

"I'd never really thought about it that way."

"So what's Michael's story?" Hazel asked, refilling her teacup.

"I don't really know. He's a very private man. I know there was some problem with his wife and that she was killed in an airline accident."

"How awful," Hazel interjected. "How long ago was that?"

"Three years last May," Denali said, remembering what Michael had told her. "Then he had some kind of problem with his business. He used to own his own architectural company, but something happened. A business partner cheated him or something like that, and the business nearly went bankrupt. But I guess Michael sold off most of his assets and honored his commitments before closing the business."

"An admirable thing to do."

"Yes," Denali agreed, "it was. I just wish I better understood his anger at God. I mean, I know what it is to be frustrated because you don't have the answers you're looking for. I even know what it is to be disappointed in how things work out. But Michael seems to genuinely blame God for something, or maybe . . ." She fell silent trying to think of the right words.

"Or maybe he blames himself and can't reconcile the situation?" Hazel suggested.

"Maybe. I thought for a time that he hated God, but he told me quite bluntly that I was wrong. I tried to get him to open up and tell me honestly what had happened to turn him away from God and Christianity, but instead of telling me, he challenged me."

"Challenged you? How so?"

Denali put down her cup and waved Hazel off as the woman leaned forward to refill it. "He told me he'd answer my question honestly if I'd answer one for him."

"So what was the problem?"

Denali smiled weakly. "I was afraid of what he might ask."

"What could he possibly have asked you that you wouldn't have been willing to answer?" Hazel questioned, eyeing her very seriously.

"I was afraid he would ask me how I felt about him," Denali admitted, taking a deep breath. "You see, I could read in his face that my feelings had been very transparent. And although I had tried hard not to let him see how he was affecting me, I knew I'd failed. I feared he would ask me if I loved him—and, Hazel, I was even more terrified of the answer."

Hazel smiled knowingly. "We often avoid the truth because of our fear of how we might have to act on that truth."

"I know that thought went through my mind. I couldn't be honest with him because I couldn't be honest with myself. I still can't."

"Oh, but I think you already have been. You just don't want to admit it."

Denali looked up at the ceiling—knowing Hazel was right. "I suppose you want to hear me admit it." She looked back to Hazel, feeling only comfort and acceptance from the older woman. "I suppose you want to hear that I'm in love with Michael Copeland."

"No, but I think you needed to hear it." She smiled and reached across the coffee table that separated them. "If that's how you really feel."

Her weathered, wrinkled hand extended, and Denali automatically placed her own against the soft, warm fingers. Hazel wrapped her fingers tightly around Denali's hand and held her fast. "He needs you to help him find his way back. Surely you can see that. God has brought you here for more than one purpose. Michael's heart is broken, and so, too, his spirit and life. You, Denali Deveraux, have brought the glue to piece it all back together again."

"But how can that be when I can't even piece my own life together?"

Hazel nodded. "Often the conflict or problem we find ourselves in is the very same one that we are most helpful to others in. Michael has a painful past that he needs to recover from. So do you. Have you ever thought that maybe you'll both heal—together?"

"You mean let him help me, as well as me help him?" Denali said, as though it were some sort of revelation.

"Exactly."

"I don't know if I can open up that much," Denali admitted. "I've pushed people away for so long that I'm not sure I remember how to let them in."

"I don't think it will be a problem where Michael is concerned. Start by stopping," Hazel told her.

"What?"

Hazel smiled and squeezed her hand. "Stop being afraid to let him see how you feel about him. Stop trying to hide your emotions, and meet them head on. Deal with Michael Copeland as he comes. If he presses a romantic interest, see where it leads."

"But what of his feelings toward God?"

Hazel let go of her hand and sat back. She grew very thoughtful for a moment. "It's my guess, but only my guess, that Michael is a Christian in jeopardy. You said he speaks of having had a relationship with God in the past. My thought is that he is drawn to you because he sees the light of Christ shining in you. He's drawn to the light because he knows very well that this is his source of strength. You irritate and intrigue him at the same time, am I right?"

Denali laughed. "That's putting it mildly."

Hazel smiled. "I think this is true because he knows the truth about God, and he knows that walking away from the truth has not brought the comfort he thought it would but instead has brought him more pain and misery. He's hurting, Denali. Just about as badly as you are.

"I don't pretend to know all the answers. And I won't say that I believe this will be a pleasant journey for either one of you," Hazel said quite seriously, "but I feel confident that Michael can and will be an asset to you in more than just business. I have a feeling that if you turn to him for help, you will find an advocate."

"I have to admit I would never have thought of him in exactly that way," Denali said, trying to imagine opening up to Michael with the truth of her feelings. "But on the other hand, it might be the answer to all my problems. After all, Michael's been with the company for the last three years." Denali suddenly felt a light go on inside her head. "He might know something. He might have been taken into my grandfather's confidence."

"Perhaps," Hazel said. "But the one thing you don't want to do is use each other. Don't make a relationship based on what you can get out of this for your cause. If you love Michael, then love him for himself and not what you can take from him. It sounds as though people have used him before."

Denali nodded, realizing that she had taken exactly the wrong impression from Hazel's suggestion. She knew it would be wrong to use Michael for information, but it seemed so natural, given the fact that no one else was willing to give her answers. Still, could she ever admit to her feelings for Michael and not wonder if she wasn't just using those feelings in order to enlist the aid of an ally?

Denali sighed and got to her feet. In some ways she felt worse than when she came, but looking to Hazel Garrison, she knew that she wouldn't have traded the encounter for all the world. "Thank you for caring enough to ask—and for sticking around for the answers."

Hazel joined her and walked her to the door. "Thank you for

trusting me enough to share the answers. I know that came at a tremendous cost to you. You don't give your trust easily, and I can't say
that I blame you. I am very choosy about whom I trust, but ever since
we first met, I knew God had put you into my life for more than the
park and resort. I hope, Denali, that we can be good friends."

Denali turned. "I'd like that a lot."

Hazel smiled and surprised Denali by giving her an affectionate
hug. "Don't forget where I live. You are always welcome here."

"Thank you," Denali said, feeling a lump in her throat.

She left Hazel Garrison standing on her front steps. Driving down
the road, Denali tried to imagine how she would deal with the things
she'd learned about herself that day. Handling the matters of vulnera-
bility and trust didn't seem nearly the oppressive issues they once were.
No, those concerns were quickly swallowed up in the face of her feelings
for Michael Copeland. Feelings she was still uncertain she could accept,
much less act upon.

Twenty

You're absolutely sure about this?" Michael asked into the receiver of his phone. He grabbed a legal pad and started to write down the information.

"As sure as you can get about these things," the man told him. "I went through all the records. She's adopted, and the revised birth certificate lists Richard Deveraux as the one to have adopted her."

"But what about the original birth certificate?" Michael questioned, thoroughly intrigued by this bit of news.

"Can't get it. All the records are sealed. Denali is the only one who could ask for them."

"Wow, I wonder what it all means."

"Well, it seems to me that if your lady was born to an unwed mother who died shortly afterward, and the grandfather and aunts were the only living relatives, there was no real need for a formal adoption. Her relatives would be the obvious choices for guardians, but maybe the adoption was made for purposes of controlling her assets or voting her stocks. You know, just making things official. It's hard to say. Maybe it was nothing more than making it simpler to file taxes. Who knows, Mike. People do things for strange reasons."

"So there's no real way to tell why the adoption took place? No court records relating a reason or anything like that?" Michael knew he was grasping at straws.

"There probably is, but so far I've not been able to get into them. I'll keep checking if you want me to."

"Yeah, that'd be good. Also find out what you can about any legal will for Rose Deveraux. Oh, and don't forget to check for a trust fund."

"Okay. I'll give you a call when I know something."

"Thanks," he told his friend and hung up the phone just as Richard

Deveraux came bounding into Michael's office unannounced. As usual.

"Michael," he said with a nod.

Michael thought Richard looked as though he'd aged about ten years in the time since Denali came to Dallas. She seemed to have a startling effect on him, and Michael couldn't help but wonder why.

"Richard," Michael acknowledged.

"Thought I'd stop by to get the lowdown on the Omni project."

"Well, Denali isn't in the office today," Michael told him as if Richard didn't already know that fact.

"Which is exactly why I am here," Richard said, his voice betraying irritation. He took a seat opposite Michael and stared at him for a moment before adding, "You are still interested in that bonus, aren't you?"

"Of course," Michael countered, wondering what game Deveraux was playing.

"Well, then, knock off with the attitude and level with me about the project."

Michael smiled. "I didn't know I had any different attitude than when you hired me on. But as for the project, it's going well. We're just about to finalize the agreement. Denali and I have been working non-stop to rework the park design. Most of the hotel designs were salvageable, so that saved us a great deal of time. And given the fact that the initial groundwork was already done by the previous team, I'd say our work has been relatively simple."

"It wasn't simple enough to get Hazel Garrison to approve the project," Richard countered.

"Well, even that was made easy. Hazel loved the layout for the park in Missouri, and with that as the starting place, Denali and I have been able to accomplish quite a bit in a short time."

"So long as the old battle-ax is satisfied and signs on the dotted line."

Michael stretched and leaned back in the leather chair. "I don't think that was ever really in question. I mean, out of all the firms she contacted and took initial bids from, yours is the firm she hired to draw up the actual design."

"That means nothing until they agree to allow you to take on the project, and you know that as well as anyone. The money paid out for plans is nothing compared to following through with the project. Your business background should tell you that much, if nothing else."

"Of course it does," Michael said, losing his patience with Deveraux. "Anyway, the job is nearly completed to the board's satisfaction, and I think it will only be a short time before we have all the paper work finished and Omni Missions' go-ahead to break ground. Denali and I have already called the specialty contractor to see how his schedule lines up. I'd say just a few more weeks at most, and we'll be done."

"Good. Then we can rid you of your partner, and you can take full charge of this project."

"You're giving this project to me?" Michael asked, leaning forward. "What about Denali?"

"She's never been intended to be permanent, and you know it. The sooner I can dispose of her, the sooner I can relax and let things get back to normal."

"I thought you looked a little tense," Michael offered, hoping Richard would confide more.

"She's enough to make anyone tense. Always prying. Always wanting answers to questions that she has no business asking."

"Some people are only centered on themselves," Michael said, trying to sound casual about the whole thing. "She probably doesn't care what it costs anyone else."

As if recognizing Michael as a sympathetic collaborator, Richard leaned forward and lowered his voice. "She doesn't care, and that's the whole point. She can ruin this family and this business, and she doesn't care. She thinks she has to have things her way." Richard grew quiet for a moment, his gaze staring past Michael to the window behind him. "I can't let her destroy what I've worked so hard to build."

"No, I'm sure you can't," Michael agreed. He studied Deveraux for a moment and thought the man almost sounded worried. He'd never known Richard Deveraux to be anything but a pillar of strength and competence, yet here he was—clearly shaken and troubled.

"The past should stay buried," Deveraux said in a voice barely audible. "There are some things that should never be brought up."

"I take it Denali is one of those things."

Richard looked at Michael as if weighing the validity of his statement. "Yes. Denali should never have been born."

Michael felt a strange chill run down his spine. Deveraux's eyes were rather glassy, almost as if he had taken on a fever. "Being illegitimate isn't that big of deal," Michael offered, "at least not in this day and age. If that's the secret you worry about, I wouldn't let it bother you."

Deveraux laughed and shook his head. "Rose never listened to reason. She had to have things her way. She could twist me around her little finger, and she knew it. Counted on it. But you have to draw a line somewhere. You know what I mean?"

Michael nodded. The conversation took a decidedly eerie turn as Richard continued. "I did what I had to do. Sometimes that happens when you're a father. You have to take responsibility even when your children have made mistakes."

"Is that why you adopted Denali?"

Richard's face paled, as if Michael's words had snapped him back to reality in the matter of time it took to blink his eyes. "What in the world are you talking about?"

Michael realized his mistake and shrugged. "I thought Denali was adopted by you."

"Who ever told you that?"

Michael glanced down at the notes he'd made from his phone conversation. He couldn't tell if Deveraux could see them, but just in case, he pretended to start putting his desk in order. "I don't recall. In fact, I'm probably mistaken. Well, obviously I am, given your reaction."

"Don't ever let me catch you speaking of such a thing again," Deveraux warned. "And if I hear anything of this floating around the office, I'm going to know that it was you who started the rumor." Richard got up from the chair and stormed to the door. "If you want that bonus, get those papers signed and that project started. I can't abide that woman in this office for much longer."

Michael nodded and didn't even react when Deveraux slammed the office door behind him.

"Well, I'd say I touched a nerve there," Michael murmured, leaning back in his chair once again, rubbing his jaw. He picked up his list of information and felt that he had to be on the right trail. There was something about Denali that Richard wanted to keep buried. Of this he was certain. Why else would he have denied the adoption? *Then again, he never really did deny the adoption*, Michael reminded himself.

Why would he adopt her and then not want anyone else to know about it?

Michael drew a penciled circle around the words *Denali adopted*, then stared at the paper for several minutes as though it might call out the answer. If Deveraux didn't want him to mention the adoption, then Denali probably didn't know about it. Perhaps that was the key to her past. If she went back to Kansas City and called up the sealed records, perhaps she would have all the answers she needed.

"Then, too," Michael reasoned aloud, "there's the matter of the stocks and trust fund. What does she know about those?" Michael stared at the paper for another moment before ripping the page from the pad and folding it carefully. "Better yet, what doesn't she know?"

Denali felt physically refreshed from her day off, but mentally her burden seemed just as heavy as ever. After her talk several days earlier with Hazel Garrison, Denali knew she had a great deal of soul-searching to do. Especially concerning Michael. Spending the day just driving around and getting to know Dallas had given her plenty of time to think. The drafting plans for the Omni project were nearly completed, and after it was finished, Denali hadn't the slightest clue as to what she was going to do.

She had always figured to go back to Kansas City, but Hazel had mentioned the idea of keeping her on board with the resort, and that idea rather appealed to Denali. To work with Hazel Garrison sounded most appealing. To remain in Dallas and get to know Michael Copeland sounded even better.

Michael. He had consumed her thoughts throughout the day. Amazing how one person could absorb your mind and make everything else seem blurred and even more confusing than it had been before! Michael Copeland had that power where she was concerned. But in spite of that power, Denali didn't feel ready to deal with her feelings for him, yet she knew she would have to face facts sooner or later. He attracted her in a physical way. She couldn't deny that. But he also held a more engulfing appeal. She felt drawn to him in a way she couldn't explain. At first she thought it was because of the pain he'd talked about with her. The sadness in his life. His distancing himself from God. His anger. But she knew now that Michael was more than a cause to her. She'd actually missed him today, and she hadn't anticipated that.

But what do I do? she wondered, making her way upstairs to the apartment. *I can't very well march into his office and say, "I'm attracted to you and just wondered how you feel about me."* She smiled at this thought, knowing full well that Michael would be the kind of guy who would do just such a thing if the roles were reversed. She giggled, trying to imagine herself very professional and businesslike approaching Michael to negotiate the terms of their relationship.

"Yes, Mr. Copeland, I find you attractive and believe that the merger of our interests might well serve both of us in future projects. Shall I have my lawyer contact your lawyer regarding negotiations toward an amicable partnership?" She laughed again.

Denali glanced at her watch as she inserted the key into the door of the apartment. She had no idea what her aunts had planned for the evening, but if she worked it right, Denali hoped she could squeeze in a quick swim before supper.

"Hello? Anybody home?"

Silence greeted her. Apparently her aunts had business elsewhere. She tossed the mail and her purse on the kitchen counter, then checked the answering machine for messages. There were none. This routine accomplished, she went into her bedroom and groaned at the sight of the laundry she should have started that morning.

"So much for the swim," she thought and gathered up the things for her first load.

As the washer hummed into action, Denali munched on an apple and read her mail. A bank statement and two advertisements offering her credit cards were all that belonged to her.

She tossed the advertisements in the trash, then finished the apple while gazing out her window at the Dallas skyline. It was a perfect day. Beautiful and sunny. She finally felt used to the heat, and now that August was upon them, it didn't seem quite so unnatural. Chrys assured her that she'd love the winter months, as it normally stayed fairly nice. But Denali liked the seasonal changes and knew in her heart that she'd miss the snow. A part of her longed to return to Kansas City as soon as the Omni papers were signed, while another part kept bringing to mind penetrating blue eyes and a sternly handsome face.

"You've got to face facts, Deveraux," she told herself. "This isn't going to just go away."

Gathering up her next load of clothes, Denali realized she didn't have many whites to wash. Rather than put the load aside until later, she decided to go in search of anything her aunts might need cleaned. She knew for a fact that Azalea had worn several simple wash and wear white blouses earlier in the week.

Rummaging around the master bathroom, Denali only managed to turn up one of the blouses in question. *Maybe they're in the closet,* she thought and went to open the door.

She found them quickly enough, spotting them on the floor near the door. But as she picked them up, she couldn't help but notice a wooden box that lay under them. Curiosity got the better of her, and, setting the blouses aside, Denali reached for the box.

Even as she lifted the wooden lid, Denali felt a current of electrical energy run up her arm. It was as if the box held some kind of charge to it. The hinged top opened easily and fell back with a muffled thud against the carpeted floor. Denali reached inside to take up a newspaper clipping and several photographs. She gasped. The photos were of her mother.

Her hands began to tremble as she pushed the photos aside and revealed a small clothbound book with the dusty pink word *Rose* written in cursive across the front. Denali felt her stomach give a lurch. Hesitantly she reached for the book, already certain that it was some type of diary. Touching the aged material, Denali felt overcome by a deep sense of longing. She opened the book and confirmed her suspicions.

" 'The two-year diary of Rose Deveraux.' " Denali barely uttered the words and noted the account began the year prior to her birth.

Feeling her chest grow tight, Denali wondered if she might actually faint. She felt so light-headed. So totally overwhelmed. The box contained articles that belonged to her mother. Yet all of her life, everyone had assured her that no such thing existed.

Why? Why had they all lied to her? Why couldn't they simply tell her the truth? What could a box of pictures and letters and diaries possibly mean to them? Why should it be wrong for Denali to have these things—things that were the last effects of her mother?

The questions kept coming. They coursed through her mind at blinding speeds. Chrys and Azalea had lied to her! She expected that from her grandfather, but not from them. They had told her over and over that they could give her nothing of her mother's—that he had insisted everything of Rose's be destroyed.

"Including me," Denali whispered. "He especially wanted to destroy me."

The sound of someone coming in the front door caused Denali to start. Fearful of being caught snooping, Denali thrust the diary and photographs back inside. She closed the lid, dropped the blouses back on top of the box, and darted into the hall bathroom just as her aunts' voices could be heard in the foyer.

"Hello!" Denali called out nervously. She fought desperately to steady her breathing. "I'm just doing laundry. Do you have any whites you want me to wash for you?" She hoped the question sounded casual enough, but when no answer came, she feared her voice had betrayed her.

And then she heard a sound that could only be described as sobbing. A chill coursed through her body. The sound of her aunts crying panicked Denali, and she instantly forgot her own misery for the moment and hurried into the living room.

"What's wrong?" she asked. Azalea and Chrys were holding each other and hardly seemed to notice her presence. Denali swallowed hard and moved forward to put her hand on Azalea's shoulder. "Please tell me what's wrong."

Twenty-one

Drying their eyes and pulling back to include Denali in their embrace, Azalea spoke first. "Let's sit down. There's something I need to tell you."

Denali nodded and walked to one of the chairs. "All right," she said, feeling uncomfortable with the tension of the moment. "What's going on?"

Chrys bit her lip and settled down on the sofa while Azalea stood wringing her hands for a moment. She appeared to be searching for the proper words, and the infinite slowness of the delay left Denali wanting to jump from her chair demanding answers. Even as she studied her aunt standing there in her flowery summer dress, Denali's mind went back to the white box. She wanted more than just an answer to her aunts' tears—she wanted answers to her life, and she wanted them now.

"We've—that is to say," Azalea began, "I have just come from the doctor."

Denali instantly lost her selfish thoughts. Her breath caught in her throat. "Why?" she questioned softly, her voice suddenly childlike.

"You knew in Kansas City that I was feeling unwell. You yourself pushed me to go to the doctor, but with the move and all, I put it off. After you left, I had some sort of spell, and they put me in the hospital—"

"I knew I should never have left you alone," Denali interrupted. She felt immediately responsible for her aunt's frail condition.

Azalea shook her head. "No, Denali. This had nothing to do with you. Even if you would have been there, the outcome would have been no different."

"What outcome?" Denali asked, knowing she wouldn't like the answer.

"I have ovarian cancer," Azalea told her. "The doctor feels I've probably been in a pre-cancerous state for years and just didn't know it."

"What does he suggest you do for it?" Denali asked, refusing to give in to her fears that nothing could be done. Her grandmother had died of ovarian cancer, but she refused to believe that in this day and age anyone should have to die of something like that.

"He's made a number of suggestions, but for the most part it's too late to do much good."

"No! I won't believe that," Denali said, jumping to her feet. "You have to get a second opinion."

"We've just come from a third doctor," Chrys said firmly, her facade of control clearly back in place. "They all say the same thing."

Azalea walked to where Denali stood. "I'm sorry, sweetheart. I hate to break the news to you like this, but we have to be strong. We have to realize that there's a purpose—even in this."

"What purpose? What good can possibly come out of this?" Denali knew she was close to shouting, but it seemed impossible to calm her fears. Azalea couldn't die! She just couldn't!

Azalea smiled lovingly and reached out to touch her niece's face. "I don't have all the answers, but I trust the One who does. I don't want to die any more than you want me to, but if that is the order of things—if that is what God's will is—then I'm not afraid. Just sorry."

"You have nothing to be sorry for," Denali said, tears welling up in her eyes. Shock quickly replaced itself with genuine grief. "I can't believe this is happening."

"Neither could I," Chrys joined in.

"It's been hard for me, as well," Azalea admitted. "There's still so much left undone."

Denali embraced Azalea and hugged her close. "Oh, please tell me this is some kind of bad dream. Tell me there's been a mistake and we will wake up and all of this will be gone."

Azalea pulled back. "You don't know how many times in life I've made a similar wish." She seemed to study Denali for a moment before offering her a sad sort of smile. "I haven't always made the right choices, Denali, but I'm going to try to correct at least one of my mistakes."

"I don't understand." Denali looked from Azalea to Chrys and back again. "What mistake?"

"Chrys," Azalea said, turning to her sister, "we have to tell her."

Chrys nodded, and Azalea turned to leave the room. Denali sat back down on the chair, almost certain she knew what was coming. They were going to give her the box. Azalea needed to make amends for keeping Rose's things from her.

Azalea appeared with the white box, and for a moment she did nothing but stand there looking at Denali. Her eyes were still wet from the tears she'd cried earlier, but they now had a certain light to them.

"A long time ago, your grandfather insisted that we destroy everything that belonged to Rose. He felt overwhelmed with his sorrow, and every time he saw her things, he was reminded of her death. The only exception he made was in allowing us to keep her room just as she'd left it.

"So Chrys and I loaded up her clothing and her stuffed animals and other knickknacks, and we sent them all away." She paused and looked at the box. "Except for these things."

"What things?" Denali forced herself to ask.

"This box contains photographs, letters, the newspaper account of Rose's death, and other little things. There's also a diary."

"A diary?"

"Yes. Rose kept it that last year and a half of her life."

Denali tried to remain calm—tried hard not to give any outward sign of knowing about the box and the diary. "Why didn't you tell me sooner?"

"We didn't want to go against Father's wishes," Azalea said, moving to take the chair beside Denali. "You have to understand, we love him very much."

"Even though we've never approved of the way he's acted toward you," Chrys assured. "You know how we feel. We've talked about it a hundred times."

"I know," Denali replied. "Still, I don't understand why it would have hurt to let me have these things. They are mine by rights. Surely even Grandfather understands that."

"Oh, he understands only too well," Chrys said, looking suddenly uncomfortable. "But you have to understand, too. The whole thing seems senseless, but this is his way of coping. In the early years, and Azalea can confirm this, we wondered if he'd survive Rose's death. He grew very reclusive and seldom talked to anyone. He would go to Rose's room for long periods of time, and he seemed totally preoccupied with anything that related to her. The business suffered horribly, but I tried to fill in for him as best I could."

"He just loved Rose more than he loved life," Azalea said flatly. "We thought perhaps he would put that lost love into you; instead, he buried it with her, and he's never been the same. Chrys and I lost our father the same day you lost your mother. We know your pain over this. We know how it feels to be left out in the cold because, whether you believe it or not, Father has never really come back to us since the day your mother died."

"I never thought of it that way," Denali said honestly. "I mean, I know he's distanced himself from you, but ... well ... I always presumed—" She hesitated for a moment and stared at the box in Azalea's hands.

"You always presumed it was solely because of your birth?" Azalea questioned.

Denali's head snapped up. "Yes. That's it exactly."

"We've tried to tell you over and over that there was more to this situation than you could ever understand," Chrys explained. "You didn't know him before your grandmother died. He's always been a hard, tough businessman. But he was a good father and husband, and his love for us remained very evident. Losing our mother took the life out of him, but he saw Rose as a way to revitalize his life. He put such store in her that he naturally assumed she'd return the favor."

"But she didn't?" Denali asked.

Chrys shook her head. "Not really. Not the way he wanted. His love for her was unhealthy. Oh, I don't mean incest—I certainly don't want to imply that," Chrys stated. "But in the sense that he couldn't see anything else. Didn't want to see anything else. Many women sought his affections and attention after the death of our mother. There were even a couple that would have probably suited him very nicely, but he'd have nothing to do with them. He focused on his daughters, then zeroed in on Rose."

"Weren't you jealous?" Denali questioned, finding relief in the fact that they would talk about the past.

"Of course," Chrys answered. "But only a little. I mean, Rose was so easy to love. She didn't act presumptuous or conceited about her position in his life."

"Oh, absolutely not," Azalea chimed in. "If anything, she regretted his obvious favoritism. I often thought that she defied him as a way to even things out."

"I thought that, too," Chrys replied. "She knew how he could be.

Bringing her gifts and not doing the same for us. Yelling at Azalea and me for minor mistakes in judgment, while overlooking major conflicts with Rose."

"How awful that must have been for all of you." Denali could well imagine the scene, and it touched her that her mother should have been so considerate of her sisters' feelings, when many children would have relished the privileged position and taken it for all it was worth.

"We loved Rose as much as he did," Azalea finally spoke. "Maybe for the same reasons. She was all we had left of Mother. I was only thirteen when Mother died, and it tore me apart. I needed her so much. You see, Chrys was always closer to Father, but Mother was my mainstay."

Chrys nodded as if to confirm this. "I threw myself into my work with Father. I was nineteen and tried to reason that I didn't need a mother anymore and that while I missed her sorely, I could easily survive. After all, everyone has to die sometime. At least that's what I told myself."

"Which brings us full circle," Azalea said, shifting in her seat to hand Denali the box. "I can't die in peace knowing that I kept these things from you. You have a right to them, as you always have, but now it's most important that I do this for you."

"I tried to speak to Father about it," Chrys said softly. "He was totally against giving you these things."

"But I thought he didn't know about them."

"He didn't—at least not for a long while. When he found out, he ranted and raved, but we held our ground. That was when he decided to split the business and move the headquarters to Dallas."

"Because of this?" Denali questioned, holding up the box.

Chrys shrugged. "I've never understood it, either. I mean, he's read every detail of everything written in the diary and the letters. In fact, he read the diary long before Azalea or I ever saw it. I don't know why it's so important to him that you be kept in the dark about your mother and father, but maybe now you can see why it's been so difficult for us. He thinks I destroyed this box. We had a long talk, and he told me how painful it was to him that I'd defied him and kept it all these years. I left him believing that I finally understood and would take care of the problem. But I couldn't. It was like destroying Rose and betraying you."

Denali hugged the box to her chest. "I've always known why it was difficult for you. You are both so good to me, and believe me—" she said, pausing to stress her point—"please believe me, I've never wanted to be the cause of conflict in this family. I don't enjoy knowing that my questions cause you grief. I don't even like knowing that I've hurt Grandfather with my prideful pursuits. But you have to understand. I'm a grown woman without a past. I don't even know who my father is—do you?"

Chrys paled and fell silent, but Azalea spoke. "We know his name. Well, we know his first name, but only because Rose speaks of him in her diary. She called him Les."

"Les," Denali said, trying the name. "My father's name is Les."

Chrys appeared to grow uncomfortable. Leaning forward she said, "Look, you can't speak to Father about any of this. Please promise me?"

Denali saw the desperation and fear in the older woman's eyes. Azalea reached out to touch her hand before she could speak.

"Please, Denali. It's important that you allow us to maintain this fragile relationship with him. He's all we have, and we're all he has. Our relationship and love is a strange one, to be sure, but I don't want to lose him. Especially not now. If he knows we've openly defied him, he'll be livid, and it won't matter how much we try to explain. Sometimes we've been able to control situations in regard to you because we know it's important to him that we stay close. However, I don't think it would work this time. Besides, I honestly think now that he's seen you and experienced your abilities firsthand at work, he may well soften. I believe it's even possible, just given some of the things he's said to me, that in time he may even come to desire a relationship with you."

These were the first hopeful words Denali had ever had in regards to a relationship with Richard Deveraux. "Do you really think so?"

Chrys looked at Azalea and then to Denali. "He does seem to show more interest in you. He's asked me several times about you. Like after the party. He wanted to know how you managed after the argument."

Denali felt a surge of hope. It was like the lights coming on after a bad storm had knocked out the electricity. She could see things, possibilities that she'd never allowed herself to imagine. But before she could shout her joy aloud, she found Azalea studying her quite seriously.

Azalea is dying, Denali thought. *She's dying, and I don't even know how much longer we can have her with us. Surely there would be time enough to . . . To what?* Denali wondered. Time to say things that were left unsaid? Time to do things they'd always planned to do? There were no plans. They weren't a family to set goals and dreams for the future.

Maybe because they were far too entangled with the past.

"I won't say anything to Grandfather," Denali promised. "I don't want to be a burden or to further upset him, especially in light of your news."

"He doesn't know about Azalea's sickness," Chrys said before her sister could speak. "We haven't told him because frankly, we're afraid of what it will do to his mental well-being."

Denali nodded. "It won't be easy for him to deal with someone else being sick."

"Much less dying," Azalea countered.

Denali turned to her, but she couldn't even find the words to question her as to the time they had left together.

As if reading her mind, Azalea whispered, "Six, maybe eight weeks. Maybe not that long."

"What?" Denali cried out. "Surely the doctor has that wrong."

Azalea shook her head sadly. "I wish he did. But already I feel the cancer eating away at me. It's worse every day. It won't be long before I'll have to be hospitalized. I want this to be as easy as possible on all of us. I don't want to spend my final days of life in death. Do you both understand?"

Denali shook her head. "No, I don't."

Azalea squeezed her hand. "You will have plenty of time to mourn me when I'm gone. I don't want to see you walk into the room with this look of dread and sorrow. I want us to spend my final days in positive thought and happy reflections. I want to discuss the things of the living, not deal with the aspects of my death and dying." She turned to Chrys and smiled. "Chrys and I have already worked out all the details of the arrangements, so there is no need to go any further with that matter. If you need to ask questions about my condition, that's fine. If you even want to share your heart with me regarding my passing, I can handle that, as well. But I don't want every day remaining to me to be spent crying."

Denali could see how important this was to her aunt. She nodded. "I can do that for you," she whispered, tears streaming down her face. "I can at least give you that, after all you've given to me." She began to cry in earnest. "But I will be lost without you. You and Chrys are the only mothers I've ever known, but especially you. You were always there for me when I had a bad dream or just needed to be held. You doctored my skinned knees and dried my tears." She paused to wipe her eyes, but it was no use. The reality of their short time was settling in. "I don't know how I will do this, but I promise to try. I love you so much." It was all more than Denali could take. Setting the box aside, she knelt at Azalea's side and put her head on her knees. "Please don't leave me. Please don't die."

Azalea soothed her as a mother would her wounded child. "Shh. It will be all right. You'll see. God has a plan, and in the midst of it, He won't forget you, Denali. He never has, even though at times it might have seemed that way."

Denali clung tightly to Azalea. She wanted so much to find comfort in her words. *Here I should be comforting her, and instead I've fallen apart.* Denali felt instantly guilty but not enough so that she could find the strength to let go. *It hurts so much. Oh, God, this can't be true. It just can't be. Six to eight weeks, maybe less. How can I find a way to say goodbye in that short a time?*

Twenty-two

Michael glanced at his watch for the third time in ten minutes. The day had seemed incredibly long, mostly because Denali had taken off to spend time with Hazel Garrison going over last-minute changes. Hazel preferred working one-on-one with Denali and had openly discouraged any further "team" meetings at the Fun, Inc. offices. Because the company was desperate to hook the Omni Missions project, Hazel's wishes were not only granted but catered to in a way that Michael had never seen in his three years with the company. Of course, when a thirty-million-dollar project was at stake, people tended to sit up and notice.

Anxious to hear from Denali and know Hazel's opinion of what Michael hoped would be the final designs, Michael picked up the phone and dialed Denali's apartment. He wondered if she would mind the call. Denali had been rather moody these last few days, and Michael wasn't exactly sure what was bothering her. He couldn't even be sure that he hadn't offended her. Nothing came to mind that should have put them at odds, but with Denali it didn't seem to take much.

After a few rings, Michael was just about to hang up when Denali's voice rang out through the line.

"Hello?"

"Denali, it's Michael."

"Oh, hello."

Michael grimaced. She didn't sound unhappy, just surprised, so he continued. "I couldn't wait to find out how it went today."

"It went well," Denali replied. "I suppose I should have called, but I figured we'd finish going over everything in the morning."

Michael tried to sound casual when he asked, "How about tonight? I know this really great restaurant, and I could pick you up at seven."

There was a long silence on the other end of the line. Michael held his breath. She was going to turn him down, he just knew it.

"I can't, Michael. It isn't that important. There's nothing here that won't keep until morning."

Michael sighed. *Strike one.*

"Well, it would certainly give me a chance to put together anything we need done before tomorrow's team meeting. We wouldn't have to stay out all night, and if seven doesn't work, we could go earlier or later."

"No. Look, Hazel is pleased. There doesn't need to be any further changes made, so relax. The meeting in the morning will be a breeze."

Michael! gritted his teeth. *Strike two.*

"All right, look," he said, trying to sound like it didn't matter. "I'd really like to take you to dinner. The business aspect is just a front."

"Oh?"

She didn't sound very convinced, and Michael really wasn't sure what he wanted to say. He felt confused about his feelings for Denali, and the fact that she wouldn't see him outside of work had really started to irritate him. Deveraux had offered to pay all of their expenses, and so far Michael had nothing to submit.

"I feel like the whole time we've been working together," Michael began, "you've avoided me regarding anything personal."

"And?"

"And I'd like for that to stop. I'm a nice enough guy, and I'd just like to smooth things over between us."

"Michael, there's really nothing . . . ah . . . that needs smoothing," Denali replied. She sounded nervous, almost hesitant. "Look," she continued, "I have something to do tonight."

"You aren't just putting me off because I insulted your faith?" he asked before he could put the question in check. Grimacing for asking it, he felt rather surprised by her response.

"Not at all. I think you have more faith in God than you give yourself credit for. I've listened to your protests and your insults, but somehow they just don't ring true. I think you're more hurt and angry at yourself and the people who caused your problems than you are at God."

He sat up rather stunned. "Why do you say that?"

She said nothing for several moments, then took a deep, audible breath. "I talked to some people, and they told me some of the details of your business failure. Why didn't you tell me that your partner ran out on you?"

"Didn't think it was any of your business," Michael said rather defensively.

"He ruined the business and cleaned you out, but you honored your commitment to your projects and didn't even prosecute him. Why, Michael? Why did you just let him go?"

Without even thinking of the implications, Michael answered, "Because he died, and suing the estate didn't seem the thing to do. After all, he had a wife and three kids." Michael shifted the receiver to his left hand. "Look, I didn't call to talk about this. I called to ask you out. It's okay that you don't want to go. I understand."

"But I truly have something going on," Denali replied. "I didn't say that just to put you off. In fact, I've got to run, but I'll see you in the morning."

"Okay, good-bye." He hung up the receiver without even waiting to hear her response. *Strike three—you're out.*

Sweat formed on his brow, making him feel foolish. He hadn't known this kind of frustration over a woman in a long, long time. He didn't like the feelings. Packing his briefcase, Michael decided he needed to do something physical. He'd go volunteer to take Dusty on a good long jog. But thinking about Dusty only served to remind him of the first time he'd laid eyes on Denali Deveraux.

Slamming the top down on the briefcase, Michael jumped when the telephone rang. Hoping against hope that Denali had changed her mind, Michael grabbed the receiver after one ring.

"Hello?"

"Michael, it's Jim Siemens in Kansas City."

Michael instantly put down the briefcase. "Have you found something out?"

"I'll say. I think I hit pay dirt—if not for me, for your friend."

"What is it?"

"I found a marriage license for Rose Deveraux."

"A marriage license? I was under the impression Denali was illegitimate."

"Well, apparently not—unless her grandfather had the marriage annulled. But I didn't find any signs of that. Of course, he could have gone elsewhere to take care of that."

"Who was she married to?" Michael asked, once again retrieving a pencil and pad.

"The name is Lester Wilson. But don't ask me anything else about him. I couldn't find anything more on the man. My guess is that he wasn't born in Missouri or Kansas. I searched through all sorts of records, but I didn't turn up anything."

"Not even a death certificate?" Michael questioned.

"Nope, not even that. Nor did I find a last will and testament for Rose Deveraux. However, I did find out about the trust fund."

"Really?" Michael was so fascinated with the fact that Denali's parents had actually been married that he had very nearly forgotten about the trust.

"Seems the mother, Shirley Fowler Deveraux, had quite a bit of money left to her by her parents. For whatever reason, she earmarked the money as a trust for her daughters. The provisions were that upon their twenty-first birthdays they would come into the money. Chrysanthemum Deveraux became eligible for her share two years after her mother's death. Azalea Deveraux took claim to hers some six years after her sister."

"And Rose?"

"Rose died when she was eighteen. She never lived long enough to lay claim to the money."

"Then the money would belong to Denali," Michael said flatly. Then, remembering the bits and pieces of conversation between Deveraux and his daughter, Michael suddenly realized that Denali knew nothing of the money.

"Well, whoever it belongs to, it's quite a sizable nest egg. I mean, the trust was established in the late fifties, and it's been sitting there gaining interest ever since."

"Wow, that is something else," Michael admitted. "Can you give me the name of the bank that holds the trust?"

"Sure."

Michael wrote down the information. "Thanks, Jim. Looks like it's time for me to do some digging from down here."

"Well, just call if you have something else. I can always use the extra money."

"Speaking of which, I just put your check in the mail. You'll have to let me know what I owe you for the rest of this."

"I'll bill you," the man said with a laugh. "And if you don't pay up,

I'll be forced to come to Dallas for a couple of weeks, soak up some sun, and do my level best to run you down."

"Sounds painful. Maybe I'll just forget where my stamps are."

"You do that, Mike. You just do that."

Michael laughed and hung up the phone.

Staring at the notes he'd just taken, Michael felt as though he were sitting on a puzzle with all the pieces suddenly starting to fall into place. Deveraux obviously had kept his granddaughter in the dark about a great many things. Denali thought her mother had borne her out of wedlock, which was clearly not the case. Unless, of course, Jim was right, and Deveraux had annulled the marriage. He wrote the word *annulled* and a question mark beside the names *Rose Deveraux* and *Lester Wilson*.

Next he wondered who Lester Wilson could be. This man would most likely be Denali's father, and Michael knew that Denali had no idea about him. He knew from their talks that even if her parents weren't married at the time of Denali's birth, no one in the history of her life had ever so much as breathed the man's name. He wrote the word *father* and a question mark beside the name *Lester*.

The trust intrigued him, but not as much as the identity of Lester Wilson. That Denali was a rich woman in her own right didn't surprise Michael. He had little difficulty imagining that even on her own, Denali had probably been frugal and cautious with money. She didn't seem the type to go off on wild spending sprees, and even the couple of times she'd admitted to losing track of time in one of Dallas's more prestigious malls, she also admitted to spending less than one hundred dollars. And, Michael smiled in remembrance, she had called that an outrageous sum of money. Renea would have dropped that in tips alone on a day of pampering and spoilage, as he called it.

Getting up from his desk, Michael reopened his briefcase and tossed the information inside. He glanced at his watch, surprised to find that so much time had passed. Everyone would be gone for the evening. No wonder things were so quiet. He thought about going home, as well, but then another thought came to mind. With Richard Deveraux in Los Angeles, and Chrys enjoying an indefinite leave of absence after wrapping up her New Orleans deal, now would probably be as good a time as any to take a general snoop around the office. Maybe he could find something—something that would give him some clue as to what else Deveraux was hiding.

"And I'm sure he's hiding something more than the identity of his granddaughter's father," he said, stepping into the hall. "I just feel it in my bones."

The silence gave evidence to Michael's desire that everyone be gone from the office. He made two sweeps through each area before allowing himself to relax. He needed facts, and he had to remember to keep focused on that and nothing else.

Richard's office seemed the obvious place to start, but Michael felt certain this would be locked up tighter than a drum. He went into Deveraux's outer office, hoping that Gladys's area might reveal something to help him. The older woman's desk sat in pristine order, revealing nothing more than a desk calendar, pen, message pad, and telephone.

He frowned and reached for the center drawer. He told himself it would be locked, but to his surprise the thing rolled right out. The order inside matched the order outside. Pens were meticulously arranged in the receptacle at the front of the drawer, while other necessary supplies were neatly positioned and ready for use. His eyes were suddenly drawn to two sets of keys. They looked to be desk keys or filing cabinet keys. Certainly not office keys, he realized, much to his disappointment.

He took up both sets and tried them in the lock on Gladys's desk. They didn't fit. Next he went to the filing cabinet and inserted first one set and then the other. The lock opened on the second try, and Michael stood back, almost in shock.

"Okay, so that one opens the cabinet," he told himself and put the set in his right coat pocket. He looked at the remaining set and wondered where they could possibly belong. Deciding to waste no more time on them, Michael put them in his left pocket and set out to explore the filing cabinet.

He would have laughed had the situation not been one of such importance to him. Gladys again left her mark in the precisely arranged collection. The files were clearly labeled and easily accessible. Color-coded labels, with client names and even dates listed across the top, made short order of his work. Thumbing through, Michael didn't even know for sure what he was looking for. These were just records of jobs performed by Fun, Inc. He opened a second drawer and then a third. The files in the third drawer looked much the same as the first and second, but with one major difference. These files dated back some forty years. On impulse, Michael pulled one of the older files and opened it.

The records indicated a design drawn up for a small amusement park near St. Louis. It wasn't anything near the magnitude of a full-blown theme park, but it brought in a tidy sum and seemed a reasonable indication of the work performed in the early years. Michael studied the papers, barely even reading the contents of the contract. He flipped through until he came to the next to the last page. Here the signatures of all parties concerned were laid out and notarized. The company requesting the park had three signatures. One from the president, and two from underlings who apparently had important enough titles to merit their okay on the project. From Fun, Inc. Michael found two signatures. Richard Deveraux and William Wilson. Both were indicated as owners.

"Wilson," Michael said the name, hardly daring to believe his good fortune. "Deveraux had a partner named Wilson. Perhaps this Lester Wilson who married Rose was a son or relative of the man."

He replaced the folder and skipped ahead several years and pulled another file. Wilson's name again appeared on the bottom of the contract. Michael repeated this procedure until he came up to the files in the early seventies. Thumbing through, Wilson's signature was given sporadically, and soon after, his name ceased to appear at all. Perhaps Wilson's son had done the unthinkable thing and married the daughter of his father's partner. Maybe Deveraux bought him out after that, or maybe the man felt badly enough about the action of his child and sold out his shares of the company to Deveraux. Intriguing! There was no limit to the number of possibilities. The biggest question seemed to be, who was William Wilson, and where could he be found?

Michael slapped the folder shut and tried to think how he would go about finding out the details. There were all manner of permits and licenses to be granted any firm, but Michael was uncertain what the rules were in the late forties when Fun, Inc. saw its inception. There had to be records somewhere, and they were probably in Kansas City.

Putting the folder away and locking the cabinet, Michael returned both sets of keys to Gladys's desk and picked up the phone. He started to dial Jim Siemens' number, then thought better of it. It would be smarter to stick with using his own phone. If the records were brought to light, he could explain away the long-distance calls from his phone. But knowing Gladys, she probably kept a meticulous record of her own long-distance calls. No doubt the woman would see the call and realize someone had used her line.

Michael made his way back to his office. His blood seemed to speed through his veins. He felt intrigued by the excitement and mystery of it all. Somehow, some way, he would learn the truth, and when he did, he would share it with Denali.

He dialed the memorized number and smiled at the sound of his friend's voice. "Jim, it's me again. Look, something else has come up."

Twenty-three

*D*enali couldn't explain to Michael that her heart's desire was to go out with him. She also couldn't explain that the cloth-covered book in her hand rendered her unable to concentrate on little but the past. The year prior to and including her birth laid etched in at times obscured, at times eminently clear notations in the pages of Rose Deveraux's diary. Denali had thought they would give her answers, and in part they did. But like so many things in life, one question answered often opened the floor to a dozen other questions.

Denali thought of Michael's call and nearly put the diary aside to call him back. She had given Michael and his circumstance a great deal of consideration, and throughout her many prayers for him, Denali felt certain that he was far from a lost cause. His words and statements simply lacked an element of truth, even though they were coming from his heart. It almost seemed as if he were saying, "These are the facts as I see them—now prove to me I'm wrong."

And she wanted to prove to him that his fears and bitterness were not in keeping with what God wanted for his life. She wanted to show him how much God cared. But she knew she couldn't. It wasn't her place to do God's job. She had interfered other times in the lives of her friends, and it simply didn't work. God had His timing, and that was that. It was a hard lesson for Denali to learn.

It was also a hard lesson to pick up the past and realize that there might never be answers for the questions she had.

" 'August third,' " Denali read aloud. " 'Today is Les's birthday. Yesterday, I decided to sneak out of the house and go shopping for a gift. I think he'll be surprised when he opens the box and finds a set of cuff links to match the same etched silver tie clip his mother gave him shortly before her death. I searched through several stores and couldn't find a single thing I liked, but then I went to the antique store, and there were the cuff links. What a find! I love him so much, and I know we're destined to be together.' "

Denali closed her eyes and tried to visualize the cuff links and her mother's proud expression upon bestowing the gift. She wanted desperately to see the scene. To see her father. But nothing came to mind. Rose never gave much of a description except to say that he was tall and handsome and that she loved his dark hair.

" 'August tenth. Les promised me we wouldn't have to wait until I'm eighteen to get married. The laws in Oklahoma are very lenient to young people, and he says we can elope right away if I want to. And I want to. Les knows that Daddy would never tolerate the idea, but we can't help it. We're in love!' " At this point, Rose had drawn several hearts and smiley faces with two of the smiley faces kissing. Denali couldn't help but feel the excitement of the young artist. Her mother made it easy to see that Les was more important to her than anything else in the world. More important than the Deveraux fortune. More important than her own father's trust and love.

She continued to read, scanning through dates of unimportant ramblings. Rose talked of working for her father and how much she enjoyed the office. Then school started, and it was Rose's senior year. She talked of working at Fun, Inc. after school. She mentioned having her senior pictures taken and the joy of giving one to Les and having him pronounce it a perfect image of her. Denali knew the photo well, and it felt wonderful to know that her mother so clearly matched the image. It meant that she and her mother were very nearly twins in appearance, and that pleased Denali very much. Of course, she'd always seen the resemblance, but to see in writing that the picture hadn't lied made Denali feel a special connection to her mother.

Reading on, Denali came to a long span of time when her mother didn't write. It happened during a two-week period in September when Rose was supposed to be on a high school music trip to New York. Her entry for September 12 read, " 'Leaving tomorrow. Daddy thinks I'm going on a school field trip. He handed over five hundred dollars without even questioning where the proper forms were. Of course, Les had made up some forms for me, and they looked really authentic. But Daddy never asked, so I never volunteered them. I figured, why risk it? Les even called school and pretended to be my father. He explained that he had arranged to take us on a trip and that I would be back on the twenty-ninth. They bought it, and Les laughed when I suggested that even God wanted us to be together. I'll be away with Les for two whole weeks, and when I come home I'll be a bride!' "

Denali found her mother's cunning and ingenuity amazing. She had created a situation in which she had all the angles covered. Richard Deveraux had been well-known for taking his children out of their private school to travel around the country. In fact, when Denali's grandmother had died, Azalea had come home permanently to school with a tutor. She knew this because Azalea had told her many times over of working with her tutor while helping care for Rose.

But even after Rose was old enough for school and Richard Deveraux had put both Rose and Azalea back on the rosters of the private school, he was often known to remove them at whim and take them with him abroad. That Rose remembered and used this idea only proved to Denali her mother's intelligence and ability for deception.

Denali skipped the empty pages, picking up the writing again on September 30.

" 'We are back home. Me to my house and Les to his. No one knows that we are married, and for now it must be that way. Father would surely have a spell if he knew, and so until I can find a way to break it to him, I must continue to play this game of the faithful daughter. I went back to school yesterday, and everyone asked me about my trip. I made up stories and dug up old postcards from last year's vacation in New York. I figured if Daddy asked, I could show him the same cards and he'd never be the wiser. Azalea seems to wonder at my happiness, but I assured her it was only that my senior year was well under way. I don't think she'll question me about the trip. I paid Stella a goodly sum to come over and make a big scene about all the fun we had on the school trip. Azalea listened to our stories about performing songs for a music festival, something we both had experience from last year when our choir truly did take a trip to sing in a state contest. We were going on and on about the songs when Chrys came home. So we told her about some of it, and no one questioned us on the details. Afterward, Stella asked me what I'd really done during those two weeks, and I told her that I'd sort of run away. I made up a story for her about needing my space, and since that's a big deal in our circle of friends these days, she totally understood. In fact, she's planning her own trip now.' "

Denali found it fascinating that Rose had manipulated so many people in order to get what she wanted. She'd lied and paid people off, all in order to have her elopement to a mysterious man named Les remain secret. But Les wasn't so mysterious. Not if the diary entries were true. Rose indicated that her father knew Les, or at least knew of him, and wouldn't approve of him dating or marrying his daughter. So once again, Denali found herself up against a wall. Unless the diary gave her any indication of her father's full name, she would have to go to Richard Deveraux for the answers she needed.

Stretching in her chair, Denali looked out over the Dallas skyline. From her bedroom, it seemed that the city might well be an artist's rendering. It seemed silent and still, not at all alive with the bustle and activity that she knew fed the very heart and soul of this town. Looking closer, she saw the activity of cars on the highway and the steady stream of airliners on their final approach into the airport. Funny, they once gave her cause to lie awake nights, and now she seldom even noticed them.

Her shoulders ached from the length of time she'd sat reading. Glancing at her watch, Denali was shocked to realize that it was nearly seven-thirty. It would soon be dark, and Chrys and Azalea would be home from their day together. She had no idea what they were out doing, but she knew it was necessary to make the most of Azalea's good days. Chrys had taken time off from work in order to devote herself to spending plenty of time with her sister. Denali knew it was important to them both, and she tried not to demand too much from either one. They needed each other more than they needed her.

Stretching her shoulders again, Denali rolled her head a couple of times to loosen the kinks in her neck, then went back to reading. From time to time, there were strange comments that made little sense. Nonsensical things, really. She chalked them off to her mother's age.

Finally on October 30, Denali read, " 'I'm worried about Les. I feel certain that Daddy is close to figuring out about us, and when he does, I know that Les will be the one he's most angry with. After all, I can't do anything wrong as far as Daddy is concerned. He loves me, but he treats me like a child, and he treats Azalea and Chrys even worse. He ignores them so much of the time, and they adore him. I love him, but I love Les more. I won't let Daddy spoil that for me. I am Les's wife, and if Daddy doesn't like it, he can just forget about ever having me talk to him again.' "

The knock on her bedroom door startled Denali, and she nearly dropped the diary. "Come in."

Azalea opened the door and smiled. "Am I interrupting?"

"No, not at all. I thought you were still out. I mean, I didn't hear you come in."

"I was very quiet," Azalea said and nodded toward the bed. "Mind if I sit for a moment?"

"Please," Denali replied. "You know you don't need to ask." She saw the weariness in her aunt's expression. Azalea had lost a great deal of weight since Denali had left her in Kansas City. The gaunt, pale face showed signs of her illness. Dark circles under sunken brown eyes aged her face by at least a dozen years.

"Did you know about Mother and Les? I mean, did you know about them getting married?"

"No," Azalea admitted without hesitation. "No one did. At least, I don't think they did. Father certainly didn't. I learned about their marriage when I read the diary. Up until that point, I had assumed that Rose and Les were on their way to elope when Father went after them in Oklahoma."

"I read about that," Denali admitted. "I read very quickly through most of it, and now I'm going over it with a fine-tooth comb. There has to be something more. Someone has to know about my father. Didn't Grandfather even tell you who he was after he brought Mother home? Didn't Mother tell you about him?"

Azalea shook her head sadly. "No. Rose barely even spoke to me or anyone else after her return. She stayed in her room and cried and cried. As I recall, Father found out about them in January. He never did say how he found out, or even why he was suspicious."

Denali flipped through the pages of the diary. "Yes, it was January fifteenth. She says here, 'Les and I are going to Oklahoma tomorrow. He has a job interview in Oklahoma City. He said I could go with him if I could find some excuse for staying away from the house overnight. I've told Father I'm spending the night with Stella tomorrow. Les and I will leave as soon as Father goes in to the office.'" Denali glanced up. "Something must have gone wrong."

"Father found out about them." Kicking off her shoes, Azalea curled her legs up under her and leaned back against the headboard of the sleigh bed. "He never even came home that night before going after Rose. I got a call from Chrys. She was working with Father, and the next thing I know, the world was coming apart at the seams."

"Does Chrys know who my father is?" Denali asked quite seriously. "I mean, I've asked her before, but she always manages to skirt the issue."

"I don't think she necessarily knows who he is. Not by name, anyway. Then again, who can tell? Chrys has always kept her secrets. We are closer than any two sisters could possibly be, but she has been known to lie to even me."

"Maybe she's lying now," Denali said, closing the book but marking the page with her finger. "My mother's diary is blank for a good month after the entry on the fifteenth. She picks it back up after her eighteenth birthday and talks about being pregnant with me."

"She apparently knew she was carrying a child for some time. Rose was no dummy. She would have recognized the symptoms and checked it out."

"But it wouldn't have been as easy in those days as it is now," Denali remarked absentmindedly.

"No, but where there's a will, there's a way, and Rose had a very strong will."

Denali smiled. "Obviously."

Azalea shared her smile. "You are so like her. Every day you grow more in her image. Chrys said Father nearly fainted at the sight of you, and I can well imagine why. He wouldn't even allow us to send him so much as a picture of you. Seeing you in person, after having no idea what you looked like for over fifteen years, must have been a shock in and of itself. That you look so much like your mother . . . well . . . that probably wreaked havoc on his finely ordered world."

"There's so much pain in this diary," Denali said, reopening the book. "Mother even writes that while she knew this should be the happiest time of her life, she's overwhelmed with misery." Denali fanned the pages and stopped after letting a good number slip by. " 'May twenty-second. I would die if I could do so without harming our child. It hurts so bad to face life without Les here beside me. Father is unreasonable. He tells me I have betrayed him and mortally wounded him. I tell him nothing. I don't even speak to him. I know it's killing him, but I want him to hurt as badly as I hurt. I want him to know that there are consequences to his actions. I will never forgive him for the shame he has put upon me and the horrible ugliness that will live with us both for the rest of our lives.' " Denali looked up and shook her head. "Do you understand this? Did she ever say anything to you about it?"

Azalea shook her head. "Not in any real sense. I held her while she cried on more than one occasion, but she wouldn't speak to me on the matter. She was stoic and rock hard at times, and other times she was completely broken."

"And Grandfather?"

"He told me he'd paid the man off."

"He paid my father off? You mean Grandfather paid my father to desert my mother and me?"

"Apparently."

Denali felt as though she'd been dealt a blow. Of course, it would be a very reasonable, very consistent action on the part of her grandfather. Money was everything to him. Money bought what he wanted and apparently disposed of what he didn't want. Denali took a deep breath. "What about Chrys? Would she talk to Chrys?"

Azalea again shook her head. "No. If she would have opened up to anyone, it would have been me. Remember, I nearly raised her from the time our mother died. As a child, I watched over her from the time she was born and guarded her jealously as if she were my own baby. When our mother got sick, she relied upon me for help, even though I was very young. I didn't mind, however. I adored Mama and I adored Rose." Azalea's eyes filled with tears.

Denali lowered her face and closed the diary. She vowed not to cry, but it was hard to keep that promise. Looking up, she found a smile on her aunt's face, her expression almost serene.

"Someday, Denali," Azalea said softly. "Someday we'll all be together."

Denali nodded. "I suppose I'll have to wait until then to know the identity of my father. Unless, of course, I can somehow convince Grandfather to tell me the truth."

Azalea shook her head. "Don't even try it, Denali. Let these final days pass in peace."

Denali set the diary aside. "I'll do my best, but I'll make no rash promises. If the opportunity presents itself and the situation looks promising, I intend to take the chance. I won't set out to make a scene or even to force this issue, but neither will I let a chance pass me by."

"Spoken like your mother," Azalea replied with a knowing glance.

Twenty-four

Richard Deveraux heard the commotion outside his office, and even before he knew what it was all about, he recognized the voice of Denali. He went to the door that separated his inner and outer offices and listened.

"Look, Gladys, I know he's in there. I have the contracts for the Omni Missions project, and I intend to sit down with him and finalize them."

"But you can't," Gladys was protesting. "He's busy with other things. Just leave the papers here. I'll see to it that he signs them."

"No," Denali answered flatly. "If I have to stay here all day, screaming at the top of my lungs, that man is going to deal with me."

At this, Richard opened the door. He stared blankly at Denali for a moment. She stood there, hands on hips, file clasped tightly in her hands. She wore a tailored suit of navy, green, and white and looked quite the part of professional career woman. She looked at him as if to imply that he would deal with her here and now or suffer the consequences. She was her mother's daughter—there was no denying that.

"It's all right, Gladys. I'll see her."

Gladys stepped back. "I tried to tell her—"

Richard held up his hand. "It's all right."

Gladys squared her shoulders and took her seat. She showed an openly hostile attitude toward Denali but said nothing more.

"Thank you, Grandfather," Denali remarked and moved toward him.

Richard quickly retreated into his office without another word. He felt as though a bolt of lightning had just struck him, and for reasons that were beyond him he felt his knees grow weak.

"Forgive me for the intrusion," Denali began.

"Forgive me, Rose. Forgive my intrusion on your life," he remembered himself saying. And although he'd tried to blot out the words that she replied, he could still hear his daughter say, *"I will never forgive you."*

"I would think you might at least say thank you," Denali said flatly.

Richard shook his head as if to clear his mind from the memory. His mouth felt dry, and his vision blurred for a moment before he focused once again on his granddaughter.

"I didn't hear you. What did you say?"

Denali eyed him curiously for a moment. "I said the signatures from the Omni Missions Board have been obtained, and now this project can move forward. First, however, I need your signature."

"Oh yes." Richard reached out for the file, hating that his hand was shaking. He looked Denali in the eyes and was instantly taken back some twenty-six years.

Leave me alone, Rose, he thought, snatching the folder and slapping it down on his desk. Opening the file, he thought he heard laughter, but when he looked up Denali was simply staring at him with a look of concern.

"Are you feeling all right?" she asked.

Richard said nothing for several moments. He was lost in the face of his daughter. *Rose. My sweet Rose. Why did you leave me to bear my guilt all alone? Why did you punish me so thoroughly? I only wanted a good life for you.*

"Grandfather?"

Richard frowned at the word and looked back down at the file. "I suppose everything is in order," he said, forcing the words.

"Yes. Michael and I both scrutinized it for any mistakes."

Again Richard heard laughter. He gritted his teeth and fought to keep his heart from racing. With his eyes focused on the file papers, he listened as Denali continued to tell him about the project.

"Hazel Garrison is great to work with. She has a real heart for this project, and I'm glad I had the opportunity to work with her. She's anxious for us to move ahead, but there is a complication."

Richard took a deep breath and let it back out before glancing up. "And that complication is what?"

"She wants me to stay on the project. She wants me in charge of setting up the contractors and overseeing the construction. I told her I wasn't really of a mind to remain in Dallas. I even went so far as to say I didn't feel very welcome to stay in Dallas."

Richard wished the dry, cottony taste in his mouth would cease. Ignoring Denali, he picked up his phone and dialed his secretary's extension. "Gladys, get me some coffee." He slammed the receiver down without waiting to hear any confirmation.

"If Garrison wants you on the project, I suppose there's nothing I can do about it. The business is too good to lose," he said matter-of-factly. Before he could say anything more, Gladys popped in apologetically with a steaming cup of coffee. She looked at Denali as if to visibly question whether she expected the same service, but Denali simply shook her head and returned her gaze to Richard.

Richard waited until the overanxious woman had exited the room before taking a long drink of the brew. It burned all the way down his throat, but Richard didn't care. He desired only that it somehow steady his nerves and boost his courage.

"So do you want me to stay on the project?" Denali asked him.

Her voice overwhelmed him. He cursed under his breath. *She even sounds like Rose.* He shifted uncomfortably. In so many ways—she was Rose. His Rose.

He felt something inside him snap. The strength and determination that had always seen him through seemed to drain from him like water through a sieve. His mind overran his logic with memories from the past. *"I refuse to live with what you've done,"* Rose had told him. *"But every time you look at my child, you'll remember and know that you are responsible for my misery. My anguish. My death."*

"No!" Richard declared, smashing a fist to the desk.

Denali startled, and her brown eyes went wide in fear. "What?" she questioned.

Richard felt himself going slowly mad. Rose had promised him revenge. She had promised to haunt him, not in a ghostly form, but in the form of her child.

"I'm sorry."

Denali's expression softened. "I think that's the first time I've ever heard those words from you."

Richard shook his head. "You can't understand."

"Maybe not, but I'd like to," Denali replied.

He looked at her again and felt a tightening in his chest. "Look, Rose," he caught himself and corrected the mistake. "Denali, there are some matters better left alone."

"Well, at least you're talking to me," Denali replied. "You've kept me at bay so long that I began to wonder if it was possible for us to have a civil conversation. Here and now, you have no audience to play to but me. Why not explain the last twenty-six years of my life?"

"How I deal with the issues is my business," he answered quickly, but his tone was gentle, almost apologetic. "I have to do things in a way that works for me."

"I just want a few answers," she countered. "I just want to know why. Why did you desert me? Why did you put up this wall between us?"

"You caused this separation, Father," Rose had told him. *"Now live with what you've done. I want nothing to do with you."*

Richard, lost in thought, replied, "I didn't mean to, Rose."

"I'm Denali," the woman across from him said.

Richard nodded. "Of course." He tried to stave off the emotions raging within him. *Rose is dead*, he reminded himself. But he had to connect to her. He had to somehow reach his daughter and vindicate himself from the past. Suddenly, Denali seemed the lifeline to that point. Maybe he had been wrong to put her away from him. Maybe he could have long ago dealt with Rose, and his guilt, by accepting her child and dealing with her.

"I was wrong," he said simply, a plan coming into his mind. The madness seemed to clear for a moment. "I was wrong to push you away."

Denali's expression changed from stoic reserve to disbelief. "You can't know how long I've waited to hear those words."

Richard fought against a wave of warning. *Don't let down your guard. Don't open yourself up to her. Rose wants revenge, and this is the way she will have it.* Richard leaned back and looked up at the ceiling. "I only did what I thought was best. I know you don't understand." He wasn't exactly sure to whom he was speaking. A part of him recognized that it was his granddaughter who sat opposite him, while another part worked to convince him that it was his daughter. In apologizing to one, he hoped to appease the other. And in that, it really didn't matter who was listening.

"You're right. I don't understand. I wish I could cut you some kind of slack in this, but I can't," Denali replied. "I've suffered my whole life for the things you've done—the way you've treated me. I can't understand how you can blame an innocent child for the mistakes of her parents."

"I didn't blame you, Rose."

"Denali."

Her voice penetrated, but Richard refused to concern himself with the matter. "I never meant to hurt you. I never meant to do a great many of the things I did." He sighed, suddenly feeling very vulnerable—something Richard Deveraux had planned never to feel again. "You can't understand the pain I've suffered. It isn't just your own loss," he finally said, meeting her gaze. He shook his head and dispelled the clouded images. "You look so much like your mother. The first time I saw you at my party, I was convinced for a moment that it was her."

"I suppose I can understand that," Denali said softly.

"You've always looked like her," Richard replied. "Even when you were little. When I saw you, it was like seeing Rose again. You would run down the stairs or get excited about something Azalea had for you, and it was like reliving those moments with her. It was so hard."

"It still is."

He saw the sincerity in her eyes. "Yes, it is, and I have a great many regrets."

"Couldn't we try again?" Denali questioned. "I mean really put the past behind us and start over."

How he had longed to hear those words from Rose. *Maybe*, he thought, *just maybe this is Rose's way of allowing me to do just that.* A wave of excitement washed over him. Perhaps he could atone for the past through Denali. It all made sense now. Rose had told him he would have to deal with her child. Maybe even then she was offering him a way out of his pain and guilt. She couldn't bear her own pain, so she wouldn't back away from her plans of suicide. But she left the child behind. She didn't kill herself while still pregnant, and maybe this was the real reason. She wanted him to have a way to deal with the past. She wanted to leave him an open door to forgiveness.

"I think you may be right," he said, his voice edged with anticipation. "Perhaps a new start would be good for us both. Perhaps it's not too late."

Denali smiled at him, and when she did, it was like he was being forgiven. Rose was forgiving him. He just knew it. He smiled, feeling the weight of the burden he'd carried for twenty-six years dissolve around his feet.

I'll make it right with you, Rose. You'll see. I'll make it right.

Twenty-five

Coming out of her grandfather's office, Denali wanted to sing and shout all at once. *He's going to start over with me. He finally sees!* Denali could hardly contain her excitement. She wanted to celebrate. The Omni project was signed, her grandfather appeared willing to forget the past and start over, and finally someone would give her the answers she so desperately needed.

She nearly danced all the way back to her office and would have if she'd thought it wouldn't have raised too many eyebrows. She felt light as a feather. The world seemed truly all right, and God was in His heaven.

"I don't think I've ever seen you like this," Michael said from the connecting door between their offices. He stood there, leaning on the open door, arms crossed against his chest.

Denali caught sight of him and flashed him her warmest smile. "I don't think I've ever felt like this." She went to her desk and let out a contented sigh. "No, I *know* I've never felt like this."

Michael laughed. "So what brought this on? You fall in love or something?"

His words momentarily startled her. She thought of her growing affection for him and wondered if she was really that transparent. Then her senses returned, and she realized that what Michael was seeing in her was totally on account of what she'd just experienced with her grandfather.

"It has nothing to do with that," she said. "My grandfather and I have just resolved our differences."

"What?" Michael questioned, coming into the room.

"It's true," she replied. "Well, maybe not in total. I mean, we haven't exactly worked our problems out, but he did agree to start over. He actually talked to me, Michael."

"What did he say?"

She thought his tone sounded suspicious but quickly decided it was unimportant. She shrugged casually. "He just said that he was wrong to push me away and that I reminded him a lot of my mother."

Michael took the seat opposite her and continued his interrogation. "And that didn't seem odd to you? I mean, after all these years he finally gets around to admitting these things, and you just float on air back to your desk and call him blessed?"

Denali frowned. Why was Michael trying to cast doom and gloom on her happiest moment? "I didn't call him blessed, I simply said he admitted that he was wrong. Which is certainly more than a lot of people will do."

Michael grew thoughtful for a moment. "I suppose I deserved that."

"Yes, I suppose you did," she said, feeling suddenly very defensive.

Michael smiled. "If I admit I've been wrong, will you react the same way to me?"

Denali heard the teasing in his voice and felt the tension drain a bit. "I might."

"And if I admit that I've been wrong, will you go out with me to dinner?"

She smiled and lowered her eyes. "I might."

"And if I admit that I've been wrong, will you let me kiss you again?"

She felt her face grow hot and was grateful not to be looking at him.

"Well?" he prodded impatiently.

"I might," she whispered.

"I was wrong," he said quickly and with great enthusiasm.

Denali laughed and forgot her embarrassment. "Yeah, right."

"I'm very serious," Michael replied. "You aren't giving me a chance. You'll give Richard Deveraux a chance after treating you badly for twenty-some years, but you won't even hear me out?"

Denali forced herself to meet his earnest expression. "All right. I'll give you a chance. What were you wrong about?"

Michael's expression hardened a bit. "I've been wrong about a great deal. You've helped me to see that much. I can't say that everything has changed, because it hasn't, but I'm willing to work on it."

"I'm glad, Michael."

He looked at her for a moment, searching her face as if for reassurance. "I'd like you to give me the same chance you're giving Richard. I want us to start over. I know I've said that before, but now it's different."

"Why?" she asked, leaning forward. Her heart raced at the implications of his words. She wanted things to be different between them. She wanted things to be very, very different.

"You've helped me to see some things—things I should have seen a long time ago."

Denali's phone began to ring, but she refused to answer it. "Let Phoebe get it," she said as if to explain her refusal to pick it up. The call transferred over, and they both seemed to let out a sigh of relief.

"Look, this isn't the place to talk about all of this. Please have dinner with me tonight. I'll make it worth your while."

"Oh?"

Michael's face brightened. "I'll take you to The Mansion," he said temptingly. "It's the best restaurant in Dallas. At least, in my humble opinion."

Denali had heard wonderful things about the restaurant and had wanted very much to have dinner there sometime. "All right," she said, seeing his eyes light up at her answer. "I'll have dinner with you tonight."

"Great! I'll pick up you up at eight o'clock," he said and got to his feet. "And no backing out!"

Denali shook her head. "I wouldn't dream of it." And she meant it. She realized without giving it much thought at all that dinner with Michael was something she very much desired.

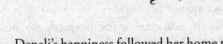

Denali's happiness followed her home that evening. Her mind overflowed with thoughts of what to wear and how to fix her hair as she came into the dimly lit apartment. She listened for a moment, then decided her aunts must have gone out for some reason. She headed for her bedroom to change into something less confining when she noticed her aunts' bedroom door was slightly ajar. Peeking inside, Denali found Azalea napping. This had become her routine, and although Denali knew their time together was rapidly drawing to a close, she refrained from waking the dying woman in order to tell her the news about Richard. Hopefully there would be time later before her date with Michael.

Going back to her room, Denali quickly stripped off her professional image and slipped into comfortable khaki shorts and a tank top. Without thinking much about it, she picked up her mother's diary and headed out onto the balcony.

The August day was warm, but the breeze blew steadily. She stretched out on the lounge and started to read.

" 'June second. The baby is due in a couple of weeks. I wish it could be over with.' " Denali spoke the words aloud, as she always did when reading her mother's diary. Gone was all pretense of joy and girlish anticipation. Her mother appeared to simply be biding her time until the birth of her child.

" 'June fifth. I thought I heard Les call to me last night. I ran to the window and opened it wider and searched the grounds below for some sign that he had come back to me. How I prayed he would. Oh, how I long to turn back the hands of time.' "

Denali read on. The words were much the same. Longing to deliver her child. Longing to be reunited with the man she loved.

The entry for June 21, the day of Denali's birth, read nothing more than, " 'She has come. My little Denali. I named her for the park in Alaska. Denali means "the high one." I pray my Denali can rise above the circumstances of her birth.' "

Denali felt her hand begin to tremble. She had browsed through the entire diary, with the exception of the final two pages. She had purposefully refused to read them until she'd read the other pages more carefully. Somehow, it seemed important to do it this way. Now, as she turned the page to read the final few entries, Denali felt as though she were losing her mother all over again.

" 'June twenty-fourth. We are home from the hospital, my little Denali and I. Father has come to see me twice already today. At first, I wasn't going to speak to him, but then it all welled up inside of me, and I had to tell him what I thought of him. I told him he had ruined my life—that he had no right to decide who I should love. I told him again that I would never forgive him for what he had done.

" 'June twenty-seventh. Denali, you are such a good baby. I wish I had the strength to stay and be your mother. But every time I look at you, I remember your father and what we had together. I know that should be enough. I know that I should save up my memories for you, but I can't. It's not your fault that I'm not strong.' " Denali felt the tears slide down her cheeks. Her mother knew the importance of absolving her child of the guilt she knew would come. " 'You are so sweet, my baby. I can't help but wonder what you will grow up to do or who you will turn out to be. I can't stay, but Azalea and Chrys will tell you about me. They will fill in the picture for you.' "

Denali shook her head. But they hadn't filled in the picture. They'd scarcely been able to bring themselves to give her the diary and photographs.

" 'June thirtieth. Father came to see me this morning. I think he'd been up all night, and I could smell liquor on his breath. He . . .' "

Denali realized that the next page had been ripped from the book. In fact, two pages were missing, and Denali had no doubt someone had purposefully removed them from the diary. After all, her mother had died on the second of July. There had to be something more that she'd said. Something vital that someone didn't want Denali to see.

"Hello," Azalea called, sliding the glass door back. "My, what a pretty evening."

"Hi," Denali said and started to get up.

"No, no. Stay where you are," Azalea told her. She slid the door back in place and sat down wearily on one of the chairs.

Denali knew she was losing ground fast. She had refused chemotherapy and surgery. The doctor had told her there was less than a ten percent chance of either one doing any good, and Azalea had decided to leave well enough alone. "Are you in pain?" Denali asked, knowing it did little good to ask Azalea how she felt. Inevitably her aunt would merely smile and say, "I'm fine."

"A little," Azalea admitted. "But it isn't so bad with the pills. Of course, the pills make me sleepy."

Denali nodded. "It's a vicious circle."

Azalea smiled. "Life's like that."

"Yes," Denali replied. *So's death*, she thought, refusing to bring up the subject.

"I see you're reading Rose's diary again."

"I've just finished it. Do you know where the missing pages are? Apparently someone tore a couple of sheets out of here."

Azalea shook her head. "It was like that when Chrys and I found it. I know, because we sat down together and read it from cover to cover."

"Do you suppose my mother tore them out? Maybe she changed her mind about the content, or maybe she just needed to send someone a note and had no other paper."

"Anything is possible," Azalea replied.

"Of course, it does just end in mid-sentence at the bottom of the last page. I can't imagine that she would tear out part of her written thoughts just to send someone a note. After all, there's half a year of blank pages she could have used—if sending a note was all she had in mind. My guess is she didn't like what she wrote there, or . . ." Denali felt a chill go down her spine.

"Or what?" Azalea asked weakly.

Denali took a deep breath. "Or someone else didn't like what she wrote there."

Twenty-six

*C*hrys let herself into her father's Highland Park home. "Father?" she called out and waited for some response. Silence greeted her, leaving an eerie sensation that Chrys couldn't quite understand.

She went into the trophy room, but finding no sign of her father, she moved quickly through and down a long corridor. She peered into each of the rooms, desperate to find him. *He said he was going straight home,* she thought. They had spoken hours earlier, and he seemed so preoccupied with issues, including something about Denali, that Chrys wanted to come and talk to him. She needed to know exactly what was going on.

"Father!" she called out again, louder this time.

She heard a slight noise coming from the den where her father was given to watching television and catching up on his reading. Chrys hurried down the hall and entered the room without announcing herself.

Richard Deveraux stood at the bar pouring himself a scotch when she spotted him. "Why didn't you answer me?" Chrys asked, coming to the bar.

"Diddna 'ear you." His words were slurred and hard to understand.

"Where is your staff? The housekeeper? The butler?"

"Sent 'em away," Deveraux replied before downing the scotch.

"I don't understand. Why would you send them away?" Chrys asked. "Why don't you set the drink down and come talk to me?"

Deveraux looked at her blankly for several moments before slamming the glass down on the bar. "You know I all ... I ..." he stammered and blinked hard as if to focus his sight. "I loved Rose. You know that."

"Yes, Father. I know you loved Rose. We all loved Rose." Chrys felt surprised and flustered—she'd never seen her father drunk before. She tried not to react in a way that would further upset him, but it didn't seem to matter.

Deveraux pushed away from the bar and staggered around the room, flailing his arms, ranting in incoherent phrases.

"Sheeez gonna forgive me," he said at one point.

"Look, Father," Chrys announced, coming to his side, "you're drunk. I'd suggest we get you upstairs to bed. You can sleep this off, and you'll feel much better in the morning."

"Rose loves me," he slurred in earnest.

"Yes, I'm sure she does," Chrys said, pulling his arm around her shoulder. She gripped him tightly around the waist, knowing that she'd be very little help if he should stagger and fall.

Cautiously, Chrys somehow managed to maneuver her father through the house and to the staircase. She tried twice to help him up the stairs before giving up on the idea. She was about to suggest he sleep on one of the sofas when she remembered the kitchen elevator. It seldom saw use but was nevertheless kept in working order.

"Let's take the elevator," she told Richard and pulled him along with her to the back of the house.

"Rose unnerstands," he rambled. "I know you unnerstand."

He was off in his own little world. Chrys didn't know how to deal with him like this. Her father had always been the pillar of strength. When others gave in to drink and wild abandonment, Richard Deveraux had pronounced them fools, then stood back and bided his time until their worlds came falling down. Finding him in this state caused more than just a mild surprise; it stood as proof that something was terribly wrong.

Managing him in and out of the elevator, Chrys struggled to help the staggering man down the long upstairs corridor and into his bedroom. She pushed the door open with one hand while trying to steady her father's tall form with the other. Never, in all her visits to the house, had she been allowed to see or enter his bedroom. And from what the housekeeper had once confided in passing, no one else was allowed in there, either.

"Come on, Father, just a little farther," she coaxed.

"Rose," he muttered, and the rest of his words rambled in a way that could not be understood.

"Here we are," Chrys said, helping her father to the mammoth, king-size bed. Doing her best to ease him to a sitting position on the side of the mattress, Chrys thought her back would actually break before she could get him to let go. His full weight seemed to cling to her, much like a drowning man would cling to a life preserver.

"You know," he said, looking at her without seeing her. "You know—truth."

Chrys shook her head. "Father, you need to sleep."

She straightened up and for the first time really saw the surrounding room. Her breath caught in her throat, and a chill gripped her. All over the walls, in every conceivable place, there were pictures of Rose. Richard started muttering again, talking to and caressing a photograph of Rose that graced his nightstand.

Chrys stepped away to stare at a huge oil painting mounted over her father's fireplace. She'd never seen the canvas before, but the artist had created a wondrous work. Rose sat smiling back at her as if she'd never known a moment of sorrow in her life.

Turning back to face her father, Chrys shook her head. "Father, what's this all about?" she asked, as if she couldn't already figure out the answer.

But Richard was lost in his own world. He spoke to Rose as if she were beside him in the room, and Chrys got the eerie feeling that in his mind's eye, Rose actually was there with him.

"Have to forgive," Richard said over and over. "Have to."

Disturbed in a way that she could not put into words, Chrys continued the task of putting Richard to bed. She untied his shoes and slipped them from his feet, then reached up to unknot his tie.

He pushed her hands away and began rambling again. "Had to," he said several times. "Had to do it. Had to keep you safe. You do know that." He reached out and gripped Chrys's shoulders, letting the silver-framed photograph fall to the floor. "Rose," he gasped, staring Chrys full in the face.

She didn't know whether it would be worse to fight his illusion or give in to it. So taking her best guess, Chrys said, "Yes, Father. It's Rose."

He looked at her for a moment as if to see the truth for himself, then nodded. "Rose."

"You need to rest, Father," Chrys told him again. "I want you to rest."

He nodded and allowed her to help him lie down. "Diddna wanna share you, Rose." He mumbled something else that Chrys couldn't understand, then grabbed at her hand and tried to pull her to him. "You forgive me?"

"Of course," Chrys reassured him. "I forgive you." Then seeing the agitation remain on his face, she added, "I always loved you and Mother more than I loved Les."

He smiled at this and fell back against the pillow. "I knew it. I knew it." He muttered the words over and over and finally let go of Chrys's hand.

She pulled a cover up from the end of the bed and tucked it under his chin. "I saved them for you," he told her, his eyes suddenly widening. "I saved the pages."

"What pages, Father?"

"The diary . . . so hateful," he said, then closed his eyes.

Chrys hoped against all odds that he'd passed out, and for a moment she thought her wish had been granted. Then he started to mutter again, only this time he kept his eyes closed.

"There . . . top drawer," he whispered. "I kept the pages. You write 'em over. Make 'em nice. Forgive me."

Chrys stared at him for several minutes before all the words seemed to finally register. The missing diary pages were in his top drawer! That's what he was trying to say. He had taken the pages out of the diary because he obviously couldn't bear what had been written there.

Chrys waited for him to say something more, but by the sound of his heavy breathing she realized he'd finally fallen into a deep, inebriated sleep. Almost fearfully, she went to the drawer and opened it. Near the front, there were several odd pipes, some old coins, and a photograph of her mother. Behind this were several loose papers. Chrys grabbed up the papers and began to scan the information.

"Oh my," she gasped, her free hand going to her mouth. "Dear God, please don't let it be true!"

Twenty-seven

The Mansion on Turtle Creek had been designed as an exercise in elegance and refined delights. The exclusive restaurant and hotel had impressive beginnings as a 1925 Italianate mansion, and from there the hotel reached heavenward, while the delectable artistry of the chef made its patrons believe they had already attained that lofty position.

Denali had never seen anything like it in all her life. She knew the pleasure of finery and elegance, but The Mansion had a mystique about it that made the evening pure enchantment. That, and the smartly dressed man at her side. She couldn't help but cast sidelong glances at Michael. He had chosen a very sleek, double-breasted suit, and the navy color seemed to darken his smoky blue eyes. He was the kind of man that a woman was proud to be seen with. Charming and handsome, Michael emitted all the signals of self-confidence and strength that Denali found appealing.

After a short wait they were seated in the main room—a point of privilege, Michael told her. But Denali wouldn't have cared if they'd stuck her in the corner and thrown her a box of crackers. The night could not possibly be ruined. Her life had finally taken an ordered turn, and it gave Denali pure pleasure and hope.

She took a deep breath and thanked God for the wonder of it all. Her grandfather had opened himself up to her, Michael had more or less apologized, and the restaurant seemed to generate a life force all its own. Who could ask for anything more? Even the remaining questions that assaulted her mind on a daily basis seemed to fade to the background of her thoughts.

"Do you like it?" he asked, scooting in to sit close beside her on the cushioned seat. The waiter positioned the table for them, and instantly the action picked up pace as smartly dressed staff buzzed back and forth to bring the necessary items to begin the experience of The Mansion.

"It seems inadequate to merely say yes," Denali responded. She gazed around the room at the rich furnishings and beautiful people. "It's simply incredible."

He laughed softly and leaned closer. "I thought you might enjoy it, given your artistic eye." He straightened and added, "Plus, the food is great."

"I'm sure it must be," Denali said, still mesmerized by the setting and the tingling sensation of Michael's nearness. From the moment she'd walked into the place, she'd been captivated by the inlaid wood, the unique winding staircase, and the massive bouquet of flowers that graced the foyer table. But seated here, in the main room, Denali found the artistry of the architectural details and styling to be most inventive. She longed to get up and walk about the place, going from room to room to inspect what lay beyond her view. More than that, she longed to touch everything—to feel the history and story behind each piece. But most of all, and most difficult to admit, she longed to touch Michael. She longed to touch his suit coat and feel the strength of his muscular arm beneath it. She found it almost impossible to refrain from putting a hand up to stroke the black hair at the nape of his neck. What was happening to her? She frowned and lowered her gaze. Had all of her sense deserted her?

Amidst the filling of water glasses and bread dishes, Denali took up her menu in silence and tried to choose from the bevy of mouth-watering entrées. "What do you suggest?" she finally asked Michael, hoping her voice didn't betray her nervousness. She glanced up to await his answer and gratefully found his gaze fixed on the menu.

"I'm very fond of the tortilla soup, for starters," he said, studying the listing very seriously. "Then the salmon or the steak—both have the most incredible seasoning and are so tender." He paused and grinned. "Well, to coin a phrase, they melt in your mouth."

Denali couldn't help but return the smile. "I see."

She let Michael choose for her and was delighted when he picked the steak. "I think you'll be pleased with the soup, too," he told her. "It's spicy but not overbearingly so."

"I'm looking forward to it," Denali said, catching the intent look in his eye. "Thank you for bringing me here."

"My pleasure," he replied, his voice low and husky. "In case I haven't told you already, you look beautiful."

Denali felt her face flush. She looked away and smiled. "Thank you, and yes, you've told me about a dozen times now."

"Well, it's true. I've scarcely seen you in anything but business clothes or jeans."

"You saw me at my grandfather's party," she reminded him.

"True, and you took my breath away."

Denali laughed softly. "Well, I had the wind knocked out of me that night, as well. But for entirely different reasons."

"Oh, so you weren't captivated by my good looks and manly charms?" he teased.

Denali instantly sobered. "I didn't say that."

This seemed to sober Michael, as well. "It seems a lot goes unsaid between us," he countered.

Denali shifted uncomfortably. She tried to tell herself it was because her floor-length gown had twisted awkwardly when she'd slid into the seat, but she knew better. To her relief, the wine steward appeared to question Michael as to whether they would care for something from the list.

She tried to battle her feelings, wondering if this evening had been a mistake. She longed to better understand this man, knew that she had undeniable feelings for him, but she was still in turmoil regarding their relationship. A part of her wanted to march right up to him and declare her feelings, while another part remained uncertain as to the depth of those feelings.

She lost herself so completely in thought that she didn't even realize the steward had gone, leaving Michael to study her most deliberately. She swallowed hard and tried not to betray her uneasiness. "If you would be so kind," she began awkwardly, "I'd like to go to the ladies' room." It had become absolutely imperative that she get away from him for a least a short time. Somehow she had to regain her composure, and this seemed the only answer.

He nodded and without a word, got to his feet and helped her up.

"Thank you," she said, feeling the warmth of his hand upon her bare arm.

He brushed his thumb against her skin and smiled. "You're welcome."

Michael watched Denali leave the room. He also noted that several other men watched her, as well. She was a striking woman in her floor-length, beaded ivory silk. He wanted to run his hands through her auburn curls and trail down the open back of her gown. Taking a long drink from his water goblet, he tried to force his focus elsewhere. He thought about the information he'd received from Jim Siemens. He wondered how he might break the news to her, or even if he should. She deserved to know the truth about her parents. There was no doubt about that. She also deserved to know about the trust fund. She was a wealthy woman in her own right—a very wealthy woman.

The thought made Michael nervous. He remembered Richard's bribe to wine and dine Denali. Money had driven his actions. Was it money that drove him now? He couldn't believe it was only Denali's fortune that attracted him. True, she was the granddaughter of Richard Deveraux, a man said to be worth millions. And true, entertaining her provided him with a hefty bonus, which, even as they shared the evening, sat in check form on his dresser at home. But it had to be more than that. He felt deep down inside that it was more than just financial.

Watching her reenter the room, Michael felt an overwhelming urge to shelter her. Protect her from the harm that he somehow intuitively knew would soon befall her. He didn't trust Deveraux. He didn't believe for one minute the man had cast aside a lifetime of anger and bitterness, even if it was to take this beautiful young woman into his life. Michael felt certain of this, because he himself hadn't been able to let go of three years' worth of anger in order to set a straight path with Denali. *If I can't deal with three years' worth of anger, how can Deveraux just cast aside a lifetime of it?*

"Hello," she said nonchalantly as she approached the table.

Michael smiled, seeing that she'd reassumed her facade of serenity and strength. "Welcome back."

They took their places once again, and when the food arrived they ate in relative silence—breaking it only to make small talk about the flavors. Michael could feel her tension. Even with a good twelve inches separating them, the nervous energy between them was palpable. It was rather like preparing to strike a match. Alone, the match would not ignite. But when friction was added, the flame would burst to life and threaten to set afire anything it touched.

"Do you come here often?" Denali asked, breaking the silence.

"No," Michael admitted. "The prices are a bit steep for a man who's trying to save money."

"Save money?" Denali asked.

Michael nodded and tried to appear quite casual about the entire matter. "Yes. I'm going to start my own business again."

"Oh, Michael, that's wonderful!" she declared.

He could see that she really meant it, and the words made him smile. "I think so. It's going to take time and hard work, but I'm sure I can do it."

Denali smiled and nodded enthusiastically. "Yes. I'm sure you can."

It was in that moment, seeing her radiant smile, hearing the joy in her voice, that Michael knew he couldn't fight his feelings for her. Denali Deveraux made him feel alive. She exorcised the ghosts of his past and gave him a feeling of accomplishment. He knew there were many obstacles between them, obstacles that strained their ability to be happy, but Michael knew determination could often overcome any obstacle.

"It's so rewarding when you stay with something you believe in," Denali told him, not seeing his uneasiness. "That's why my spiritual beliefs have always been so important to me. I've always known that God had a specific plan for my life."

"Me too. Only His plan for me was destruction."

"How can you say that?" she asked, her voice indicating offense at his words.

Michael played at spearing a tiny new potato. "I say it because it's true. I had plans and goals. I thought they were pretty good ones, and I trusted that God felt the same way. At least, He'd never come right out and said they weren't any good."

"Did you bother to listen to see what He had to say?" Denali asked rather hostilely.

"Look, I don't want to ruin the evening by having us argue over religion," he replied.

"Religion has very little to do with what I'm saying," Denali countered. "Michael, there is this deep hurt inside of you. I see it in your eyes every time you look at me. I feel it in the things you say. I know you've had tragedy in your life. I just wish you would open up and talk to me about it."

"Why?" he asked, unable to stop the question.

"Because I care." She looked down, biting her lip as if she wished she'd not made this declaration.

Michael put his fork down and studied her for a moment. "All right. What do you want to know?"

Denali's head snapped up. "Everything."

Michael was taken aback for a moment. He drew a deep breath and forced a grin. "That entails more than a single dinner conversation can contain."

"So start out with current affairs, and we'll worry about the rest later," she suggested. "Tell me about your wife."

Michael couldn't keep from frowning. He knew the harshness of his expression was one Denali was used to dealing with.

"That's hardly current affairs, but all right. Renea and I were high school sweethearts," Michael said, feeling the memories unwind. "It wasn't love at first sight, but rather, it grew out of a mutual admiration for each other. She was talented and beautiful and had a large following of admirers. I was shy, quiet, and had my nose in a book most of the time. We were thrown together on a project for art class and became friends." He paused and forced a smile. "Am I boring you yet?"

Denali shook her head. "Not at all."

"Well, we dated through high school and college and got married right after I received my master's. We had saved a sizeable amount of money toward establishing an architectural firm. Renea worked as an interior design consultant, so it made a nice coupling for the business as well as our personal life." Michael played with the silverware and tried not to appear overly nostalgic about the memories. At one time they had cut him like a knife, but sharing them now with Denali didn't seem so bad.

"I had to work hard, especially those first five years. I was putting in twelve to fifteen hours a day at the office, and Renea grew bored. Her interior designs weren't really taking off, and she was often left at home with nothing to do, and she resented it. She also resented that I put all the profits back into the business. She wanted a nice house, a showplace that she could make over in her own image, so we moved to LaTour. It strained the budget, but after a while I landed some very lucrative contracts. Rather than put the money back in the business, I paid off the debt on the apartment. Renea wasn't even happy with that, however. She thought it foolish and chided me for not having some fun with it.

"So with the next big contract, I decided to have some fun. I bought the Mercedes, took Renea to Hawaii, and let her refurnish the apartment to her heart's desire."

"But that still didn't make her happy?" Denali questioned.

"No," Michael admitted. "I never did figure out exactly what Renea was looking for." He grew thoughtful, remembering how hard he had tried to please her. "She never seemed happy. I was gone too much of the time or came across as too consumed with projects when I was home. Then I suggested we have children, and she went ballistic."

"She didn't want to have your children?" Denali asked in disbelief.

Michael wanted to hug her for the way she looked at him. It was as if to say the thought was so outrageously unbelievable that she couldn't even comprehend the meaning. "No, she didn't want my children or anyone else's. Renea didn't want to be saddled down with kids, nor did she want to share the wealth with children."

"How sad," Denali said, appearing to try to imagine it all. "I want a dozen," she added, then laughed and blushed at her words.

"You'd make a good mother," he told her. Then, remembering the birth certificate and marriage license, Michael wondered if he should change the subject and offer her the truth about herself.

"So what happened?"

"What?" Michael's reflective thoughts were broken.

"Why was she flying to New York?"

"Oh yes," he said, nodding. "Well, there's a bit more of the story before we get to that. I figured Renea's biggest complaint was my over-extending myself. I thought she was genuinely worried about me, and when she suggested an old friend be brought on as a partner, I gave in and allowed him to invest in the company. Ralph came in and shared expenses and responsibilities right down the middle." Then his voice lowered and his jaw tightened as he added, "I just didn't realize I was also sharing Renea."

Twenty-eight

*T*he night air was actually cool and lacked the normal humidity that Dallas was famous for. Michael signaled the valet to bring his car, then turned to Denali. "I'm sorry about all that."

Denali looked up to meet his gaze. His eyes were clearly filled with pain and anguish. It appeared he was doing battle within himself, and with every passing moment, he was losing ground. "I asked for it, remember?"

He studied her for a moment and gave a brief nod. "I think you got more than you asked for."

Just then the valet brought Michael's Mercedes. Michael tipped the man while yet another valet helped Denali into the car. She sat there wondering what she could possibly do or say to prove to Michael that her interest was genuine. She finally felt that she understood some of the mystery behind the man, and she didn't want to lose it now.

Michael maneuvered through the crowded entryway and merged into traffic without saying a word. As he headed the car back in the direction of LaTour, Denali finally got up her courage.

"Do we have to go right home?"

He glanced over at her, then shrugged. "No. What did you have in mind?"

Denali smiled. "I just thought it might be nice to take a drive. The weather's so perfect and the night so beautiful, I thought maybe we could continue our conversation."

"Are you sure you want to do that?" his tone echoed in deadly seriousness.

Denali grew marginally uncomfortable. "Why shouldn't I want to?"

"I don't know," Michael said, making a turn in the opposite direction of LaTour. "I just answered a lot of personal questions and spilled my guts for you. I guess the way I figure things, it's your turn."

Denali swallowed hard. "You already know quite a bit about me."

"Not nearly as much as I'd like to know."

She let the words fade into silence between them. Staring out at the passing scenery, she wondered if she could be open and frank about the way Michael affected her. *If he asks me about my feelings*, she thought, *I can honestly say that I'm confused. What harm can there be in that?* Then the perfect excuse came to mind.

"But I'm not through hearing your story."

Michael merged onto the interstate, and Denali was grateful for the light traffic. She wanted him to be able to concentrate on the things he said to her. She wanted him to unload and share the details of his heart with her. Whether or not he would do that was anybody's guess, but she hoped he would.

"There's not much else to tell," he said, sounding tense.

"How did you find out that your partner was having an affair with your wife?" Denali boldly questioned.

Michael gripped the steering wheel tighter, but except for this he made no other outward signs of discomfort. "There were a lot of little things that came together at the end."

"Such as?"

"Such as they were both on the plane to New York." He said nothing for several moments as he exited the interstate and took off in a familiar direction toward the Omni Missions property.

After several minutes passed in silence, Denali realized that Michael's intention was to find a place where they could park and be alone. She began to question the sense of asking for this little after-dinner drive. Perhaps she was getting more than she'd bargained for. She felt a trembling start deep inside her. What if Michael pressed her for answers she wasn't yet ready to give? What if she spoke out of haste and embarrassment and later regretted her words?

Just as she had presumed he would do, Michael pulled the car onto the long, private drive. When they reached the end of the road, the very place they'd stopped on their site visit, Michael parked the car and turned off the engine. Blackness enveloped them, making Denali very uncomfortable.

As if reading her mind, Michael switched on the interior lights, then turned to her. Denali could see the tension in his expression as he spoke. "I'm going to tell you something that I've never told anyone else. I'd rather it stay between the two of us."

"Of course," Denali said, barely allowing herself to speak for fear of betraying her own anxiety.

"You asked about Ralph and Renea," he said, then leaned back against the car door. "I guess there were all sorts of warning signs, but I missed them or ignored them. I even joked with them both prior to their New York trip that it was very convenient for me to have Ralph on the same flight as my wife. I admonished him to look out for her, and of course he promised me he would be happy to do just that." Bitterness crept into his voice. "I just didn't realize exactly how happy he intended to be."

"But being on the same flight isn't proof of an affair," Denali said, caught up in Michael's misery.

"No, but the things that followed the accident gave me all the proof I needed."

"What things?"

He grimaced. "I got a call that night forwarded from the office telephone. It was from the hotel where Renea had made reservations. They wanted to know if Mr. and Mrs. Masters were still en route to the hotel, or would they be cancelling their reservations. I, of course, tried to explain the situation, and they were notably embarrassed and sorry for the inconvenience. I was still trying to get word about the crash, and no one was saying much of anything. I couldn't be sure they were both dead, but from the news reports it sounded like there would be no survivors. And even at the point when the hotel called, I still didn't want to believe they were having an affair. I mean, it sounded plausible that it was just some sort of mix-up, right?"

"What happened after that?"

"The bank called me on Monday morning. See, the flight was on Friday night, and, after the official word came in from the airline, I didn't want to sit home by myself. I didn't want to think about anything, so I threw myself into my work. I spent all weekend at a job site, putting in over fifteen hours on Saturday and another thirteen on Sunday. My wife and business partner were dead, and that left a very big hole in my organized world." He paused, as if realizing his rambling. "I've digressed. The bank called. They were concerned because a large check had come through on the business account, but there weren't enough funds to cover the amount due. I told them it must be some sort of mistake, but that until we cleared it up they could draw the money from my savings account."

Denali watched as his face contorted and his breathing quickened. "You don't have to go on if you'd rather not," she offered.

His look suggested disbelief. "I wouldn't dream of stopping now. You wanted the truth, and I'm giving it to you."

Rather than argue with him, she nodded. "So what happened next?"

"The bank official took down the numbers to my account, then went to check on the transfer. It was only a matter of minutes before he was back telling me that I no longer had a savings account nor a personal checking account. I told him I'd be right down, and when I arrived I was taken into a private office and shown the facts. Ralph had cleaned out the business account—"

"And Renea had cleaned out the personal accounts," Denali interjected.

"Exactly. Worse yet, they had taken the money in cash. I couldn't even get the bank to stop payment on a check or reverse the transfer of funds. I promised the bank to make good on the check, asking them to give me twenty-four hours to scrape together enough money to cover everything. Then I went home and sat down to think. Even then, even knowing what they had done, I still didn't want to believe that Renea had left me and that Ralph had swindled me."

"What convinced you?" Denali asked softly.

"The letter."

"A letter? From Renea?"

Michael nodded and closed his eyes. "Apparently she'd mailed it from the airport. It took until Monday afternoon to get to me, and by that time I knew she was dead. I had my suspicions about her and Ralph, and of course, that whole bank issue was staring me in the face. I toyed with that letter for I don't know how long. You see," he said, opening his eyes again and looking at her as if to make sure she was still listening, "I had already convinced myself of the worst, and this letter would either confirm my fears or alleviate them. I wasn't sure I could deal with the truth."

"But you opened the letter?" Denali asked.

"Yes. It finally got the best of me. I opened it and read all my worst fears in the lines Renea had written."

"Did she give you a reason?" The question sounded lame even to Denali, but she wanted to know. She herself had faced rejection and desertion, and the haunting question of "Why?" lingered even now in her mind.

"Oh, she gave her version of the reason. Told me I was boring, not lively enough to suit her needs. She likened me to Dallas. A city operating behind the guise of a masquerade costume. All show—pretentiously playing one part while underneath being something entirely different. She said I made all the proper moves to maintain an outward appearance of being the loving husband, when in truth I was nothing of the kind. As far as she was concerned, my costume disguised the reality of my workaholic nature. I was all business, and Renea decided there was no hope of me being anything more. But Ralph had what she was looking for. She told me that Ralph made her feel needed and loved. Ralph understood her loneliness and longings."

Denali didn't know what to say. She was afraid of sounding as though she felt sorry for him and knew he would only resent pity. She searched her own feelings for some word of consolation, but nothing came to mind.

"So there you have it. That plane crash took everything—my wife, my business, my partner, the money. Everything. I thought it rather a harsh blow by God. I guess I still do."

"Why not let Ralph and Renea be responsible for their own actions? I doubt very seriously that God desired such behavior," Denali replied, trying to choose her words very carefully.

"Maybe not, but He could have put a stop to it. I mean, it wasn't just me. Ralph had a wife and children. Thankfully, she never knew about the affair or Ralph's plans. He apparently was going to notify her later. So she lives on as the grieving widow, believing her husband to have been fully committed to his family, while I have to carry the truth around inside, realizing the lie I live every time I happen to cross paths with her. Do you know what it does to me to have to face that woman? To have to listen to her go on and on about how hard it's been without Ralph? What a good father and husband he was—how unfair that he had to be on business when his life was snuffed out?"

"But you're a good man," Denali said, realizing the cost he'd paid. "You aren't the kind of person to save your own conscience by destroying someone else."

"For all the good it does me."

"Michael, just because people have failed you is no reason to believe that God has done the same. I've lived with a lot of deception and desertion in my own life, but God is all I've had to count on when the times got really bad. It doesn't stop me from wanting answers, nor does it keep me from searching to learn the truth, but it does give me hope."

He looked at her as if weighing the truth of her statement. Something in his expression suggested he was keeping something from her. Denali wondered if he wanted to condemn her beliefs but didn't have the strength to fight. Feeling a deep need to express her concern for him, Denali knew words were useless. Instead, she reached out across the seat and put her hand on top of his. Pushing her fingers down between his, she was gratified when he curled his hand up to tighten his hold on her.

Neither one spoke a word. Both were wounded by their past experiences. Both knew the pain of losing someone close to them. But in the silence something changed between them. Denali felt it and knew within her heart that she had crossed some kind of threshold. She cared about this man—cared about his wounds, his bitterness, his suffering. Where it took her from here she had no idea. But one thing she did know: Things would never be the same between them again.

Twenty-nine

D enali had actually looked forward to seeing Michael in the office on Monday, but it wasn't to be. Azalea had awakened Sunday to announce that it was time to take her to the hospital. She had approached Chrys and Denali with such calm, clear resignation that there were no questions asked and no tears shed. And so for the week that followed, Denali sat with Chrys and Richard at the hospital and waited for the only mother she had ever known to pass away.

Richard remained ever the stoic figurehead. Chrys and Azalea had only managed to break the news to him a week earlier and probably wouldn't have bothered even then but for Richard's observation of Azalea's weight loss. He had taken the news in his normal calm fashion, but everyone was certain he had been just as devastated as the rest of the family. For all his strength, little things betrayed the breaking down of his mental well-being. When he appeared at the hospital, he came with a bouquet of yellow roses and a box of Azalea's favorite candy and spoke of her recovery. It was as if she'd come to give birth to a child rather than die. And when Denali approached him in greeting, he called her Rose.

In spite of this, Denali took the opportunity to be near her grandfather. She listened to him speak of matters related to past events. He talked of Azalea and Chrys and even Rose as though life had never dealt him the painful blows he had known. At one point they even shared a chuckle over a family camping experience when Denali's mother was fifteen. Azalea seemed grateful that they should come and regale her with stories. She thanked them over and over—telling them all how much she loved them. Then she surprised everyone by asking them to leave.

"I'm tired," she said softly. "I know you all must be tired, as well.

Go home and rest. God has all of this under control."

Denali leaned down to kiss her forehead. "I love you. I'll be back first thing in the morning."

"I'd like you to stay for just a few minutes," Azalea told her, taking a weak hold of her niece's hand.

Denali exchanged a glance with Chrys and was strengthened by her reassuring nod. Richard didn't seem to notice or to mind. He appeared to be his old, reliant self at this point. He kissed Azalea on the cheek and allowed Chrys to escort him from the room. They were already talking business by the time the door closed behind them.

"What can I do for you?" Denali asked Azalea. The heady hospital smell was already getting to her, making Denali long for a walk outdoors. Still, if Azalea needed her to stay, then that was exactly what Denali would do.

"I've been wanting to talk to you. To tell you some things," Azalea replied.

Denali reached a hand up to stroke back some of the graying hair. "You should probably save your strength," she told her softly.

"It takes no strength to die," Azalea countered with a weak smile. "We both know why I'm here—we just don't know when. But I feel it will be very soon, and I didn't want to die without telling you that I've mentioned you in my will."

"Oh, Azalea," Denali whispered, patting her aunt's hand, "you've already given me so much, and I'd trade all my material wealth if it could just restore your health."

Azalea nodded wearily. "As would I. But we both know that wishing it so won't make it happen."

Denali felt herself weakening. She had worked so hard to be strong for Azalea. "I don't want you to spend your final days worrying about me," Denali finally said. "It's hard enough to face the truth of what's happening without knowing that you're worried about me."

"That's another reason I asked you to stay. I want you to have this." Azalea weakly grabbed a large manila envelope from the table beside her and handed it to Denali.

"What is it?" Denali questioned, already opening the flap. She pulled out the papers and gasped. "The deed to Cambry?" Her eyes misted with tears. "This can't be true—is it really the deed?"

"It is. I purchased Cambry for you. That's why the place sold so fast. I just couldn't bear that you should have to leave the home you loved so much. The furnishings and everything you cherished are still there awaiting your return. I bought it all and retained two of the staff to keep the place in order. It's all yours now. You needn't be bound by Dallas or by your grandfather."

"I don't know what to say." Denali was suddenly blinded by her tears.

"Just promise me you'll be careful where Father is concerned. I know he's made an effort to open up to you, but Chrys and I are both worried. His mind doesn't seem strong, if you know what I mean."

"Maybe he needs me," Denali countered.

"Maybe. But he needs to reconcile himself to the past and to God. Reliving happier days through you won't change the present or the past."

"And you think that's what he's doing?" Denali asked seriously.

Azalea licked her lips and drew a ragged breath. "I do."

Denali stared at her aunt for a moment. She had never once done anything but seek to protect Denali from harm. And even though Denali faulted the actions that sometimes caused her grief, she knew confidently that Azalea wasn't capable of self-serving motives.

"I'll be careful," Denali promised and leaned down to kiss her aunt one more time. "I promise." Seeing Azalea nod in satisfaction, Denali straightened. "Thank you for Cambry. I'm so touched, and I can't even find words to speak what's on my heart. You have truly given me something precious. I won't ever forget that you've done this out of love for me."

"It was all out of love for you, Denali," Azalea whispered weakly. "It was always for you."

She later learned that Azalea died before Denali had even had a chance to get to the parking lot of the hospital. Chrys gave her the news the minute she walked in the door.

"The hospital called," Chrys said, her eyes red from crying.

"She's gone, isn't she?" Denali questioned matter-of-factly.

"Yes."

"I think I already knew," Denali admitted. "I just felt as though I'd never see her alive again. I think she knew it, too." Denali held up the envelope. "Did you know about this?"

Chrys nodded. "She had me bring the papers to the hospital. She wanted very much to give you the deed rather than have it be a part of her will."

"I'm glad she did. I want to remember Cambry and Azalea and all the good things. I don't want to dwell on what comes to me from a will."

"She made provision for you there, as well."

"Yes, I know. She told me. She didn't say what she had left me, only that she wanted me aware of the fact that she was naming me." Denali smiled sadly and put the envelope on the counter. "I need to go for a walk. Do you mind? I mean . . . if you need me here—"

"No," Chrys replied. "I completely understand."

Outside the air held a hint of fall. It was still plenty warm, but something about the feel of the day made Denali long for her colorful Kansas City autumns.

Walking with purpose, Denali crossed the street and made her way to the small cemetery. So often she had sought her solace here. How appropriate that she should seek it here now. She shoved her hands down into her blue jeans and tried to imagine life without Azalea. The weeks she'd spent in Dallas prior to Azalea's joining them definitely lacked an element of comfort. For all of her life, Denali had relied upon Azalea to be the nurturer and care giver. Chrys had her career and the link to Richard, but Azalea had always made it clear that she was there, if not solely, then very nearly exclusively, for Denali.

Sitting down on the stone bench, Denali tried to sort through her jumbled thoughts. Azalea had cautioned her to be careful of her grandfather. She was worried that his mind wasn't strong.

"But what does that mean?" Denali questioned the air. Did Azalea and Chrys honestly believe the man was losing his mind? Or did they just worry that the grief of reopening the past would be too much for him to handle?

Denali lost track of time as she sat contemplating this thought and praying for guidance. She didn't even hear the man and dog approach her until they were directly in front of her.

"I've missed you."

Denali looked up and smiled. "Michael." He stood there in his jogging clothes, Dusty obediently sitting at his heel. "I see you and Dusty are making the rounds again," she said.

"Yes, well, we were both rather cooped up this week. Dusty's owner had to fly out on business, and my partner has been out of the office all week."

She smiled. "Sorry about that. I promise to do better next week."

"How's your aunt?"

Denali took a deep breath. It wasn't until meeting Michael's sympathetic expression that she felt the tears come to her eyes. "Oh, Michael," her voice broke, "she just died."

Michael's expression sobered. "I'm so sorry, Denali." He led Dusty to the stone bench and sat down beside Denali. Dusty seemed to sense her sorrow and jumped up to put his front paws on her knees.

"It's so good to see you," she managed to say. Struggling to rein in her emotions, Denali stroked Dusty's head and thought of what she should say.

"It's good to see you, too," Michael said. Without attempting to pull her close or make any other move, Michael slipped a supportive arm around her shoulder. "I know you're hurting, but I want you to know that I'm here for you."

Denali took a deep breath and blew it out softly. She wanted so much to be strong. "Thank you. It means a lot."

"Will you have to help with the arrangements?"

"No. She and Chrys took care of everything before she died. She even took care of my needs."

"How so?" Michael asked.

"Remember my house in Kansas City?"

"Your ancestral home?" Michael inquired.

"Yes. It's called Cambry. Anyway, when Grandfather demanded it be sold along with most of the furnishings, I was very angry. That house and its things were all I had left of my mother. My entire life had been spent in that house, and I loved it very nearly as much as the members who lived there." Denali looked up and met Michael's searching eyes. "Azalea knew how I felt. She might have been the only one to truly understand because she didn't want to leave it, either. Anyway, she bought it before joining Chrys and me here in Dallas. She bought it and the furnishings and everything that was so dear to me, and she gave me the deed just minutes before she died." Denali fell silent for several moments before shaking her head. "Right up to the last minute, she was thinking of someone other than herself. I wish I could be more like her. I'm so self-centered and pushy. I demand answers that no one feels comfortable giving, and I chalk it all up to my right to know. Now that dear woman is dead, and her last words were to tell me that she'd done everything out of love for me." Denali's emotions were rapidly taking over. "Look, can we talk about something else? I'm still sorting through all of this."

Michael gave her shoulder a squeeze. "As a matter of fact, there is something else I want to talk about."

"Good," Denali said, trying to give him a smile. "Problems at the office? The place fall down without me?"

He smiled. "Not exactly." He reached down to unhook Dusty. "Go ahead, boy," he encouraged the dog to take his freedom.

"Won't he get away from you?" Denali asked, her voice filled with concern.

Michael shook his head. "Nah, this is our routine anyway. I usually give him some time off the leash if I'm not in too big a hurry."

"Which you usually are," Denali countered, remembering the first time she'd encountered Michael Copeland.

"Usually, but not today."

His words were soft and alluring, and Denali found herself slipping under their spell. He was so handsome, so kind and attentive. *Oh, Michael, why can't I tell you the truth about how I feel? Why can't I even figure it out for myself?* But now was hardly the time to dwell on such things.

"I've done a great deal of soul-searching since our date last week," Michael began. "Which, by the way, was the best evening I've spent since . . . well . . . it's been quite a while."

"Thank you for saying so." Denali saw the serious intent in his eyes and began to tremble. She hoped against hope that he wouldn't notice.

"I thought about the things you said, about not blaming God and about Him not having deserted me. I've considered everything you've said to me from the start, and I have to say I've never been quite so overwhelmed with the thoughts and feelings that came out of my contemplation. I wanted so much to believe that everything was God's fault. His doing—not my lacking. I wanted it all to be His responsibility so that I didn't have to feel guilty for the actions of my wife and partner." He looked out across the gravestones and dropped his hold on Denali. She immediately missed his touch but said nothing.

"I was so hurt by what she'd done, Denali. I felt that I must be less than a real man if I couldn't even keep my wife happy. I'd given her everything I could think of, and still it wasn't enough. I took a chance with Ralph, even though I didn't know him very well, and all because I trusted Renea to look after my best interests as I looked after hers. To have put that kind of trust in her, only to have her destroy it, has taken a real toll on me. I wanted to hate everyone and everything."

"I know," Denali finally whispered. She looked down at her feet, the breeze blowing her cinnamon hair across her face like a veil.

"But then you came to Dallas. You were forced upon me, just as I was forced upon you, and I really resented that. I'd owned my own business and had been responsible for an impressive clientele list, yet I had to be partnered with the boss's granddaughter." He chuckled. "And then when I saw you and realized that you were the woman I'd been so rude to . . . well . . . let me tell you, I've never cared for the taste of eating crow."

Denali laughed. "I could have died when I saw you walk into that office. It was bad enough having to deal with what had transpired between us that day when we collided, but then I had to deal with your attitude toward Christianity."

"I know, and I know that I wasn't easy to deal with. But you have to understand, I didn't want to be dealt with. I didn't want anybody approaching me or getting close enough to see inside. I still don't. Well, that's not entirely true. I make an exception where you're concerned."

Denali swallowed hard. He was opening up his feelings for her. He was saying the very things that she knew deep inside she had longed to hear. Licking her lips, she pushed back her hair and looked at him. "What about God?" she barely breathed the question.

Michael got to his feet, and for a moment Denali was afraid she'd offended him. She quickly jumped up and put a hand out to touch his arm. "I'm sorry. You don't have to answer that."

He turned to look at her. His expression was one of total surprise. "I know I don't have to answer, but I want to answer."

"You do?" She felt her heart pounding furiously as she waited for him.

"I feel like I owe it to you to answer. After all, you helped me find my way back through the darkness."

"Does that mean. . . ?" She couldn't finish the sentence. It was almost too much to hope for.

He nodded. "I set things right. I searched inside of myself and faced the beast head on. God and I are at peace again."

Denali felt her chest tighten and her eyes grow hot with tears. "Oh,

Michael, that's wonderful news. I'm so glad for you."

"I'm glad for me, too," he said in a lighthearted manner that helped Denali regain her composure.

"It's always good to bare your soul and come clean about the things you've been lugging around with you for so long," Denali said, wiping her eyes. The intensity of the moment was almost too much, and Denali looked for some way to change the subject. "Where's Dusty gotten off to?"

She turned as if to go in search of him, but Michael pulled her back and into his arms. "You're good for me, Denali," he whispered before covering her mouth with his.

Denali yielded to all the pent-up emotions that she'd worked so hard to bury. She allowed him to pull her tightly against him, relishing the way his strong embrace made her feel safe, protected, loved. And she wanted to believe that he might love her. Even if she couldn't allow herself to be honest about her feelings for him, she wanted very much for him to be honest with her. But did that honesty include love? Or had she simply transferred her longing for her grandfather's affection to Michael?

The kiss deepened as if in answer to her unspoken question, and Denali wrapped her arms around Michael's neck in response to his passion. It was only her second real kiss, and she wanted it to last forever. She wanted him to kiss away the past and the pain. She wanted him to kiss away Azalea's death and the concerns she had about her grandfather's mental health. Mostly, she just wanted to go on kissing Michael—because Michael made her feel whole.

When he finally pulled away, Denali was afraid to open her eyes. She didn't want the illusion to end.

"Look at me, Denali," Michael said softly, lifting her chin with his finger.

She opened her eyes and was reassured by the expression on his face. "You've given me a reason to believe again," he told her. "To believe in God. To believe in people. To have hope for the future. I want you to know how grateful I am. You were the only one to go the distance with me, and yet we were virtually strangers."

"That's hardly the case now," Denali managed to say, suddenly feeling very shy.

He grinned. "Very true, Miss Deveraux." He took hold of her hand

and tucked it in the crook of his arm. "And I think we should definitely pursue this matter further."

They walked in silence for several minutes before Dusty came bounding across the graves to bark enthusiastically at their feet.

"Someone or something is always interfering with my serious discussions," Michael said with a laugh. He reached down to reclip Dusty to the leash. "Guess I should get you back home for your supper."

"I need to get back to Chrys," Denali said, suddenly remembering the real reason she'd come to seek solace in the cemetery. "Will you come to the funeral on Wednesday? I mean, would you be there for me?"

Michael nodded. "Absolutely. Just let me know the time."

"Thank you," Denali replied and turned away quickly in order to fight the urge to kiss him again. She touched her fingers to her lips and sighed. *Now what do I do, Lord?*

Thirty

Azalea's funeral was a stately and quiet affair. There were only a dozen or so in attendance, and Denali thought it sad that more people couldn't have known her aunt. Azalea had lived a very private life, and it wasn't until she stood at her aunt's graveside that Denali realized most of that private life had been devoted to her. Azalea had filled her own mother's shoes to provide loving care to Rose, and then filled Rose's shoes to provide care for Denali. She had thrived on being a nurturer and a care giver, and never once had it entered Azalea's mind that she might not be fulfilling her own potential. At least, if it had entered her mind, Azalea had certainly never said so.

"We are on this earth but for a short time," the stoic minister said. "Our lives are fleeting, our endeavors—even more so."

But Denali disagreed. Azalea had endeavored to give Denali the things that truly counted. Love, friendship, security. *Funny,* Denali thought, *I had so much of what I was searching for, but never really saw it.* She determined that Azalea's endeavors would not be fleeting.

Denali, mindless of appearances, tightly gripped Michael's arm for support. Very little passed in conversation between them, but Denali knew that touch held the same importance for Michael as it did for her. She knew without a doubt Michael understood that words were unnecessary for her comfort, but his supportive touch was imperative to see her through this sorrow. He understood her need, and that meant the world to Denali.

⌒

Relaxing in the apartment after the burial, Denali contemplated what she should do with her life. She had to deal with her feelings for Michael; there was simply no way around that matter. She also had Cambry to consider and Hazel Garrison's job offer. Then, too, her grandfather had agreed to start a new relationship. It was all so overwhelming. Suddenly, many of the things she'd dreamed of were standing at her door. Why, then, did she feel so confused and uncertain about the direction to take?

"I'm sorry to tell you this," Chrys said, coming into Denali's room unannounced, "but I have problems in New Orleans and I have to fly out right now."

"What? But you've just buried your sister. Surely they would understand—"

"No," Chrys said, shaking her head. "This is too big to wait even a day on. I'm sorry to leave you by yourself, especially at a time like this, but believe me, I have no other choice."

"I understand," Denali replied, even though she wasn't really sure she did. "When will you be back?"

"It's hard to say. This could be handled in a day, or it might take a week. I just can't be sure. I'll head for home at the first possible moment."

"Do you want me to drive you to the airport?"

Chrys shook her head again. "No. I've already called for a cab."

Denali watched Chrys bustle around the apartment until finally she stood at the door with bags in hand. "Please be careful," Denali told her.

"I will. I promise." And then she was gone.

Denali closed the door and felt the overwhelming emptiness of the apartment. Azalea was gone. Now Chrys. It was the first time she'd had to face life on her own. Even when she'd first come to Dallas and Chrys had flown off to New Orleans, Azalea had been as close as the telephone. "I suppose I should have tried it long ago," she chided herself aloud. "But it never seemed necessary."

She took herself to the balcony and stared out on the city skyline. Azalea's dying had taken much of the sorrow out of her death. Having watched her linger in pain and misery, seeing her life ebbing away, caused Denali to feel a sense of relief in her passing. She might be gone, but she no longer had to bear the burden of her illness.

"Gone, but not forever parted," the minister had said.

"Oh, Azalea," Denali whispered, "I'm only afraid that it will feel like forever." She felt the sadness wash over her. Maybe Chrys had the right idea. If she threw herself into business, then she wouldn't have time to dwell on her losses. She also might not have to think of her gains. After all, she held even more confusion over the issues between her and Michael.

"What do I do with you, Michael?" she whispered. If she stayed in Dallas and took the job Hazel was offering, her relationship with Michael might well continue to develop into something serious. But then there were other issues to be dealt with. Would she stay with Fun, Inc. or work for Hazel? Would she find a way to get the answers to her questions regarding her mother and father? Then again, did they really matter in the face of losing Azalea? Her aunt had reminded her that knowing the truth wouldn't change the truth—it would only alter Denali's perception. Was that really worth the risk of alienating the remaining two members of her family? The jumble of thoughts twisted and raced through her head just as the telephone rang. Stepping back inside, Denali picked up the call on the fourth ring.

"Hello?"

"I began to wonder if you had gone out," Richard Deveraux stated in an almost harsh manner.

"I was on the balcony," Denali explained. "Chrys just had to leave for New Orleans, but I suppose you know that."

"Yes," Richard replied. "That's part of the reason I'm calling. I thought rather than have you there by yourself, you might come spend some time with me."

Denali bit her lip to keep from gasping aloud. She swallowed down the lump in her throat and replied, "I must say this is a surprise. Are you sure?"

"Of course I'm sure," he nearly roared back at her. "I don't extend invitations unless I'm sure. Look, we've just buried Azalea, and I figured it would be good for both of us."

Denali smiled. "I'd like it very much. When should I come?"

"Right now. Come right this minute."

"I'll need to pack a few things, but then I'll be over," Denali told him. Her heart nearly overflowed with happiness. This was an answer to prayer. Finally she would have a chance to spend time getting to know her grandfather. Maybe now she'd have some direction about the future.

Denali arrived some time later at the house on Beverly Drive. She stared at the two-story home for several minutes before getting out of the car to go in. Would she learn the truth in this house? Would she start a new relationship of love and hope with her grandfather? Would she finally know peace? She hoped the answer to all three questions would be a resounding "yes." She wanted so much to fit all the pieces of her puzzle together and see the picture clearly.

With bag in hand, she climbed out of the car and made her way to the house. She knew a nervous trembling in her body and felt like a skittish, uncertain child. She prayed a third time for strength, then knocked on the front door. "Please let it be all right," she whispered, eyes turned skyward.

The door opened, and Richard Deveraux stared at her hard for a moment. "You made it in good time," he told her gruffly, then backed away in order to allow Denali entrance into the house.

Denali smiled. "You don't know how much I've longed for this."

He stared at her strangely for a moment. "I suppose that's understandable." He took her bag and motioned to the stairway. "I've fixed your room up just the way you always liked it."

Denali frowned but followed him up the stairs. He couldn't possibly have any idea how she liked her room. A strange sense of foreboding overcame her. Maybe this wasn't the great idea she thought it was. Azalea's warning to be careful came to mind.

"You're going to enjoy it here. Cambry was a fine home, but this place is much more to my liking. I hope it's to your liking, as well. It's important to me that you be happy here."

"I'm sure I will be," Denali told him. "But I'll probably only stay a few days."

He turned on the top step and looked down at her. "I'm hoping that you'll consider staying here permanently. In fact, I intend to talk to Chrys about the same thing. I should have all my girls under one roof." With that, he turned to the right and motioned Denali down the hall. "It's this way."

Denali followed after him in slow, deliberate steps. She'd never been to the second floor of her grandfather's house, and she didn't want to miss a single thing. Gawking around like a tourist, Denali noted an inlaid wood table at the top of the stairs. It was narrow and long, maybe as much as six feet, with a red brocade runner that graced the length of it. Atop this, a hand-painted vase with fresh flowers stood in the middle, with silver hallmarked frames trailing down either side. Denali glanced quickly at the photographs inside those frames, noting that most were of her aunts and mother. *His girls*, she thought and moved on.

Beyond this, the hallway was fairly barren. The hardwood floors were covered with a runner that appeared to be Persian. Denali found herself wondering how they ever kept the thing in place against the highly polished finish of the oak flooring. But she had little time to even consider the matter.

"Here we are," Richard said, pushing open the first door on the right. "I hope you're pleased."

Denali entered the room and gasped. "Why, it's just like the one in Cambry," she said without thinking.

"Exactly," her grandfather countered. "Does it please you?"

Denali didn't know what to say. The room was an exact duplicate— not of her own bedroom, but of Rose's. "Mother would have loved it, I'm sure."

Richard smiled. "She always wanted to keep her little garden girls happy."

Denali hesitated, then asked, "Why do you say that?"

He shrugged. "It was just her way," he replied, as if not understanding Denali's real meaning behind the question.

"I tried to replicate everything in detail. I'm just so happy you've agreed to come here. To give me a chance to make things up to you," Richard said, his eyes filled with an unmistakable chilling sincerity.

He seemed so genuinely happy that Denali found it hard, but not impossible, to ask the question that had haunted her mind since his telephone call. "Does this mean you're willing to talk to me about the past?"

Richard's expression grew serious. "Things happened back then. Things I'm not proud of. You have to understand. I want you to forgive me. I want to rewrite the past. But you alone hold the key."

"I'm not sure I understand. Why do I hold the key?" Denali questioned earnestly.

Richard moved toward her several inches. "I want to explain things, but it's not going to be easy. Some things are better left unsaid. It's important that you see this."

"But I need to know about my mother and father," Denali countered. "Will you be willing to answer my questions honestly?"

Richard's expression contorted a moment and then became one of confusion. "It's . . . it's like this . . ." he stammered. "I want to be honest . . . I do. But you have to respect my desire to protect you."

"Protect me from what?" Denali questioned. "Surely you needn't protect me from the truth."

Richard shook his head and muttered something unintelligible. "Just did what I had to do. Just protecting you." Denali reached out to touch his arm, but he drew back sharply. "I know," he said, staring at her, but not seeing her. "I know."

Denali felt that sense of foreboding return. She shuddered, unable to hide her reaction from Richard. "What do you know?" she questioned softly, hoping he would somehow snap out of the trancelike state he was in.

He looked at her then, but still Denali got the feeling that his mind had taken him elsewhere. Maybe staying here with him wasn't such a good idea. Maybe she'd call Michael and get his opinion. She thought of the message she'd left on the kitchen cabinet for Chrys. Maybe it would be better if she gave Chrys a call tonight and asked for her advice rather than seek out Michael for his.

"I want you to understand," he told her, then turned abruptly for the door. "I want to make things right between us, Rose."

Denali called after him, but he'd already closed the door behind him, and Denali wasn't at all certain that she wanted to pursue him, given his state of mind. He'd called her by her mother's name again, and Denali couldn't help but wonder if he had completely given himself over to seeing her as her mother's representative.

"Maybe he thinks my mother has somehow come back to him through me," Denali said, sitting down on the edge of the bed. For the first time, she began to seriously contemplate the mental health of her grandfather. Maybe this was what Azalea and Chrys had seen all along.

"He keeps calling me Rose," she whispered to the room. Then looking around her, Denali's skin goose-bumped, and she shivered. "Does he really think I'm Rose?"

Thirty-one

The telephone was ringing when Michael stepped out of the shower. He hurriedly wrapped a towel around his dripping body and made a mad dash for the extension in his bedroom.

"Hello?" he answered anxiously.

"Michael, this is Chrys Deveraux."

He frowned. He'd hoped it might be Denali. He'd not talked to her since the funeral, and that had been almost two days ago. "What can I do for you, Chrys?"

"Michael, I just got back from a business trip to New Orleans. Denali left me a note, and I'm worried about her."

"Worried? Why, what's wrong?"

"She's gone to spend some time with my father. I tried calling over there, but the line seems to be disconnected or off the hook. Look, Michael, I don't want to talk about this on the phone. Can you come up?" Her voice sounded fearful.

"Sure. Just give me a minute to get dressed. I'm afraid you caught me in the shower."

"I'm sorry. I know it's late."

Michael frowned at the obvious worry in her tone. "I'll come right up, Chrys."

And in record time, he did just that. His black hair still hung damp from the shower, but he was dressed in jeans and an ancient polo shirt. His main concern was not appearance, but rather, why it was that the normally stoic Chrys Deveraux had voiced such an emotional appeal.

"Thank you for being so quick," Chrys said, letting him into the apartment. "I know this must seem like absolute madness to you, but I'm afraid for Denali."

"So I gathered. Why don't you tell me about it," Michael suggested.

Chrys led him to the living room and motioned him to sit. She took her place in one of the chairs opposite the sofa and twisted her hands in her lap. "You know that things have been strained between my father and Denali. I mean, he did hire you to keep her out of his hair."

Michael nodded. "But that's not the reason I spent time with her. I want that understood right up front."

Chrys looked at him strangely for a moment. "That isn't important right now. I'm afraid for her, Michael. My father isn't well. I've noticed his mind slipping. He's not the same man he was before Denali came to Dallas. I think she's had a positively overwhelming effect on him, and he can't deal with it."

"Why do you say that?" Michael questioned, his nerves stretching taut. If Denali was in real danger, the last thing he wanted to do was sit here and make small talk with this woman.

"I'm going to bare the family skeletons to you, Michael. Not because I want to, but because I think Denali may well need me to. I know you understand some of her background. You've spoken to me about it before, and I asked you not to bring it up again, but now I'm going to bring it up because I think it's imperative that I do so."

"Go on," he encouraged.

"Denali's mother, my sister Rose, fell in love with our father's business partner, William Wilson. His real name was Lester William Wilson, but most everyone knew him as Bill. Rose called him Les, for what reasons I'm not sure. It might have been to hide his identity as she wrote about him in her diary. It might have been because she didn't like the name Bill—I just don't know. But the fact is, she fell in love with him, and he was nineteen years her senior. She knew our father would never, ever tolerate the romance, but nevertheless she involved herself and got pregnant with Denali."

The pieces were starting to fall into place for Michael. He thought of the information he'd received on Rose and Lester's marriage and asked, "Did anyone know about them getting married?"

Chrys looked at him in stunned silence for several moments. Then, without a word, she got up and went out of the room. Michael feared that he'd overstepped his bounds, but when she returned with a handful of papers, he knew Chrys was ready to divulge everything.

She handed him a copy of Rose's marriage license. "I don't know how you found out about this. I wouldn't know about it myself, except

I'd read of it in Rose's diary. I never was convinced they had truly married until recently. I went to my father's house not long ago and found him very drunk. When I put him to bed, I found his bedroom entirely devoted to Rose. Her pictures were everywhere, and he even had a huge oil painting of her hanging at the foot of his bed. I found these papers." She sat down hard and shook her head. "I still can't believe it."

Michael began to understand her fear for Denali. Richard was obviously obsessed with his dead daughter. Perhaps now he would transfer that obsession to Denali.

"So your sister married your father's business partner. When did your father find out about it?"

"It wasn't until they'd been married for several months," Chrys admitted. "Rose used to help father and me out at the office. I guess she was alone too much of the time with Bill . . . Lester. Azalea and I found her diary some weeks after her death, and it was all there. I thought maybe she'd just made up the part about getting married. You know, wishful thinking on the part of an overly romantic mind. Especially in light of the fact that she was pregnant. I put two and two together regarding who Les really was, but Azalea never knew."

Michael nodded, wishing she'd hurry and share the rest of her information with him. "What about the adoption? Richard adopted Denali. Why?"

Chrys paled. "How did you find out about that?"

"It isn't important, but your answer might be."

"He didn't want anyone to know about Rose and Lester. Lester had no family—at least none who were still alive. In fact, he really had no friends to speak of. Father was basically his one and only companion until Rose came along. When Denali was born, I presumed the birth certificate was issued listing an unwed mother and unknown father."

"But that wasn't true, was it?"

"No." She handed him another record. "This is Denali's original birth certificate, and here are the papers of her adoption. She was never told. She presumed her name was Deveraux because her mother had been unmarried, but, in truth, her name was Wilson at birth, and Father changed it."

Michael mulled all of this new information over in his head. Little by little he sorted it into acceptable piles. Denali was born the legitimate daughter of Lester and Rose Wilson. But if that was true, then what had happened to her father?

Michael looked up at Chrys. "Where's Les now?"

Chrys gasped for breath and exhaled nervously. She shook her head from side to side and handed Michael two more pieces of paper. "These are the torn-out entries from Rose's diary. Denali has the diary and has only recently learned of her father's name. I lied to her and told her that I didn't know any Les. I told her I didn't know who her father was."

Michael took the pages. The look on Chrys's face told him they would reveal the final solution to this puzzle. He began to read, even as Chrys started to explain.

"Rose was supposed to be spending the night with a friend, but Father found out she wasn't there, and he went into a rage. He went to her room and tore it apart looking for something that would clue him in to where she'd gone. He found her diary and read that she and Les were going to Oklahoma. He had some kind of job interview. This doubly grieved Father. He went after them. I thought at the time that they had eloped and that he was going to stop it. When he returned with Rose, she wouldn't even speak to us. She stayed for weeks in her room, and then we found out she was to have a baby."

Michael tried to concentrate on both the words on the paper and the woman's near-hysterical explanation. Rose's spidery handwriting was smudged in places where Michael could only presume her tears had fallen on the paper. " 'I will never forgive Father for what he's done. I will have this baby and I will find a way to leave him forever.' " Michael read on, feeling the bitterness and anguish of the young girl who'd written them. " 'I cannot forgive him for taking the life of the man I love—for killing my baby's father.' " Michael stopped reading and looked up to find Chrys in tears.

"Is this true? Did Richard kill Lester Wilson?"

"I don't know," Chrys said, her voice breaking. "I wish I did. No, on second thought, I'm glad I never knew. We knew something had gone horribly wrong, but we always presumed Father had paid Lester off. We figured he had bought him out of the business and sent him on his way, because from that day forward we never saw him again. The business continued as usual, only the name William Wilson was removed from everything dealing with the business."

"And no one questioned this?"

"No," Chrys replied. "Father told everyone that he had decided to get out but told me privately that he had paid Lester off. I never doubted for a minute that it was true."

"Obviously no one else doubted it, either," Michael said, hardly able to believe it. "But if everyone bought into this so easily, why worry about what Denali knew? Why not at least answer her questions enough to keep her satisfied? Maybe if Denali knew about her mother and her father, she would have been much easier to contend with, and Richard wouldn't have this obsession with the past."

"He couldn't tell her. He couldn't tell anyone for one very good reason." She reached out, giving Michael one rather official-looking document and then another piece of Rose's torn diary. "That's the last will and testament of Lester William Wilson. As you can see, it was drawn up around the time he married Rose."

Michael looked over the information. "He bequeathed everything to Rose, including his thirty percent of Fun, Inc."

"Yes. And as you will see on that other piece of paper, Rose wrote out her own will and left everything in turn to Denali. Rose already held ten percent of the stock, and with Lester's thirty, that gave her forty percent."

"An equal share to Richard," Michael said. It was all becoming so clear. "Richard couldn't risk Denali finding out about the stock because then she'd have power over him and the company. And if not power over him, then at least equal to him."

"Not only that, but now Azalea has died, leaving her ten percent in the company to Denali, as well. Denali now owns controlling interest in Fun, Inc."

Michael felt a sensation much like a blow to his midsection. "And does Richard know this?"

Chrys nodded and barely whispered, "Yes, and this, along with a trust fund that Father never bothered to tell Denali about, makes her a rich and powerful woman. At least in Father's world." She got up and paced nervously. "Now you know everything. Michael, I think he might well do something to her. He's so lost in his mind, and I'm not sure he'll ever be on solid footing again."

Michael jumped to his feet, letting the papers fall where they would. "I'll go get Denali, and you can explain all of this to her. She deserves to know the truth, and Richard will just have to live with the consequences of his actions."

Chrys followed him to the door. "Be careful, Michael. It's the middle of the night. My father might not take kindly to your barging in there without warning."

"Denali's life may be on the line," he told her frankly. "I don't much care what Deveraux thinks or feels on the matter."

Thirty-two

*D*enali found herself lost in a swirling haze. She felt herself drawn forward, as if being pulled by some unseen force, but she couldn't see what she was being drawn toward. Fear gripped her in a way that warned her to turn around and run, but try as she might, she couldn't manage such an action. She felt a cold hand reach out to take hold of her arm.

"Denali Rose," the voice said in a low, ominous tone, "you are called to account for your actions."

"But I've done nothing wrong," she mumbled, trying desperately to make sense of the scene.

The unseen companion tightened its grip and pulled her toward what appeared to be a black abyss. Denali wrenched away and tried to run, but instead found that she was shackled to the place where she stood.

"Help me," she cried out, and just when she felt certain that her doom was imminent, she awoke with a strangled cry. "No!"

Sitting straight up in bed, Denali panted for breath. Her heart pounded furiously, almost as if she'd been running a race. Sweat trickled from her brow. Staring into the darkness around her, Denali remained fearful and uncomfortable. Reaching out for the lamp, she switched it on and leaned back against the headboard of the bed.

"It's just a nightmare," she told herself.

She remembered other nightmares. Bad dreams that had haunted her as a child. Azalea had always been the one to offer her comfort and concern when the dreams had come to wreak havoc with her sleep. But of course, Azalea couldn't come to her now. In fact, no one, with the exception of her grandfather, could come to offer her comfort on this night. No one except Chrys knew where she was, but Chrys was apparently still in New Orleans. The office knew her to be on funeral leave. And Michael . . . She hadn't allowed herself to call Michael, even though it had been her deepest heart's desire. She wanted to do this on her own. Face the past and her grandfather and all that went with it— all by herself. Call it pride or stupidity, she didn't care. It was important to Denali to be self-sufficient, and if that meant putting Michael on a back burner somewhere, then so be it.

She relaxed a bit, thinking on her decision to set Michael aside. It seemed important to deal with the past before embarking on an adventure bound for the future. It hardly seemed fair to Michael that she should bring so many unresolved issues into a relationship. He knew in part about her dilemma—that much was true—but there was still so much that neither one of them knew. Things that Denali needed to understand before she could make a new start.

Oh, why does this have to be so hard? she wondered. *I want so much for my life to be normal. I just want to be happy.* She hugged her knees to her chest and rested her chin. She felt like a little girl again. Like the times when she'd sneak into her mother's bedroom in order to feel close to the woman she'd never known. *Mother, if you could only understand what you did to me. You may have needed to take the easy way out, but you left me here to pick up the pieces and to face the anger of those you left behind. I have so many questions, and now that I'm here with Grandfather, I'm more certain than ever that those answers are never going to be given to me.*

She shuddered. For the first time, she realized the truth in her thoughts. Richard thought she was Rose. Of this she was certain. She thought of the diary entries and the closeness that Rose had shared with her father. No doubt Denali's grandfather had been unable to take rejection and deception from the child he'd always assumed felt as much loyalty to him as he felt to her.

Her fears somewhat abated, Denali realized she was very hungry, and the thought of sneaking downstairs for a midnight snack suddenly outweighed any haunting reminders of her nightmare. She had passed up dessert at supper that evening, and now the luscious-looking strawberry cake sounded quite appealing. Besides, being scared was for little girls, she told herself. "I'm a grown woman, and I need to start acting like one."

She slipped out of bed and pulled a white cotton robe on over her nightgown. Securing the belt at her waist, Denali cautiously opened her bedroom door and listened. Shrouded in darkness, the silence of the hall did little to offer her encouragement. Denali's eyes could make out the basic shape of things, but little more. Taking a deep breath, she forced herself to go forward. It was rather like the dream she'd just had. The darkness, the cold, the foreboding.

"I'm being silly," she told herself and picked up her pace.

She stubbed her toe against the hall table and barely suppressed a cry. No sense waking up the whole house and having to explain about her midnight foraging session. The household staff lived in the apartments over the garage, so she knew they weren't of any concern. But Richard was a different story. She had no idea if he might be a light or heavy sleeper. Or even if he'd concern himself with such matters should he be awake and hear her in the hallway. She simply knew very little about the man.

Grabbing hold of the stairway bannister, Denali felt relieved to make her way downstairs. *I'll turn on a light in the foyer*, she told herself and had very nearly reached the point where she could do just that when headlights flashed across the trophy room windows. Someone had just pulled into the driveway.

Anxious to see what was happening, Denali went to the window and tried to look out without giving herself away. The Mercedes in the drive looked familiar, but it wasn't until Michael emerged from the driver's side that Denali realized who the visitor was.

Hurrying to the door, she pulled it open and snapped on the outside light just as Michael made his way up the walk. Before Denali could even question his presence, he reached out and took her into his arms. He held her tightly—almost possessively, desperately. Denali felt both shock and elation at the action. He obviously had sought her out, but it was the middle of the night.

"What in the world are you doing here?" she questioned as his hold on her loosened. Then suddenly she thought of her aunt. "Is something wrong with Chrys?"

"Not exactly," Michael replied, his voice heavy with concern.

"What are you saying?" Denali asked.

"Look, some things are going on that you need to be aware of. I've come to take you back to the apartment where Chrys and I can talk to you." He reached up and pushed back a strand of her hair. "You look so beautiful," he murmured, appearing to have completely lost track of the real reason for his visit.

"I don't understand," she said, pushing him away. "Michael, you aren't making any sense. It's the middle of the night, and frankly, the only reason I'm awake to greet you at the door is because I'm headed to the kitchen for a midnight snack."

"More like a one-thirty snack," he said lightly, but the seriousness of his expression told her otherwise.

"What's wrong, Michael? Just tell me right now." Denali watched as he appeared to consider her request. What was it that he had to say? Why did she suddenly feel so frightened?

"This isn't the best place or time," Michael replied and, nudging her back through the open doorway, stepped into the house. "Look, just go get dressed, and we'll go back to the apartment. Chrys has sent me here, in case you're worried about my intentions, but honestly, I would have come anyway. I was starting to worry about you."

"Why?" Denali asked. He wasn't making sense, and she desperately needed something to fall into order and be clear for once.

Michael again reached out for her, and Denali went into his arms without protest. She could feel his heart racing beneath her hand as she reached up to put a barrier between them. She wondered if the cause was fear for some unspoken problem or if his feelings for her matched her own for him. Feelings that she still couldn't seem to come to terms with.

Hesitantly, she looked up into his face. "Michael, please tell me what's wrong. Why are you here?"

He lowered his mouth to hers and kissed her into silence. He took his time, kissing her long and lingeringly until Denali had very nearly forgotten her protest. Her hand no longer separated them but instead had found its way upward to play teasingly with the hair at the nape of his neck.

"I care about you more than I realized," Michael whispered as he allowed the kiss to end. "There are things going on here that might well have put you into jeopardy."

"What things? I don't understand," Denali replied anxiously. "And what do you mean about caring for me more than you realized?"

Michael shook his head. "I can't explain everything—I mean, not just yet. I need to get you out of here. Chrys believes there's a definite danger to be faced from your grandfather. She showed me some papers this evening. Papers that explain a great deal about your past and answer the questions you've been asking for so many years."

"What papers?" Denali asked in disbelief. "Everyone has always told me there was nothing that would give me the answers I sought." She pushed away, feeling strangely betrayed by Michael's words. "What papers are you talking about?"

Michael's eyes seemed to plead with her for understanding. "Just trust me on this one, Denali. I don't think it's wise to discuss it here and now."

Denali folded her arms tightly against herself. "I'm not going anywhere until you explain what this is all about."

Michael sighed, realizing he had no choice. "Remember your mother's diary?"

"Yes," Denali replied suspiciously.

"And remember the missing pages at the end of it?" Michael questioned.

"Yes." Her voice betrayed her fear.

"I've seen those missing pages," he responded matter-of-factly. "They were torn out by your grandfather. He didn't want anyone to read what was written there because it incriminated him."

"What are you saying?" Denali asked, backing away from the man. "Tell me what you mean."

"Rose blamed your grandfather for the death of Lester Wilson—your father. He was also your grandfather's business partner."

Denali felt herself go numb. Her breathing quickened to counter the dizzy, lightheaded feeling that washed over her. "I don't understand," she said, her voice sounding childlike.

"Your mother married a man nineteen years her senior. He was the business partner who shared Fun, Inc. with your grandfather. Richard couldn't deal with the matter and went after your mother and Lester one night when they were headed to Oklahoma."

"He had a job interview," Denali muttered.

"Yes, that's right. Chrys said your grandfather felt deceived and betrayed by both Lester and Rose, and he went after them, presuming that they had eloped."

"But they were already married," Denali replied, her throat dry and tight.

"Yes, but he didn't know that until he caught up with them. It was then that things turned ugly."

Denali shook her head. "Chrys knew all of this? She's always known? Why didn't she tell me? Why couldn't someone be honest with me?" Tears were streaming down her face. "My father is dead? Is that what you're telling me?"

"Not only that, but your grandfather probably murdered him," Michael said, reaching out to take hold of Denali.

"No," she said, slapping at his hand. Her voice edged on hysteria. "Don't touch me. You've all been lying to me."

"I'm not lying now," Michael said seriously.

From the dim glow of the outdoor light, Denali could see the concern in his expression, but she didn't care. He'd just said that her grandfather was a murderer. Not only that, but that he'd willfully killed her father—the father she'd never known and now would never know.

"Why is this happening?" She hugged her arms to her body, trying desperately to ease her trembling. "Why is God letting this happen to me?"

"Denali, come with me. Don't even bother to change your clothes. You've got to get out of here before Richard wakes up. He doesn't even know Chrys knows the truth—at least, she doesn't think he does. He got drunk one day, and she found the papers in his bedroom—a room, I might add, that he's utilized to focus on his obsession with your mother. Chrys says the walls are covered with photographs and paintings of Rose."

"He thinks I'm Rose," Denali admitted, trying desperately to regain her composure. "He put me in a room that looks just like her room back in Cambry, and he calls me by her name."

Michael's eyes widened, and his jaw clenched down tight as he reached for her once again. This time Denali didn't fight him. The truth was finally beginning to sink in. Her grandfather had told her there were things he had done out of protection for her. Things he wasn't proud of—things that he had felt no choice in. Did that include murder?

Denali stared up at Michael, a hundred questions coming to mind at once, but just as she would have spoken them, the foyer light snapped on and Richard Deveraux stared down at them in complete rage. Denali watched him fearfully, suddenly convinced that everything Michael had told her was true. This man had killed before. What would stop him from doing it again?

"Rose!" Richard Deveraux bellowed out the name and stared with narrowing eyes at Denali's trembling form.

She backed up against Michael, not at all comforted by his presence.

He had taken a firm grasp of her arms and held her fast against him, but Denali could only see the livid rage in her grandfather's expression. Was this what her mother had seen on that fateful night? Was she reliving the past?

"Rose Deveraux, I demand you come away from him."

Only then did Denali see the gun in his hand.

Michael saw the gun and in one fluid motion whipped Denali around behind him and began backing toward the door.

"Put the gun down, Richard. You don't want to hurt her."

Deveraux started down the stairs. "Get away from her. Get away from my Rose."

"This is Denali, Richard," Michael reminded the old man.

For a moment, Richard halted on the steps. He waved the gun back and forth as if trying to choose which one of them to focus the weapon on. Of course, Denali was fairly well protected by Michael's broad-shouldered frame, but the gun in Deveraux's hand was a .357 Magnum, and Michael knew that if he fired the weapon, the bullet would go right through him and into Denali. His only hope was to bring Deveraux back into the present.

"Richard, it's Michael. Remember me?"

Deveraux grew even more confused. He shook his head and seemed to blink his eyes several times, as if trying to focus on the scene more clearly.

"Copeland," he finally said, taking another step down. "What are you doing here? We had an agreement about Denali. You won't get that bonus if you don't carry out your part of the bargain." Richard's words were exacting and laced with obvious malice.

"What agreement?" Denali questioned, edging to the side of Michael. "What are you talking about?"

Richard's expression contorted as once again he seemed unable to put the scene together. He appeared confused and at times allowed the the gun to be pointed to the floor rather than at Michael. "I did what I had to do. You were foolish, Rose. Foolish to marry a man so much older than you. A man with no future except for that which I gave him."

Michael realized Deveraux was hopelessly insane. His guilt had eaten away the working portions of his brain, and now reality and his illusions from the past were melded together in a way that he couldn't figure one from the other. Michael's only hope was to get Denali out of there before Richard decided to ease his guilt and kill them both.

"You're just seventeen," Deveraux began again, and Michael backed up another step, hoping Denali would perceive his reasoning and take it upon herself to head for the door.

"You're a child—he's a grown man. You can't do this to yourself. I trusted you," Deveraux said, coming down another couple of steps. "And you," his voice lowered to a near growl, "you knew better." His hate-filled expression focused on Michael. "You stole my child from under my nose. Did you think I would let you get away with that? You took my Rose. The last gift my wife gave me. Our precious child—you took her and spoiled her so that no one else could have her. You can't expect me to let you live after doing that." He raised the gun again to aim it squarely at Michael's chest.

"Denali," Michael barely breathed the name. "Get out of here. Run!"

He pushed at her and started for the door, but Deveraux fired, splintering the wood of the open door. "Coward!" he declared. "You can't run from me. She belongs to me—not you. She's my daughter, and you had no right to take her from me."

Michael stopped in his tracks. He could no longer feel Denali behind him and could only hope that she had wisely chosen to run from the nightmarish ordeal. Working hard to steady his own breathing, Michael considered for the first time if Deveraux would kill him. He stared hard at the nickel-plated revolver, wondering seriously if he might charge the old man and deflect the path of the bullet before Deveraux took another shot. Somehow it didn't seem likely.

Michael met the old man's eyes. They were cold and lifeless, lost in the past. The past! That was the key to survival. "Richard, think about what you're doing," Michael finally said. "You can't do this to Rose. Think of how she'll feel afterward. She'll blame you, Richard. You'll never know a moment's peace."

This seemed to do the trick. Deveraux frowned and shook his head. He muttered several incoherent words and stared for a time at the gun in his hand. It almost seemed to shock him for a moment. Michael decided to take advantage of Deveraux's hesitation. He turned ever so slowly to the side, fully intending to make a rush for the door, but instead he found Denali frozen in place, a look of utter horror on her face.

Apparently Richard saw her, as well, because it was to her, or rather the ghostly image of her mother, that he spoke. "I'm sorry, Rose. You'll come to understand in time. You can't be married to this man." He raised the gun again. "I have to end this now."

Thirty-three

*D*enali could only think of the lives that had been lost because of this scenario so many years before. She threw herself with amazing speed in front of Michael, and when he tried to move her, she wrapped her arms back around his and stood her ground. As if given strength beyond her means, Denali remained unmoved even as Michael protested aloud and tried to turn her away from her grandfather.

"I won't let you kill Michael," she declared. "You'll have to kill me instead. Do you understand?"

Richard looked at her strangely. Once again he appeared confused. "This isn't how it's supposed to be, Rose. You go wait in the car—like last time. You go and wait."

"No. I won't let you kill him!"

"You're my daughter and you'll do what I say," Deveraux roared. "You'll see. This is all for the best. We'll have the marriage annulled, and no one will ever know. No one!" He stressed the latter words. His voice contorted as if some sort of inner battle raged within him.

Denali realized he was completely lost in the past. He would never see the truth of the situation. He only knew her to be Rose Deveraux, and perhaps that was the only way in which she could reach him. With this thought came an eerie sensation that somehow she was about to have all the answers. The puzzle was finally going to be finished. *Oh, God, help me*, she thought.

Just then it came to her that while the scene might well be very close to the actual one carried out so many years ago, there were several elements of the truth at that time that were never exposed. Believing them her only hope, Denali dropped her hold on Michael and stepped forward just a few inches.

"Father," she began softly, determinedly.

Deveraux looked at her, and his expression softened. He very nearly smiled. "Be a good girl, Rose. Do what I've told you and you'll see. It's all going to work out. We'll just forget about all of this once he's gone."

Denali shook her head. "We can't do that, Father." She gambled their lives on her next statement. "I'm going to have a baby. His baby."

Richard's face showed stark disbelief. Denali had altered the past with that simple statement, and it was clear that her grandfather was struggling to somehow put this bit of information into an acceptable form.

"No," he muttered. "It didn't happen that way."

"But it's the truth," Denali told him softly. Again she tried to reach into his mind. "Father, I didn't want to tell you. I knew you wouldn't understand. But I love Les and he loves me, and we're going to have a baby. Your grandchild. Your granddaughter." Denali pressed on. "I'm going to call her Denali. You know how much I love that park in Alaska."

Richard nodded, but his eyes seemed to glaze over. "Denali," he whispered.

"Yes. The baby is going to be born in June."

"That's right," Michael suddenly declared, easing his way beside Denali. He put a supportive arm around her shoulder. "I've already rewritten my will, Richard. I've left everything to my wife—to Rose. She'll get my thirty percent of the company. She already has ten percent, Richard. If you kill me, she'll have forty percent, just like you."

Richard and Denali both looked at Michael. Denali wondered why he was saying these things. Was it true? Was this yet another portion of the truth that Chrys had divulged?

Richard began muttering incoherently, and Michael moved from Denali to step toward him. "Think about it, Richard. Rose won't be able to live without me. She'll kill herself, Richard. Can you live with causing her death? She'll die, and then she'll leave her forty percent to Denali. Denali will own the same amount of stock as you—you'll no longer have controlling interest."

Richard's mind was unable to absorb the news, and without warning, Michael took advantage of his confusion to jump forward and wrestle the gun away from him.

Denali stood back in shock. It took only a matter of seconds and seemed rather anticlimactic. Now Michael stood with the gun in hand, and outside the sounds of sirens could already be heard. No doubt someone had heard the gunshots and had seen the lights on in the Deveraux home.

Richard sank to the bottom step of the grand staircase. "I only did what I had to do, Rose. You have to understand. I had to kill him. I had to. Why didn't you just go to the car like last time? Why didn't you just wait until I'd dumped his body in that abandoned well? Bill can't hurt us anymore." He put his hands to his head and pressed hard as if to squeeze the images from his mind. "I had to do it."

Denali suddenly realized she was crying. Watching her grandfather's tortured soul bare the truth of his actions was almost more than she could deal with. So much had come to light in one very startling moment that Denali wasn't all that sure she herself could contend with the truth. Her father had been murdered by her grandfather, and her mother had never been able to abide the truth of the matter and in turn had killed herself. And in their passing, Denali had inherited their stock in Fun, Inc. Could it be true?

"Are you all right?" Michael questioned, coming to stand beside her.

"I don't know," she admitted. "I don't think I really understand what's happened here tonight."

But there was no time for Michael to explain. Just then two squad cars pulled up in front of the residence, and already the slamming doors alerted them both that company was well on the way. With the flashing red-and-blue lights still revolving, Denali looked to find her grandfather's face swathed in the pulsating glow.

"She loves me," Richard muttered and rocked back and forth on the steps. "She loves me."

For reasons beyond Denali's understanding, she could only think of the game of plucking flower petals. *She loves me. She loves me not. She loves me.* She wanted to go to Richard and comfort him, assure him that she did love him—that she always had. But Michael held her fast.

"Police," a voice rang out.

Richard's head snapped up, the look on his face ranging somewhere between panic and horror. Then he turned to Denali, and the look changed to one of anguish and betrayal.

She loves me not.

His countenance seemed to say it all, and it depleted Denali's resolve. Putting her face in her hands, she began to weep tears that spanned generations. She cried for her mother. For her father. For herself. Even for Richard. One possessive action, one regretful, misguided judgment had forever changed their lives. Knowing the truth didn't change a thing that had happened in the past, but maybe it would alter the course of the future.

After plugging the telephone back in, Denali called Chrys while Michael told the police what had happened. Richard sat mumbling and shaking his head, methodically pulling at his shirt as if trying to pick off unseen debris.

"I'll be home soon," Denali told Chrys. "You might want to talk to the police officer and see what's to be done with Grandfather." Denali heard Chrys's tearful apology begin once again. "Look, don't apologize. We can talk about all of this later. Grandfather needs us to be strong for him. I think he's going to need some long-term care, and then there's that whole affair about him killing my father." Denali motioned to a nearby officer and held her hand over the receiver. "This is my aunt, Chrys Deveraux. She should be the one you talk to about the arrangements for my grandfather."

The man nodded, and Denali announced him to Chrys before handing over the phone. She breathed a sigh of relief, then looked up just as two uniformed police officers were helping Richard to his feet. She wanted to say something or do something that would somehow make the situation less critical, but there was nothing to be done. This man, her grandfather, had taken it upon himself to control and ruin the lives of those around him. Now his mind could no longer deal with the stress of those decisions, and while Denali felt a form of compassion for his well-being, she felt an even stronger anger at the way he'd cheated her out of so much.

He alone became the reason that her parents were dead. Richard Deveraux had, in many ways, killed them both. She suppressed a shudder. He'd tried to kill her, too. Well, maybe not exactly—maybe not physically, but he certainly had worked at killing her emotionally, and holding a gun to her and Michael had been enough of a physical threat to make her feel rather hostile toward the old man.

The police officer hung up the phone and came to where she stood watching her grandfather being led away. "Your aunt is going to meet us at the station."

Denali nodded. "Thank you."

"Do you live here with him?" the officer asked, glancing around the place.

"No," Denali replied. "I live with the woman you just spoke with. I'd come to spend a few days, but I'm leaving here as soon as you give the okay."

"Then by all means," the man motioned toward the door. "I'm sure you've had a rough night and would like to get some sleep."

"I'm not sure sleep is possible, but yes, I'd like to leave."

"Just make sure my partner has all the information on you that he needs."

Denali nodded, walked to the door, and found herself intercepted by Michael. One look at his face told her everything she needed to know. He loved her. She felt confident of that now more than ever. She didn't resist when he pulled her through the doorway and led her to his car. She reached for the handle, but Michael turned her around and wrapped his arms protectively around her.

"I thought he might hurt you," Michael whispered against her ear.

"I thought the same about you," Denali said softly.

Michael pushed her away just enough to see her face. Denali lifted her gaze slowly and found him studying her quite intently. "Why?" he asked. "Why did you throw yourself between us? Richard might have killed you."

"True, but I didn't think there was much chance of that. After all, he thought I was Rose." She thought carefully about her words and wondered if she dared to say what she really felt. There were still many unanswered questions, and Denali needed to be very clear on everything before taking a chance on Michael Copeland. "I guess I care more about you than I realized," she offered as an afterthought.

Michael laughed and pulled her tight again. "Well, that's a good thing, lady. Because I'm certain that I have fallen in love with you, and it would be very helpful if you returned those feelings."

Denali moved away from him as though the words he'd spoken had offended her. "You what?"

"You heard me," he replied. "I know we've had our rocky moments—"

"That's putting it mildly," Denali said with feigned sarcasm.

"But the fact is, I do love you."

"And not just because my grandfather paid you to say that?" she questioned, remembering Richard's earlier reference to paying Michael for some arrangement regarding her.

"Look, I want to come clean with you on that. I don't want there to be any lies between us—nor unspoken issues," Michael began.

Denali could see by his expression that he appeared to be under great conviction for the things he'd done. "All right. Come clean."

"I'm not sure where to start."

Denali laughed nervously and crossed her arms. "How about the beginning?"

"Of course," Michael replied. "It's just that it seems like a long time ago." He opened her car door. "Why don't we drive somewhere else, maybe get some coffee, and talk this over in private?"

"I'm hardly dressed for the occasion," Denali said, looking down at her robe. "Chrys is going uptown to help with Grandfather. Why don't we just go back to the apartment and discuss it there?"

Michael nodded. "I suppose that would work best."

Denali, reattired in jeans and a soft cotton blouse, brought Michael a cup of coffee and picked up another mug for herself before settling down on the sofa. She curled her legs beneath her, hoping to hide the nervous anxiety that settled over her. What would Michael tell her? She needed to know the truth about everything, but it remained a mystery as to how that truth might affect them.

"I have to start by telling you that I'm not the same man you dealt with in May."

"I know that," Denali replied, keeping her glance on the mug of steaming coffee.

"Good, because that man made bad choices and let his greed and self-centered plans make decisions for him." He took a long drink before setting the cup down and turning his full attention to Denali. Still, Denali refused to look at him.

"Richard came to me and asked me to keep you out of his hair. He didn't say why, just that you were somehow a problem to the family, himself in particular, and that while he had to bring you on board because of Hazel Garrison's request, he didn't want to have to deal with you." He took a long breath as if waiting for the news to sink in.

"Go on."

"He offered me a huge bonus to come into the project with you, but only if I managed to keep you away from him. The night you showed up at his party, I thought for sure I'd blown it."

Denali laughed and finally threw him a quick glance. "Yes, I remember you being quite concerned that I not pester Grandfather."

Michael shrugged. "I wanted to get my business back. I needed money, and that was all I could think about. Deveraux told me to wine and dine you but to keep you away from him. He promised to pay all the expenses and throw in a hefty bonus to boot."

"So you took him up on it and pestered me to go out on one date after another."

"Yes."

Denali started to feel uneasy about the times they'd shared together. Had it all been a lie? The looks, the words, the shared sorrows and memories from days gone by? How could anyone treat another human being with such a callous attitude?

"So I meant nothing to you but a way to get back your business."

"In the beginning," Michael said, reaching out to touch her leg. "But only in the beginning. From the first time you really started to open up to me, it changed everything. I couldn't focus on anything but your needs, and let me tell you, that was something I found very disturbing."

Denali couldn't help but smile. "Yes, I can well imagine."

"No, I'm not sure you can. My entire nature and course of living directed itself to one issue and one need. My business. After Renea's deception, I fully intended to never love another woman again. It became the business at all cost. But focusing on my self-centered needs nearly destroyed me."

"Yes, but my life was also self-centered. My course was set upon exposing the ugly truth about the past." Denali put her cup down and turned to face him. She looked into Michael's blue eyes, then let her gaze travel up to his tousled black hair and then back down to his sensuous lips. Her attraction to him seemed an obvious chink in her armor.

"I love it when you look at me like that," he whispered low.

She met his eyes. "Like what?"

"Like you're memorizing every detail. Like you enjoy what you see."

Denali glanced down to the place where his hand still touched her leg. His touch began to feel quite warm, and beneath the covering of her jeans Denali thought her leg might well be glowing red from the heat. She couldn't find the words to deal with him. She didn't feel ready for this. There were still things she needed to sort out in her head. In her heart.

"When did you change your mind about me? When did you stop approaching me on behalf of my grandfather?" she asked softly.

Michael reached up and touched her jaw very gently. "I don't know. I suppose that sounds like a cop-out, but it's the truth. I headed into the project intent on doing what Richard suggested. But little by little you chopped holes in my plans and set my theories adrift, and before I knew it, I was falling for you in a big way."

Denali closed her eyes and tried to focus on his touch. His thumb began gently stroking her cheek. "I've changed, Denali. God has straightened me out again, and I'm back on course. I know He has a plan for my life, and I believe that plan includes you."

Her eyes snapped open at this. "You do?"

He laughed and leaned back against the couch. Immediately, Denali missed his touch and nearly leaned forward to follow the absent nearness.

"But there are still some other matters that you need to hear. I don't want you to mistake my feelings for you. And if there's any question about how you feel, I'd rather you take your time and deal with it before we say anything more about a future together."

Denali stiffened. "What things? After everything that has been said and done tonight, what else could possibly come between us?"

"You're a very rich woman, Denali," Michael began. "Before your aunt finally broke down and told me the truth about you, I had already begun my own investigation."

Denali's eyes narrowed, and she felt a tightness in her chest. "Why would you do that?"

"Actually, I did it for you. I had no way of knowing that I'd ever get any cooperation out of Richard or your aunt. I knew you wanted answers, and I found it impossible to believe that there weren't any out there to be had. I hired an old friend to do some snooping."

"And what did he find?" Denali asked, her voice shaky and uncertain.

"He found proof that you'd been adopted, but your records were sealed, and only you had the power to get into them."

"I was adopted? By who?" Denali questioned, confused by the turn the conversation had taken.

"Your grandfather. See, your original birth certificate contained the names of your parents. Deveraux hadn't counted on that. You were born Denali Rose Wilson, and Richard knew that if you were to find out, if anyone was to find out, they would have to question Lester's disappearance. So after your mother's death, Richard hid the wills of both Lester and Rose and adopted you so that he could lie and tell everyone that you were born to his unwed daughter. It worked beautifully. You never questioned it, and neither did anyone else. And apparently Richard took care of all the legal details surrounding anything to do with Lester. He might even have had Lester's power of attorney, for all I know."

"So after he killed my father, my mother inherited Lester's stocks in Fun, Inc.?" Denali questioned, making certain she understood all the details of the situation.

"Yes. And what Richard didn't know was that Lester had changed his will to leave his stock to Rose rather than Richard. And what further thwarted Richard's plan was that Rose had made out her own will, albeit a very simple one. That will left everything to you. Everything, including what Lester had left to her."

"And Grandfather knew all of this and realized that I now held equal shares of stock in the company with him."

"Exactly. Not only this, but your grandmother had left each of her daughters a trust fund."

"What? I never heard about this," Denali said, seeing that the depth of her grandfather's deception had still not yet been fully realized.

"I know. But Chrys and Azalea knew about it because they'd both come into their money at age twenty-one. Rose never reached her twenty-first birthday, so therefore the trust passed to you. But when you came of age, Richard wasn't about to hand over the money, and he swore everyone to secrecy."

Denali suddenly felt very angry. "He knew that money would have set me free. I wouldn't have needed him anymore." She balled her fists and smacked at her thighs. "But why? He never wanted me to need him anyway."

"I think he did. I think he was desperate to have you need him, but he feared that you would turn out just like Rose. He'd lost his wife and his daughter, and putting stock in you just didn't seem wise."

Denali jumped up. "He could have had my undying devotion, but he didn't want it."

"Calm down, Denali," Michael said, leaning forward. "Getting angry at that crazy old man isn't going to change anything."

"He cheated me out of my parents and my life. I had a right to know about those things," Denali said, pacing the floor in front of Michael. "It was cruel and inhumane, and he knew it."

"Yes, probably so. But in his own warped perspective—and believe me, I'm not trying to advocate what he did—it probably seemed his only hope. His mind is warped, Denali. It may well have been that way for a long, long time. After all, he murdered a man. And not just any man. He murdered his daughter's husband, the father of her unborn child. A child he didn't know existed."

"Would it have made a difference?" Denali questioned, her voice raising. "Murder is still murder."

"Agreed, but Richard thought he was protecting Rose. That's all he saw. That's how he justified it. Then when your mother announced her pregnancy and produced you, it was probably like being accused all over again. You were Lester's daughter. Then Rose killed herself and left you behind. You then became the haunting reminder of both parents. The two people whose deaths he could clearly hold himself responsible for."

Michael got up and walked toward Denali, but she wanted no part of it. "Please don't touch me. I have so much anger inside right now, and I don't want to be touched."

"I thought touching was important to you," Michael said with a half smile.

"It is, but not when I feel like this. I'm afraid my anger would just destroy anything—anyone I touch."

Michael nodded. "But you have to let go of that anger. Remember the things you told me. Remember how anger and bitterness take possession of you. Take control of your life. Look what it did to your grandfather . . . to me."

Denali knew he was right, but it hurt so much to realize the truth about her life. She was defeated and totally drained of energy.

"I love you, Denali, and I want you to let go of all this and be happy."

His expression softened, and his eyes lit up in a way that Denali had never seen before. He actually looked happy. She had no words to give him in return, however. She knew for herself that she loved him, too. She'd realized it as she had reflected back on her actions at her grandfather's house. She wouldn't have jumped in front of the gun had she not loved Michael enough to try to save his life.

Michael stepped closer but still honored her wish that he not touch her. "I want you to believe me when I say that my feelings have nothing to do with your money. I came into our relationship because of my greed, but I don't feel that way anymore, and I don't want to ruin my chances with you by leaving you with any doubts in that regard. In fact, I tore up the check from Richard, and I'm giving up the idea of re-starting my business. I'm happy to go on working for Fun, Inc.—as long as you believe that my intentions are honest and true. If not, then I'll quit and go work elsewhere, but I don't want to lose you."

Denali's anger abated with this heartfelt declaration. Instinctively, she knew he spoke the truth. His sincerity was evident and clear. "I do believe you, Michael. But I'm going to need time to sort this thing out."

He smiled. "I can wait. I'm good at waiting."

Denali shook her head and rolled her eyes. "Since when?"

Thirty-four

October was a pleasant month and a perfect setting for the ground-breaking of the Omni Missions resort. Denali stood with Chrys and Hazel Garrison, while Michael appeared otherwise occupied with several of the other board members. Quite a crowd had gathered for the celebration. Hazel had wanted the moment to be a memorable one and created a most festive atmosphere. Huge canopied tents had been erected, with hundreds of tables and chairs arranged beneath their shaded awnings. Caterers stood ready with tables of mouth-watering treats, and there was even a band playing a wide variety of music.

"It's nearly time for you to make your speech," Hazel said suddenly. "I'll leave you two alone to collect your thoughts a bit." She smiled broadly at Denali. "I know you'll do a good job."

"Thank you," Denali replied. Her mind, however, wasn't on speechmaking as she spied Michael's handsome face. She intended to tell him what he wanted to hear—what he'd been desperate to hear for the last six weeks. She loved him. And while there was never any real doubt about that point, Denali didn't want to cheat either one of them by coming into the relationship without first putting the past behind her.

"Your smile suggests something other than the pleasure of speech-making," Chrys said with a laugh.

Denali nodded. "I suppose you know me well enough to figure that out."

"Look, before you go up there—before you do anything else—I want you to know how much I love you," Chrys said, tears forming in her eyes. "I made stupid choices. I listened to Father when I should have listened to my heart. I know we've talked about all of this before, but I'd like you to forgive me."

"Of course I forgive you," Denali said, tucking the speech papers under her arm. She reached out to hug her aunt and added, "Forgive me, too."

Chrys pulled away. "You did nothing wrong. You were born to this family, and that wasn't a fault of yours. You were entitled to so much more than you received."

"I received love and kindness from you and Azalea. I knew a mother's love in both of you. I missed out on many things, I know that. But I also took for granted many of the very real and evident things that I had. If I've learned one thing in this whole affair, it's that often we don't appreciate what we have because we're too busy pining for what we've never known. I don't intend to let that happen anymore."

Chrys nodded toward Michael, who by this time was surrounded by a sea of people. "Does that include him, as well?"

Denali smiled. "Yes. Especially him."

"Look, there's something else I want to say. I just finalized things with my lawyer, and I want you to know that along with Azalea's stocks, I'd like you to take charge of mine and Father's, as well. Obviously, Father is never going to be able to manage the company again. We both know the doctor's prognosis for him isn't good. But I didn't tell you that he gave me his power of attorney a long time ago. As I see it, I hold responsibility now for his forty percent and my ten percent. I want you to be in charge of it all. You have a good head on your shoulders, Denali. You know this business as well as I do, and I have the utmost faith in you to make it succeed. I'm giving you control over the entire matter because I know it's what I'm supposed to do."

"But you could stay on and work with me. We could share the responsibility," Denali protested.

Chrys shook her head. "I intend to retire. I've been working since I was a child, and now I want to have some fun. Besides, I met a man in New Orleans."

"Chrys, that's wonderful!" Denali exclaimed and hugged her aunt again.

"I think so," Chrys replied. Her countenance radiated her joy. "I think it's about time I stopped worrying about Fun, Inc. and Father and started thinking about my own future. I'm not a young woman anymore, and I don't intend to let any more opportunities slip by me. I don't think you should, either," she said, nodding to Michael's approaching figure. "He's a good man, Denali."

"Yes, he is. And don't worry," Denali said, patting her aunt on the arm, "I don't intend to let him slip away."

"You know," Chrys said, turning to leave, "if you want a good partner, I'd say Michael Copeland is your man."

Denali laughed. "Are you talking business or pleasure?"

Chrys glanced over her shoulder just as Michael reached them. "Both."

Denali laughed softly, and Michael raised a quizzical brow. "What was that all about?"

Just then Hazel Garrison called the crowd to order and began to make her opening statements about the theme park and resort. She had instructed Denali that her statement would be brief and that Denali would then be asked to come forward and make her own comments on the project.

Michael leaned down and again questioned her. "Is something going on that I should know about?"

Denali looked up and nodded. "Definitely."

" . . . And so it is my pleasure," Hazel told the crowd, "to introduce the young woman whose vision for this park helped to make this ground-breaking possible. Denali Deveraux."

The crowd began clapping, and Denali realized this was her cue to come on stage. She stretched up to whisper in Michael's ear, knowing that she couldn't go before the crowd without telling him how she felt.

"I love you," she said, then pulled back and made her way to the stage.

She could see from the smug look on his face that her words had been clearly understood. He stood there, arms crossed, grinning from ear to ear as though he'd won some sort of contest. Her heart swelled with pride at the thought of spending a lifetime with this handsome, intelligent man.

Denali made her speech without really even hearing her own words. She avoided looking back down at Michael, fearful that if she did, she'd never finish her task. After telling everyone what a pleasure it was to be a part of the Omni project, Denali concluded with remarks regarding the future of the project and her great happiness to announce that she would be staying on to see it through to completion. She left the stage amidst a hearty round of applause and walked right into Michael's awaiting arms.

He drew her away from the crowd, just as she had known he would.

Arm in arm, they walked back through the wooded area where she'd tripped on their first site inspection. Stopping there, under a canopy of tree boughs, Denali and Michael embraced.

"I knew you'd come to your senses sooner or later," Michael whispered before kissing her briefly on the mouth.

"So now what?" Denali questioned, reaching up to run her hands through Michael's hair.

"You tell me?"

Denali glanced skyward. "Well, there is this whole Fun, Inc. thing. Chrys just informed me that she's giving me legal control of the entire company. It seems she has Grandfather's power of attorney, and along with her own stock, she's giving it all over to me in order to retire and start up some love interest with a man in New Orleans. I believe she's thinking about marriage."

Michael tightened his hold on her, and Denali cherished the possessive way he held her. "Chrys is a very smart woman. Perhaps you should follow her example."

"And start up a love interest with a man in New Orleans?" she asked impishly.

"Not hardly."

"Oh, then, did you mean I should think about marriage?" Denali questioned, trying hard not to reveal the nervousness she felt. They were moving awfully fast, and while it was exactly what she wanted, it still frightened her just a bit.

"Yes," Michael stated, his expression quite serious.

"I have thought about that," Denali said, trying to act nonchalant. "I've also thought a lot about the business. Fun, Inc. is a big responsibility, and even with it consolidated to Dallas, it's going to require a great deal of expertise and know-how. I'm going to need a partner in this, Michael, and you have all the right qualifications to make it work."

"I agree," Michael replied, his voice seductive and low, "you do need a partner."

Denali licked her lips and let her gaze meet his. "And you would like to be that partner?"

"Yes," he whispered, then added, "but I'm not just talking about the business."

Denali felt a tingling sensation travel the length of her body. "Me either."

Michael smiled. "Good. Just so long as we both understand each other. It's very necessary that we be clear on the details of this partnership."

Denali nodded. "I suppose we should draw up some sort of formal agreement."

"Yes. We need to make it all legal and binding."

She swallowed hard. "When?"

"The sooner the better," Michael replied. "We can sit down and negotiate the terms of our agreement this afternoon, if you like."

"Like who will be responsible for what, and how conflicts will be resolved and questions dealt with?"

Michael laughed. "That, along with whether or not you tolerate people drinking right from the milk carton, and whether you plan to root for the Dallas Cowboys or the Kansas City Chiefs whenever they play each other in football games."

Denali laughed. "That's easy. Drink out of the milk carton if you like, and I'll root for whichever team needs my help. I'm more concerned about whether or not we'll be able to tolerate each other on a twenty-four-hour basis."

Michael pressed his lips against her ear and then let his kisses travel down her neck. "I think I can stand it just fine," he murmured.

Denali playfully pushed him away. "I'm serious, Michael."

He grinned roguishly. "So am I."

She shook her head and sobered. "What about Cambry? I love that house. I just don't know what I'm going to do about it. I really didn't have in mind to live in Dallas the rest of my life."

"Who said we had to?" He reached out and brushed back a piece of windblown hair. "Look, we have our entire lives ahead of us. The past is resolved and we're looking forward. Agreed?"

"Yes."

He linked his arm through hers and pulled her snugly to his side. "I vote that we let God take controlling interest of the future and that we devote ourselves to thinking only about today."

"Let tomorrow take care of itself—is that it?" she questioned, looking up with pride at the man she'd chosen to spend the rest of her life with.

"Exactly."

She put her head on his shoulder and sighed. "I second the motion. All in favor say 'aye.'"

"Aye," Michael murmured.

"Aye," Denali countered with firm resolve. "Those opposed?" She let the silence linger between them for a moment. "The motion carries. Controlling interest goes to God."